PRICELESS

PRICELESS

MARNE DAVIS KELLOGG

ST. MARTIN'S PRESS   NEW YORK

www.stmartins.com

Library of Congress Cataloging-in-Publication Data

Kellogg, Marne Davis.
　　Priceless / Marne Davis Kellogg.—1st ed.
　　　　p. cm.
　　ISBN 0-312-30381-5
　　EAN 978-0312-30381-5
　　1. Americans—Europe—Fiction. 2. Married women—Fiction. 3. Jewel thieves—Fiction. I. Title.

PS3561.E39253P75 2004
813'.54—dc22

2004041817

First Edition: July 2004

10　9　8　7　6　5　4　3　2　1

For Daddy

Happy trails, until we meet again.

ACKNOWLEDGMENTS

For many authors of fiction, writing is something they are compelled to do but they find no pleasure in it. For me, writing is a constant source of joy, like drinking good wine and eating dark chocolate cake. I can't wait to get to work every morning and see what's happened overnight. Perhaps that's because my books are about luxury—Kick Keswick wears cashmere pajamas, steals fabulous jewelry, and her capers take place in some of the world's most beautiful locales, to which my dearest darling, Peter, takes me for research. We cherish our happy, romantic times at the Hôtel Ritz in Paris and the Hotel Splendido in Portofino researching this book.

Priceless was also fun to write because of the talented people I am privileged to work with. In particular, I thank Sally Richardson, publisher, St. Martin's Press, and Jennifer Enderlin, associate publisher and executive editor. Working with Jennifer is rich and rewarding—her vision, creative input, and enthusiasm are awesome and energizing. I also thank her assistant, Kimberly Cardascia, who is surrounded by artistes and remains organized and unflappable, and art director Anne Twomey for branding Kick so elegantly.

I'm so grateful to my agent, Robert Gottlieb, president and

CEO, Trident Media Group, and Kimberly Whalen, vice president and managing director of foreign rights. Kim is always available, interested, and thinking. I am very, very fortunate to be represented by such an outstanding, committed team.

My continued thanks for guidance in the beautiful world of gems, jewelry, and jewelry-making remain first and foremost to Bob Gibson at Raymond C. Yard, Inc., in New York, and to Brien Foster at Foster & Son, in Denver. Both gentlemen are always generous with their time, knowledge, and expertise, and any mistakes that have been made are mine. Thank you, also, to Lana Lee of Neiman-Marcus Precious Jewels, Denver; Harry Winston, New York; Graff, London; and Van Cleef & Arpels, Place Vendôme, Paris.

Priceless makes mention of many exquisite French and Italian wines—some available and affordable, some rare and stratospheric—selected by our friends Blair and Suzanne Taylor, owners of the glorious Barolo Grill in Denver and Enotec Imports, Inc., one of the country's leading importers of fine Italian wines. They also assisted with the Italian translations for the book.

Armel Santens, French-born general manager of the historic Brown Palace Hotel in Denver, graciously took the time to make the French in this book idiomatically correct. Any mistakes are mine.

I thank God every day for my family and friends—I am blessed by their loyalty, steadfastness, and support for my writing. My love and undying thanks to: Mary and Richard, who have bottomless bottles of rum and scotch and invite me to dinner even when they'd probably rather not, especially when they're occupied with trying to get their sons married off to a couple of crackerjack girls; Mary Lou and Randy, who thrilled us all by getting married and still found the time to throw a sensational launch party; Marcy and Bruce, who not only have thrown spectacular parties for my books in Denver, but also got their friend Susan Parker in Oklahoma City to throw one, too; Mita Vail and the Norfolk Book Ladies, who whip up major champagne-driven literary fêtes at the drop of a hat; Pam and Bill, whose faith and courage provide us with rock-solid love, continuity, and tequila; Sally Rippey, for her doggerel and her dogged support; Judith; Susan and Doug; Frank and Jane; the ladies of the Denver Debutante Ball; and the cowgirls of the National Western.

My family is amazing—we are a tight group. I am so grateful for all the Connecticut Kelloggs and the Colorado Davises; for my mother's grace and dignity; Hunter, Courtney, Duncan, and Delaney; Peter and Bede; our wire fox terrier, Kick, who makes me laugh all the time, and, of course, for my beloved husband, Peter. Next stop, St. Moritz.

Marne Davis Kellogg
Denver, Colorado

PRICELESS

PROLOGUE

The St. Honoré Room at the Hôtel Bristol in Paris, one of the most elegant private dining rooms in the world, thundered with applause as Cécile Everett rose to accept the Legion d'Honneur honoring her late husband, industrialist Cameron Everett. Soft light from the crystal chandeliers and the candles on the tables and torchères in the garden bathed the darkened room, while on the podium, Mrs. Everett stood still—the spotlight sparkling off her jewelry and honey-colored hair—and prepared to receive the ribboned sash from the president of France. Once the black-tie crowd of international industrialists and celebrities quieted, the president spoke.

"Your husband was a visionary," he said. "His talents helped fashion the future of French industry."

Mrs. Everett kept her smile firmly in place, posture perfect, hands at her sides. She had a lot of experience at this sort of thing, standing by Cameron when he was being presented with honors and, now, standing alone to receive his posthumous recognition. She knew the president would go on for several more minutes and then she would receive the sash and say a few words. Finally, she would be able to return to her suite and call it a day.

She was a very beautiful, very well-kept woman. How old? Maybe sixty, or seventy, or eighty. Cameron had taken such poor care of himself that by the time he fell dead in midsentence at a board meeting at age eighty-two, he looked every year of it. But with Mrs. Everett, it was hard to tell, her plastic surgeons had been so skillful, and the investment in the care of her skin and body over the years had been so huge. She had magnificent skin on her face—pale, translucent, pampered. Her midnight-blue satin gown was long-sleeved, high-necked, covering up telltale spots and sags on her arms and décolletage that might give better clues as to her actual age. The skin on her hands was white and spotless. Her oval nails short and bright red.

In spite of Cécile Everett's beauty, what really drew the eye was her jewelry. To be sure, her pink diamond and pearl drop earrings, and the stones in her rings and bracelet, were extraordinary, but they all paled in comparison to the brooch pendant attached to her necklace—the Pink Elephants. It was a large piece of three elephants walking in a row, Papa, Mama, and Baby—with Mama and Baby following tail to trunk. They were solid pink diamonds, set invisibly in platinum with sapphire eyes and smiling ruby mouths. On the lead elephant's head was a crown of rubies with a diadem: the fabulous Pink Elephant Diamond. The largest, most perfect pink diamond on earth, twenty-seven brilliant-cut carats of sparkling cotton candy. Cartier had designed and fabricated the piece for Mr. Everett as a twenty-fifth anniversary gift for Cécile—he had given it to her long ago in a tent at Tarangire National Park in Tanzania where they were on safari, surrounded by real elephants and spear-toting Maasai warriors. They'd toasted each other with shots of gin out of stainless steel coffee cups.

Cécile smiled at the memory as she turned to face President Gérard.

"It is my honor to present this award to you on behalf of the French people." The president draped the blue-white-and-red sash over her head where it made a striking contrast against her gown, as she knew it would. He kissed her elaborately on both cheeks.

"Thank you, Mr. President. Cameron always had deep affection for the people of France and this award would have meant more to him than any other. I'm sorry he isn't here to accept it in person. I am proud to accept on his behalf." Mrs. Everett turned to face the room and smiled as the heartfelt applause from her husband's friends and colleagues buffeted her. Then, President Gérard helped her down from the podium and escorted her back to her table. He offered his apologies about having to proceed to his next official engagement and made a quick exit via a side door.

"Excuse me," Mrs. Everett whispered to her seatmate. "You've been so helpful to me all evening, may I ask one more favor?"

"Of course."

"Do you mind walking me back to my room? I'm feeling a little overwhelmed."

"Not at all. It would be my pleasure."

It took several more minutes to make her way through the crowd of well-wishers and into the cool, uncrowded lobby.

"You're so kind to do this," Cécile said. "I'm sorry to take you away from the party."

"Please, Mrs. Everett," her escort replied, holding her steady by the arm, and guiding her into the opulent, old-fashioned elevator cage. "I'm happy to see you safely upstairs. That was a beautiful tribute to your husband."

Cécile nodded. Her eyes were slightly glazed. "I suppose. These evenings just seem to go on for hours. I imagine he's glad he's dead and doesn't have to attend."

They both laughed as the ancient contraption jerked its way to the eighth floor, and the equally ancient operator slid open the door.

"I had almost nothing to drink but it just seemed to hit me. I think I need a good night's sleep." She wobbled slightly as they made their way down the corridor. The companion held her more securely and slid the key into the lock.

"Here we are." The door swung open easily to the exquisite Suite Panoramique with its antiques-filled living room, wood-burning fireplace, sumptuous bedrooms, huge white marble bathrooms and private fitness studio. Outside, the lights of the Tour Eiffel and the Sacré-Coeur twinkled across the rooftops of Paris. Below, the traffic on the Faubourg St. Honoré passed in a silent stream.

Dim lights burned on the desk and beyond in the master bedroom.

"Do you need anything? Would you like a nightcap?"

"That sounds wonderful," Cécile answered. "A little scotch, please. Lots of ice."

Ice cubes tinkled in crystal tumblers and single-malt splashed on top. "Is that enough?"

"Perfect, thank you. *Salud.*" She held up her glass and they clinked.

"*Salud,* Mrs. Everett."

They stood comfortably, side by side, admiring the view of Paris as they sipped their drinks.

"I'm so glad the evening's over," Cécile said. Her words came out in a slur. "Oh, dear, that's a sign it's time for me to go to bed." She swayed as she placed her drink on a side table.

"Are you all right? Can I help you?"

"I'm fine. Just so, so tired. Thank you again." She turned and headed toward the bedroom. "Good night, dear. Lovely to see you."

"Good night, Mrs. Everett. Sweet dreams."

Cécile Everett was so concentrated on trying to make it to her bed, she didn't notice that her escort was still on the premises and had casually taken both of the cocktail glasses into the kitchen and was washing them out, drying them carefully to remove all fingerprints, and returning them to the bar. Cécile's head spun, as though she were very, very drunk. She pulled off the jewelry while she walked—earrings, bracelets, rings, necklace—and dropped it all with a clatter onto the glass-topped table in her dressing room. She reached behind her head and unzipped her dress, stepping out of it on her way to the king-sized canopy bed that beckoned like a soft puffy boat.

The companion gave her two more minutes before entering the bedroom and tucking her in under the covers. Cécile was unconscious. She never made a sound or opened her eyes. The rest went like clockwork. It really was ridiculous how easy this was, how trusting these women were, these widows and divorcées. And how helpful that little extra something in her drink was. As usual, it worked like a charm and had the added benefit of being an amnesiac: Mrs. Everett would not be able to remember anything past leaving the party. Furthermore, she would be too embarrassed, too prideful—too frightened of what had become more and more frequent lapses of memory—to admit she'd lost track of the Pink Elephant Diamond.

The array of pink stones lay like a pile of make-believe, dress-up jewelry on the dressing table. Each piece extremely valuable in its own right. But this was a big-game hunt. Any hack could steal jewelry from an incapacitated widow, but for this thief, only the finest trophy, a priceless piece, would do. The Pink Elephant brooch was easily unhooked from its diamond rivière necklace. It went into one pocket and out of another came a small, slightly battered bouquet of shamrocks tied with a satin ribbon. And a note:

The Shamrock Burglar

The thief left the suite—cautioning the maid in the hall with a finger to the lips that Madame was sleeping—returned to the party, and danced until two.

ONE

"Kick," my husband said.

"Yes, Thomas?" I shook the tablecloth and it floated to the grass like a fresh sheet.

"If this is what you're doing for our six months' anniversary, I can't imagine what you've got in mind for six years."

"Six months of sheer pleasure." I smiled. And that was the truth.

There is so much to be said for love when you're grown. I learned years and years ago—I won't get into exactly how many years, just "years and years" will do—that a point comes in your life that when you open your eyes in the morning, there'd better be more going on in your bed than matinee idol good looks and a strong libido, because if you're going to make it for the long haul, at some point you're going to need to have a conversation. And if that conversation isn't interesting, well, forget it.

Thomas and I weren't quite yet "Love Among the Ruins," but, thank God, we weren't children with stars in our eyes, either. Let me put it this way: We were experienced. We had the good sense to appreciate the subtleties and refinements of life: when to speak, when to stay silent; the rich satisfaction of enjoying each other's company over excellent food and fine wine; sharing common interests in books and art and music; the pleasure and intimacy of love without any silly show-off acrobatics; long, quiet walks. And finesse. Ah, yes, finesse—the ability to do something grand without appearing to have done anything at all.

"Where do you want me to set the pie?" He'd carried it carefully from the house. I think it was the most perfect lemon meringue pie I'd ever made.

"Here, I'll take it." I placed it in the center of the cloth. "Why don't you open the wine?"

"With pleasure." Thomas slid one of the mildly chilled bottles of Chinon from a wicker basket.

"This is lovely," he said, "Clos Varness '98. Nicely done, Kick."

The late May sun sparkled through the apple tree's lime-green leaves, my apple tree on my beautiful little farm in Provence—La Petite Pomme—just outside of Éygalières. I'd owned the farm for several years. It was as close to paradise on earth as one can get—several acres of crops, sometimes sunflowers, sometimes lamb's lettuce, flower, herb, and vegetable gardens, and an apple orchard whose trees produced little pink apples, slightly larger than crabapples but smaller than normal. A rocky, olive tree-lined lane meandered its way to the little yellow farmhouse with its hyacinth-blue shutters and jasmine espaliers.

I moved here, permanently, from London over a year ago, happily single, wealthy beyond my wildest dreams. Ill-gotten gains to be sure, but now I'm in the process of trying to rectify all that. I live a completely respectable life, one without secrets. Well, with fewer secrets at any rate. I have so many, it would be impossible to abandon them all at one time.

My name is Kick Keswick and I am—or rather *was*—the Shamrock Burglar—revered in the annals of London's criminal archives as the finest, most successful, most talented, and most notorious jewel thief in all history.

TWO

Jewels and jewelry have always held the preeminent place in my affections. I have a natural feel for them. I have the touch. Not only do I love and appreciate the security they provide, but also I love the pleasure their beauty brings me. I never tire of looking at stones through my loupe, staring deep into their mysteries—the icy power of a perfect diamond; the heavenly, unfathomable blue of a Kashmir sapphire; the bottomless green of an African emerald. I never fail to be dazzled by the artistry of great jewelers, the creative and intricate fabrications of Cartier; the perfect quality of the stones and exquisite construction of Raymond Yard; the smooth, seamless detail of Van Cleef; and the enormous, look-at-me gems of Harry Winston and Graff. I can only describe the pleasure and warmth I receive from jewelry as intense, intimate, erotic. They gave me a very good life, and I, in return, gave them my undivided, undiluted love.

I'm retired now. I waved good-bye to my prestigious daytime career as the doyenne, chatelaine, and arbiter of taste at London's distinguished Ballantine & Company Auctioneers, climbed on an Air France jet, and vanished into the blue with several million dollars' worth of gems hidden in my bra and stacks of Euros packed into special pockets in my suit coat and skirt. Not to put too fine a point on it, but I am a good-sized woman. Not obese by any means, but full-figured. Let me put it this way: I have more surface area to my body to store treasury notes and gemstones than a slimmer woman has. Consequently, during my long career, depending on the market price of precious gems—diamonds, sapphires, rubies, and emeralds—and metals—gold, silver, and platinum—I've stolen and stashed enough to live in comfort for several hundred years.

Ironically, my husband, Thomas Curtis, has left behind a highly decorated career as the Commander of New Scotland Yard's Investigations Branch. His white hair and blazing blue eyes had made him a recognizable media figure, present at every major bust, arrest, and announcement. He was respected as one of the Yard's most talented senior detectives. But, come to find out, there was more to Thomas than met the eye. Much more. He had almost as many secrets and was as notorious as I. In his off-duty hours he stole unprotected, important, and sometimes even priceless works of art from the homes of people who had informed the police they would be out for the evening or out of town on holiday! It really was unfathomable to think such an upstanding, law-abiding, *law-enforcing* citizen as Thomas would do such an unscrupulous thing. But he performed these robberies as a service: The paintings would quickly and mysteriously turn up, unharmed, at nearby police stations in the wee hours of the morning with notes from the elusive "Samaritan Burglar" warning the owners to take better care of their valuables lest a real thief get his hands on them.

Everyone in London was wild about both of us—the Shamrock and the Samaritan, their hometown celebrity burglars. They adored us. Ourselves included. I loved reading about his exploits over my breakfast, seeing the words "Samaritan Rescue Turns Up in Mayfair Police Station," stamped on the TV screen. And, in spite of the fact that New Scotland Yard was humbled by its inability to catch me, Thomas later admitted to me he loved hearing about my escapades, each robbery elegantly complemented by my signature, a lovely, crisp bouquet of shamrocks tied with an ivory satin ribbon in place of the missing goods. Who knew who either one of these dashing villains was? No one. Certainly neither one of us.

I had no clue who the Samaritan Burglar was—I'd suspected a fellow who visited the auction house only when we had sales of major paintings and looked like David Niven with a pencil-thin mustache, a debonair, country-gentleman style, and a knack for befriending elderly aristocratic strangers. I'd kept my eye on him for years—he never bought a single thing and only bid while things were lively and therefore kept him safely out of the running. But as far as I knew, the police had never noticed him and I certainly wasn't going to tip them off about my suspicions, being unwilling to draw any attention to myself from the constabulary. When I moved away from London, the true identity of the Samaritan Burglar was still a mystery. And so it is to this day. Except to me. And Thomas, of course.

And as I've already mentioned, nobody, Thomas included, had a clue who the Shamrock Burglar was, either. They never even got close. But, now, that's why I was the best. I was pro-not re-active, setting my terms and conditions. I planned and executed my robberies meticulously and never took any chances.

Thomas and I met and grew fond—I shall say for lack of a better word—of each other when there had been a murder, followed shortly by a bombing, at Ballantine & Company. He had been in charge of the lengthy investigations. During the course of these investigations, he'd invited me out twice—once to a concert, another time to see the Raphael cartoons at the V & A—such civilized and tempting invitations to someone like me who'd spent a highly sheltered lifetime within the walls of Ballantine & Company. My lifetime had been dedicated to studying and appreciating the finest life had to offer, never venturing socially at all from my own little world, with the result being that not only am I a jewelry expert and a master jeweler, but I can also spot a fake painting or piece of furniture in a heartbeat. Everyone at Ballantine always remarked on my "natural" eye for quality and authenticity. In a perfect and proper world, Thomas and I would have been "naturals" for each other as well, but I'd turned down his invitations. Then one thing led to another and it was time for me to leave permanently for France without telling him, or anyone else for that matter, good-bye.

I settled very happily into my life of retirement as an unmarried woman. I had lots of friends, lots of invitations, two fast cars—a Jaguar XK convertible for fair weather and a small Mercedes wagon for foul—and a tiny, snow-white Westie named Bijou for companionship.

But I'd been unable to get Thomas Curtis out of my mind. I wasn't obsessed with him, nothing of the sort. He just simply

drifted to the surface every now and then and made me wonder if I'd made a mistake not getting to know him better. He'd
been such a fine, distinguished, cultured, solid, unmarried
man. The kind that's hard to find.

Thomas had not been able to forget me, either, and after he
retired, he set out to track me down, using the only clue he
had: Late one afternoon, he'd come to my flat in London to dis-
cuss the bombing case. He admired the Van Gogh above my
fireplace, and I mentioned how much I loved Provence. That's
all there was to that part of the conversation. Months later,
we bumped into each other in Les Beaux at a cocktail party at
my good friend Flaminia Balfour's farm—Ferme de la Bonne
Franquette—and, corny as it sounds, fell in love right there on
the spot. It was an authentic *coup de foudre*.

Later that same evening, back at my house—while I was
making a tarte tatin, and he'd poured us each a glass of Château
d'Yquem—he called me to join him in the living room and
thereby subtly informed me that not only was he the Samaritan
Burglar, but also that he knew I was the Shamrock. He imparted
this knowledge by hanging a special painting over the fireplace.
I recognized it immediately. *Polonaise Blanche* by Renoir. The
only painting he'd stolen and been forced to keep because, un-
beknownst to each other, we'd been robbing the same house at
the same time and I'd had to tap him unconscious over the head
with my little rubber mallet. He'd regained consciousness just in
time to escape by the skin of his teeth, but was too late to get to
the police station where he'd planned to leave the painting during the hubbub of their shift change.

"It was at that moment I realized the Shamrock Burglar was a woman." He smiled. "And I surrendered myself to you completely."

"What do you mean you knew the Shamrock Burglar was a woman?" I was amazed.

"Only a woman would be so thoughtful as to use a rubber mallet. A man would have garroted me or broken my neck. You simply gave me a hard thwack in exactly the right place to make me fall like a stone and made your escape."

"Of course I wouldn't break your neck. I'm interested in jewelry, not murder."

After a small wedding in the little Anglican church in St. Rémy and a beautiful seated dinner for twelve at Flaminia and Bill's, we settled nicely into our country-life marriage, setting a solid course to become good, rehabilitated citizens. I taught English at the St. Rémy library four days a week and he helped deliver meals to senior citizens. We were a model couple.

We'd even hosted a charity benefit—a picnic in the orchard for two hundred—for the hospital to purchase a new ambulance. All the leading citizens came, thereby endowing us with their imprimatur of social acceptance and respectability.

Still, I'd be lying if I didn't admit that I occasionally miss my former life, the thrill of the perfect heist, the payoff of feeling beautiful gems cascade through my fingers like smooth pebbles from a stream, listening to their distinctive bright, reverberating click. Occasionally I get the itch to test my skills, keep them sharp, because I've dreamt that I've gotten rusty and gotten caught, and I wake up so out of breath I'm sure I'm having a

heart attack. I miss the solace of being by myself, of indepen-
dence, of having exclusively my own agenda, and I miss my
privacy. But even that had improved drastically since we'd added
a small wing onto the house so Thomas could have his own
study and bath. It helps keep the romance in our marriage.

As the afternoon grew warm in the orchard, we settled across
from each other on the shady ground cloth and Thomas poured
the white burgundy. I set the cold chicken—a roasted poulet de
Bresse—on a platter and arranged chilled artichokes, asparagus,
and tapenade-stuffed tomatoes around it. I laid out napkins that
matched the cloth, pale yellow with red roosters and hens.

"You shouldn't have gone to all this trouble, Kick." He handed
me a glass of wine. There was an edge to his voice but—there it
is again, the wisdom that comes with maturity and experience—thank God I'm now old enough to know enough about
men to know that usually whatever the edge is, it has nothing
to do with you. Usually the preoccupation has to do with
changing the oil in their cars, or did their shirts get picked up
at the laundry, or in Thomas's case, making sure his shoes were
perfectly shined.

"You know it's no trouble." I raised my glass. "To us, Thomas
Curtis."

"To us, Kick Keswick. I absolutely adore you."

We leaned across the lemon meringue pie to kiss. Just as I
closed my eyes, it seemed to me that a look of sadness crossed
his face.

THREE

Two mornings later, bands of sunlight filtered through the shutters and warmed my face and I stretched my arms and legs in all directions as far as they would go before opening my eyes.

It was the first time since we'd gotten married that I'd had my bed, our bed, all to myself. And it was quite wonderful.

Yesterday, Thomas went down to Marseilles to have lunch with an old friend, the chief of the Marseilles police, and to attend an afternoon art auction. I spent the entire day experimenting in the kitchen, trying to perfect some little chewy, gooey chocolate cakes I'd invented and had dubbed "bagatelles" because they were shaped like giant, three-hundred-carat, emerald-cut diamonds. I sealed in their moistness with a covering of silver leaf—an extremely intricate undertaking. Silver and gold leaf are the devil to work with, very fragile, temperamental, and nerve-wracking. And when nicely done, very rewarding. I've found that a glass of champagne while you're working with the foil has a steadying effect. Two glasses of champagne is even better. Three? You simply say to hell with the foil and eat the cakes. I love to be in the kitchen. Almost as much as I loved stealing jewelry. I thrive on beautiful food. Years ago I gave up worrying about my waistline. It's part of my charm.

Thomas called at dinnertime last night to say the auction had gotten off to a delayed start and was going longer than expected. Did I mind if he spent the night and wasn't home before lunchtime today?

"Of course not," I said. "Has that little Chaumière come up for bid yet?"

"Next group."

"I'd love it if you could get it."

"I'll see what I can do. I'll be home by noon."

So now, I had to fight the urge just to lie here all morning in my beautiful pale yellow and white bedroom and finish up the bagatelles or get up and make us some sort of welcome home lunch that we could spend the major part of the afternoon enjoying and then go to bed and forget about dinner.

It was completely quiet. I could hear the bees buzzing in the lavender beds right outside the window and the distant hum of a tractor.

I reached across to Thomas's pillow and grabbed a handful of warm fur and a cold nose and kisses from Bijou. I opened my eyes. It was late. Past nine. Thomas would be home in three hours.

I took a hot shower, fixed my hair and makeup—I always get totally put together before I do anything because you never know what's in store and you don't want to have a big opportunity or encounter come your way and not look as though you're ready for it. To tell the truth, even though I'm retired,

I can't seem to accept the fact that I don't need to be ready at all times to have my mug shot taken. That my capture and incarceration are right around the corner. And we've all seen how bad those pictures can look if you don't have your hair combed and your lipstick on.

And when it comes to cooking? I'm artist-as-chef, and what artist wants to work on a less than perfect canvas? The conditions must be ideal and I certainly couldn't put together a proper meal wearing my bathrobe, even if it is washable silk, salmon-pink, my favorite color.

I'd thought up an ambitious menu in the shower: cold cucumber and watercress soup, similar to vichyssoise, and as labor-intensive as a chilled soup can get, what with all the peeling, chopping, boiling, and puréeing required; lamb's lettuce with garlic, olive oil, lemon and crunchy crystals of Fleur de Cel; cheese soufflé, and one of Thomas's favorites: a rum-soaked pineapple upside-down cake. Oh, and a bottle or two of Domaine Tempier Bandol '96, Cuvée Paradis, the softest, most elegant red you can drink with a cheese soufflé.

I dressed in loose persimmon silk slacks and a comfortable faded cotton shirt, pearl necklace and earrings. White espadrilles and a crisp, snow white apron.

The kitchen was cool and hushed. The blue and white tiles, gleaming and spotless. I started a pot of coffee, fed Bijou her breakfast, and poured myself a glass of grapefruit juice. My caretaker, Pierre, had left the morning paper—the *International*

Herald Tribune—a *pain au chocolat,* and a fresh baguette, but they would have to wait until I got the lettuce rinsed, the cake in the oven, and the soup in the refrigerator. The soufflé was all last-minute.

It's hard to describe how I feel about my kitchen in Provence without sounding a little New World, or whatever it's called. You know—the people with the crystals and wavy music and so forth. Whether I'm standing at the sink washing dishes or at the counter chopping vegetables, I feel rooted right down to the center of the earth. It's extraordinary. A sense of peace and complete rightness fills me. This is my one perfect spot on the planet. This is where I belong.

Outdoors, morning was well under way—all the earliness was far gone and it was starting to get warm. Not only were the bees hard at work, but Pierre had already accumulated a large pile of weeds and trimmings on his tarp from the beds along the front of the house where Thomas thought he might like to put in a rose garden.

"Bonjour, Pierre," I called out the window.

He turned and gave me a little salute. "Bonjour, madame."

I turned on the TV set. Giovanna McDougal, SkyWord's best-known tabloid reporter, was doing a story on the latest royal scandal. I switched it off and put on Glazunov's *Seasons* ballet, *Printemps,* full-throttle. The *Zephyr of Spring* roared around me as I chopped up the watercress and cucumber for the soup, peeled the potatoes and put them on to boil, and assembled ingredients for the cake.

There are a number of ways to make a pineapple upside-down cake, which incidentally was invented by the Dole Pineapple Company in the 1940s, not—as we'd all like to imagine—by a desperate galley master aboard Captain Cook's ship, wondering what on earth he was going to do with all those goddamned pineapples and coconuts that were rolling knee-deep around the deck.

Some cooks use regular cake pans but I prefer to bake mine in a heavy cast-iron skillet, the sort everyone's grandmother used to use for everything. I like the density and heft of the skillet, the way it cooks evenly, and I also like the old-fashioned aura it gives to the presentation. There's something very satis fying about pulling a sizzling hot skillet from the oven and turning out a caramelized cake or a round of skillet-bread. I unhooked my pan from the wall rack and set it on a hot burner and cut in a stick of butter. Then I crumbled in a cup of brown sugar, let the mixture bubble together for a minute or two, pressed drained pineapple slices onto the warm syrup, and proceeded with the batter. There are two secrets to this cake: You must use good, strong, dark rum, and the egg whites for the meringue must be beaten to stiff peaks before you begin to add the sugar, which must be done one tablespoon at a time, all the way to the end, no cheating.

A few busy minutes later, maybe ten, I poured the golden, rum-scented batter onto the brown sugar and pineapple—it looked and smelled like a ribbon of planter's punch—and then eased the skillet into the hot oven very gently so as not to star-tle the eggs.

I got everything tidied up and finally—by now I was

starving—picked up the *Tribune* and went into the garden for a cup of coffee and a bit of breakfast. I'd just opened the paper and taken the first bite of my *pain au chocolat* when the sound of a car turning onto the gravel drive came around the house.

Thomas.

Bijou gave a couple of halfhearted barks before returning to the rabbit hole she'd been unsuccessfully excavating for several weeks.

I dashed into the kitchen, pulling off my apron, smoothing my hair. At the kitchen mirror I pulled a lipstick out of my pocket and freshened that up, pinched up my cheeks to give them a few roses, and went to welcome him home.

"*Bonjour,* madame," the Federal Express man said.

"*Bonjour. Merci.*" I signed and accepted the overnight envelope. While the truck sped back down the road, I looked at the airbill. It had come from T. Curtis, New Scotland Yard, London.

I turned it over and over in my hands. I didn't want to open it. My head began to ache, a sharp pain bolted through my eyes from temple to temple like an electrical arc.

Inside was a sealed envelope on official stationery. I tore it open and removed the handwritten note:

My precious Kick—By the time you read this, I'll be in London. I've gone back to the Yard to help work on a case that has resurfaced. I couldn't tell you in person. I don't know when I'll be back. Please don't try to contact me. Forgive me.
Thomas.

FOUR

I called his cell phone.

"This is Commander Thomas Curtis of New Scotland Yard. Leave your name and number and I'll return your call as soon as is possible. If this is an emergency, call 999 or the main office at 020-7230-1212."

I hung up. What had happened to his cheery, "Thomas, *ici*"? What did it mean, "Commander Thomas Curtis of New Scotland Yard"? He'd retired. And what sort of message could I leave? I couldn't get my breath and a roaring filled my head, a horrible haywire clanging, like fire bells.

I stared across the field. Tears flooded my eyes. I'd never felt abandoned before in my life, although I had been often, starting at an early age. But now the incredulity that filled me was like a giant void. A vexing I'd never experienced. I sat down on the bench next to the front door and in spite of my efforts not to, I began to cry.

Pierre approached me, his stance slightly canted, unsure of himself. "Madame?" he said.

I handed him Thomas's note, now a soggy wad. "Monsieur is gone."

"*Il est mort?*" Pierre looked horrified.

"No." I shook my head. "Not dead. Just gone. From me. From us."

He was relieved. "*Non.*" He shook his head. "He will come back."

"I don't think so, Pierre."

"You'll see, madame. He adores you."

"I don't think so, Pierre."

"Then he's a fool."

"*Oui.*" I buried my face in my hands.

Pierre pulled a freshly pressed checkered handkerchief out of his back pocket and offered it to me.

"*Merci,*" I said. I mopped my face with the cloth. "I'm fine. You go back to work. I'll be fine. Really."

Inside, the timer buzzed and buzzed. The pineapple upside-down cake was done. Shortly it would start to burn.

After a while, I'm not really sure how long, except the smell of caramelizing sugar had crossed the road from irresistible to bitter, I went indoors. I took the blackened cake out of the oven and set it next to the sink, where it smoked and sputtered, and then went into my bathroom and repaired my face. Crying wasn't going to accomplish anything. I needed to think.

I poured a fresh cup of coffee and took it into the living room and sat down at my desk, a long, book-covered table beneath the windows. I'd spent many hours at this table looking out the window, contemplating various aspects and actions of my life. It was where I'd made the final decision to retire for good because I loved my life so much, I didn't want to get caught and spend the rest of it in jail just dreaming about it. So my window table was a natural spot for me to retreat to now. Outside, far across the valley, Les Alpilles—the Little Alps— were scarcely visible through the noonday haze, while inside, the living room remained dim and cool. I turned and stared at the painting over the fireplace. The *Polonaise Blanche*. The Renoir Thomas had given me the night we fell in love. A painting of ice skaters waltzing in the snow.

Suddenly a chill ran up my spine and I caught my breath. What if? What if?

I got up and crossed to the bookshelves on the opposite side of the room and removed a section of fake books to reveal a wall safe. There was a knot in my stomach as I spun the dial. The tumblers fell into place and the safe door clicked free. I swung it open. The safe was empty. Gone—all the jewels were gone.

"Son of a bitch."

FIVE

To have your husband leave you is a bad thing. To have your husband leave you *and* take your pile with him is worse. It's contemptible.

The contents of the safe weren't everything I had, far from it. But it held all the jewelry that Thomas *thought* I had, including the Queen's Pet—a diamond bracelet I'd stolen from Lady Melody Carstairs's estate and that originally belonged to Queen Victoria—and a ring I'd fabricated with one of my ten-carat Kashmir sapphires. I'd framed it with three emeralds, carved like leaves. The sapphire looked like a big blue grape waiting to be plucked. I still had sizable bank accounts in Switzerland, as well as safety-deposit boxes packed with cash, gold, silver, and platinum ingots, and millions in stones, none of which I'd ever told Thomas about. But it was the *principle* of the thing. I would have told him, in time.

God damn you, Thomas Curtis. God damn you for making me love you.

I closed the safe, replaced the section of books, and returned to my bathroom where I took the precaution of locking the door. The headache had disappeared, replaced by focus. And a sort of dreadful curiosity. I pressed on a small invisible button imbedded in the wall underneath the windowsill and then folded back the bathroom rug to reveal a large section of floor tiles that had been unlatched when I pressed the button and was now slightly elevated. I knelt down on the cold floor and slid aside the secret panel, revealing a safe with an extremely sophisticated electronic lock. As far as I knew, Thomas didn't know about this hiding place, or any of the other secret stockpiles I had throughout the house and grounds.

This particular safe contained twelve good-sized safe-deposit boxes packed with gems and cash, including almost three thousand perfect diamonds separated by color, weight, and cut; over two hundred fifty thousand U.S. dollars in cash, as well as two hundred fifty thousand in Euros. One box held several sets of fake identifications—credit cards, driver's licenses, license plates, passports. I had dozens of options, dozens of contingencies—all developed over decades of imminent discovery and flight—that I'd meant to throw away but had never gotten around to.

I punched in the combination, and after a five-second delay, the locking bars withdrew and clicked into place. I pushed my hair back and leaned over to heft open the vault door.

I felt calm and cool as a cucumber. This wasn't the end of the world—it was, instead, a re-entry into a familiar byzantine world I thought I'd left behind.

Methodically, I slid out each box and inventoried its contents that I knew by heart. It didn't take long to see that everything was there.

"*Bon.*" I closed the safe, replaced the floor panel and pulled the rug back into place.

I threw away the pineapple upside-down cake—I've never cared for it as much as apple cake anyway—and uncorked a bottle of Pol Roger, non-vintage. As the bubbles effervesced and danced in the crystal flute, I leaned against the counter and tried to get a handle on the situation.

I was beyond shocked that Thomas had left, but more than that, I was floored that he'd stolen the jewelry. What was he going to do with it? He had plenty of money of his own. How could I have misjudged him so totally?

Maybe he didn't steal it. Maybe one of the workmen had while we were adding on the wing. We hadn't done anything lately that required pieces as dressy as these, so I hadn't had any reason even to look in the safe for almost eight weeks. So just because he left me, I told myself, didn't mean he'd stolen from me. And, why did he leave me, anyway? We love each other. I re-read his note: ". . . gone back to the Yard to help work on a case that has resurfaced. I couldn't tell you in person. I don't know when I'll be back. Please don't try to contact me. Forgive me." All right. Maybe it really was a big secret and he really couldn't tell me.

I called his cell phone and left him a message. "Thomas. Call me up."

Well, hell. My stomach growled. It was past one. I stopped to think. What did I used to do when I had no agenda? No husband's plans I had to take into account? What were all those things I used to do that made me so happy? I didn't want to stand around the kitchen and drink champagne all day. That would accomplish nothing, and I didn't especially feel like making the cheese soufflé. I could take the dog for a walk but she'd actually been back and forth to visit Pierre at the far end of the garden a few times and taken herself for as much of a walk as she wanted or required. I could read a book or a magazine. I could do whatever I wanted. Why didn't that make me happier?

I picked up the phone.

"Balfour residence."

"Good afternoon, Carole," I said to Flaminia's housekeeper. "Is Madame Balfour in? It's Kick."

"I'm sorry, Madame Keswick, she's gone to Paris overnight. She'll be back in the morning. Shall I have her call you?"

"Please."

There were a number of other people I could have called and invited to dinner, but actually, the minute I heard Carole's voice, I'd regretted making the call and was relieved that Flaminia wasn't available.

I took my glass of champagne into the garden and put it on the table alongside my now dried-out breakfast and newspaper and went to work on the crossword puzzle.

I've found that sometimes it's just easier, and better, to pretend everything is fine than to deal with it straightaway.

SIX

The day paced itself along as they always do, no matter how quickly or slowly we think they should go, they follow their course. It grew hot, then cloudy, then cooled off.

I took a long afternoon walk through the fields and climbed up to the abandoned ruins of an ancient church and down into the next village for a light late lunch. Before I left home, I quarreled with myself about taking my cell phone along, in case Thomas called.

"To hell with him," I concluded and left the phone at home and took my dog and my book instead.

The restaurant had a lovely view of Les Alpilles and between bites of cassoulet and sips of burgundy, I stared at them as though their chalky outcroppings and cliffs could provide me with some answers. They were ancient, tired mountains. Tired of their burden of stone, sagging beneath the crushing weight, longing to lay down and rest. I knew exactly how they felt. I paid my bill and walked home in the deepening twilight. The mountains and I commiserated with each other until it was black and the stars cooled them off and put them to sleep and I was alone.

Now that it's just me, and night has fallen, I have a lot of time to tell you my story.

I was living proof of a person's ability to change her or himself if the desire was strong enough. If someone who started under such diminished circumstances as I could do it, anyone could. Not to gild the lily, but I was born as the chronically overweight daughter of a chronically alcoholic, Oklahoma-oil-field camp-follower mother. My father was unknown, to both of us. Through sheer determination and a number of breaks, I remade myself into a comfortable, happy, successful, entirely different person. It wasn't luck and it wasn't magic. I made a concerted effort to change until virtually no trace of my roots remained. Well, except one. One that I'd welcome with open arms if the opportunity presented itself: my abandoned child.

I got pregnant when I was fifteen, had the baby in a home for unwed mothers outside of Omaha and never even looked at its face. It's hard to believe, but the truth is, I really have never even known if I had a son or a daughter. But it was the early 1960s and things were so different then when it came to illegitimate children. And now, I'd give just about anything to find out what became of that baby of mine. In spite of registering on all the Internet adoption sites, no one has come forward to claim me.

It was then, when I was fifteen, that I grew up. I was on my own and had nothing to lose. I'd been turned down for a job by Homer Mallory in one of his jewelry stores because—according to him—I was too fat and had no class, so I turned to a life of crime and became a jewel thief. Being young and idealistic, I naturally viewed my forays as crusades, not crimes, on behalf of all overweight girls and all downtrodden people everywhere who were cruelly and insensitively insulted by the ruling class. A version of that ethic followed me throughout my career—I only robbed people who had enormous means yet still felt compelled to lord it over those who had nothing and could not defend themselves.

I started with small, cheap items—lavalieres and flimsy engagement rings made of silver-plated metal, set with diamond chips so tiny you had to squint and use your imagination to see them. I quickly advanced to stealing fine jewelry from fine jewelry stores—specifically Mr. Homer Mallory's fine jewelry stores. I was successful enough to buy myself a little yellow Corvair convertible for my sixteenth birthday. I got the big head, of course. I've never been short on ego, which I prefer to think of as self-confidence, but we all get a little ahead of ourselves sometimes, and so I got caught. After a humiliating handcuffing in front of Homer himself, I ended up in reform school and found myself surrounded by what I considered to be white-trash losers, teenage girls doing time for stealing hair spray or hubcaps and who wanted nothing more from life than to get married and have babies. I had much more in mind for myself—I intended to be someone.

Then one Saturday night, the one night a week when they showed movies at the school, I saw Doris Day in *Pillow Talk,* and it changed my life. She wasn't married, she didn't have any children, she worked hard at a job she was paid handsomely to do, and she wore beautiful clothes and had her own apartment. That was the life for me. But how to get it?

Reform school didn't reform me in the way it was intended to. Instead, for me, it was akin to attending business school. I planned and planned. I spent hours in the school library studying great museums of the world and English manor houses and using my imagination to figure out ways to break into them. I pictured myself as successful. When I walked out the gates of the Oklahoma Detention School for Girls and into Oklahoma State University, thanks to a scholarship for less than fortunate young ladies, I was changed. I had a goal and ambition: I would become the greatest jewel thief in the history of the world.

The break I'd dreamt about came two years later on a junior class trip to Europe. It was one of those mind-numbing, whirlwind bus tours where you get dragged around to twenty cities in thirty days and finally have no idea where you are or where you've been except by looking at the stamps in your passport.

In London, when the bus pulled out for a morning stop at Shakespeare's house in Stratford-on-Avon before heading north to Edinburgh via Stonehenge and Balmoral, I wasn't on it. I was breakfasting on hot buttered crumpets, cherry preserves, and thick hot chocolate at a little café on Carnaby Street, watching the rain pour down and waiting for the shops across the street to open and thinking I was pretty much the smartest bird on the face of the earth.

The Mary Quant cosmetics shop opened first, so I had my

makeup done—I was pretty sure I looked exactly like Twiggy. My false eyelashes were as big and wooly as caterpillars. Then I traded my prim Oklahoma State sorority sister clothes—the Kappas would have had a mass fainting spell if they'd had a clue they'd let a juvenile delinquent, a reform-school girl into their ranks—and all my money for a psychedelic mini-dress and hot pink go-go boots.

"Ooooo, aren't you the looker," the shop girl had said. She had platinum hair, black-rimmed eyes, and platinum lipstick.

Of course, once I was out the door, the stupidity of my actions hit me like a sledgehammer: None of this was me. I wasn't Doris Day. I wasn't Twiggy. I was Kick Keswick from Oklahoma City, Oklahoma, and now all I had was this stupid dress and no money. Even my luggage was on the bus bound for Edinburgh. I wobbled down Carnaby Street, filled with self-recrimination and crying my eyes out in a drenching rain that not only made the dress cling to my delectable well-rounded body like Saran Wrap on a platter of popovers, but also threatened to make my glamorous new eyelashes come unglued.

And then . . . just like in the movies . . . my deus ex machina appeared in a Rolls-Royce Silver Cloud. Sixty-year-old Sir Cramner Ballantine invited me out of the downpour and into his car, exactly the way Cary Grant did when he invited Doris Day into his limousine in *That Touch of Mink*.

"Get in, miss," he'd said. "Get in out of the rain."

This was how my real life began.

Sir Cramner was managing director of Ballantine & Company

Auctioneers, founded by his ancestors in 1740. He gave me a job and set me up in a spacious flat in Eaton Terrace, one of London's most envied addresses. He schooled me in manners and tutored me in discernment, teaching me how, thoughtfully, to seek out, identify, and appreciate fine things. We adored each other, and in spite of his day-to-day obligations to his wife, Lady Ballantine, and his family, we were as inseparable as a man and his mistress can be. He came for dinner at least once a week, sometimes twice. He was the only person I'd ever loved and I loved him until the day he died at age ninety-two, five years ago.

Sir Cramner never would have abandoned me the way Thomas had.

Thomas.

Why did he leave me? I didn't get it. We were having such a good time.

SEVEN

The next morning when I woke up, Pierre had already come and gone—I hadn't heard him but my *pain au chocolate,* baguette, and morning paper were on the counter. I fixed a tray and went outside.

I decided to keep pretending that everything was normal, because basically it was. It was back to the way it'd been for years before Thomas. Everything was familiar.

I blended my café au lait, carefully pouring streams of rich dark coffee and hot milk that met just above the cup and foamed together into the bowl. I spread a bite of baguette with sweet butter and *fraises de bois* preserves, opened the paper, and saw the headline. My heart lurched.

"What?!"

LONDON'S NOTORIOUS SHAMROCK BURGLAR SURFACES IN PARIS.

"What?!"

I read it again. It said what it said the first time: LONDON'S NOTORIOUS SHAMROCK BURGLAR SURFACES IN PARIS.

I could not believe my eyes.

Last night, the cat burglar who operated for years in London's swank Mayfair, Chelsea, and Kensington neighborhoods, stealing hundreds of millions of pounds' worth of jewelry from many of England's most prominent individuals and families, suddenly reappeared in Paris after several months' absence, making off with a necklace said to have belonged to the Empress Josephine. The piece, a collar of large diamonds, emeralds, and sixteen-millimeter Oriental pearl drops, has a 255-carat cabochon emerald pendant, known simply as l'Empresse. The necklace was stolen from the Musée Montpensier, a small private museum, owned by the DeBussy family. The museum, on rue de Montpensier, houses a small, very fine collection of jewels from the Bourbon and Bonaparte dynasties. L'Empresse was considered the centerpiece of the collection.

The article went on to say that the piece had been replaced by the Shamrock Burglar's signature: a small bouquet of fresh shamrocks tied with a gold satin ribbon.

"This is absolutely ridiculous. And they didn't even get it right. It's an *ivory* satin ribbon—not gold."

I started to laugh. "Oh, my God. Wait till Thomas sees this. What am I saying? He's probably already seen it. Oh, my God. I hope he doesn't think *I* did it."

I stopped laughing, and the more I thought about it, the actual gravity of the situation sank in. This was not even slightly funny.

I knew I couldn't do anything about whatever it was Thomas had going on but I could, and must, do something about the impostor. Aside from the more superficial issues of ego and professional prestige—I was, after all, a superstar, a celebrity, practically a household name, and I wouldn't let some second-rate hack besmirch it—there were real issues at stake that could jeopardize my entire world. I couldn't let them go unaddressed. And Thomas, of all the people in the world, knew without a doubt that I had been the Shamrock Burglar. As the big picture became clearer and clearer, I realized I could be in legitimate, serious jeopardy.

I sorted through all the possibilities of who this thief could be and came up empty, unless it was Thomas himself but that was highly unlikely. He would have used the proper color of ribbon.

No one came to mind who could pull off a burglary such as this with any style at all. No one was as good as I was. Any knucklehead could rob a museum, but this was someone special. It took someone with a little panache and sangfroid, a sense of humor if you will, to leave a calling card blaming it so neatly on someone else. Possibly a hotel burglar.

The most skillful "working" thieves are those who specialize in hotel burglaries because they require enormous flexibility, class, and cold-blooded seat-of-your-pants thinking. These robberies are seldom made public—only about twenty percent of the time do they come to light. Usually, the matter is handled privately between the guest and the management—the ladies being as eager to protect their reputations as the hotels, because more often than not, there was some sort of indiscretion involved that would embarrass an important customer. I'd had an opportunity to learn more about hotel robberies than most people. Frequently ladies in distress came to the auction house and discreetly asked that we help them replace certain items that had been stolen while they were on vacation. They didn't want to tell their husbands or their insurance carriers. They simply wanted us to find similar pieces and leave it at that.

There are always a number of these cat burglars lurking around great hotels and expensive resorts, preying on rich, lonely women. They're like lemmings, following the seasons, from the French and Italian Rivieras to Palm Beach and Aspen to the Saratoga races.

Almost always dashing Casanovas posing as aristocrats, these men are charming, good dancers, beautifully mannered, and oh so my-oh-my in bed. And they vanish into the night along with all their mark's prettiest jewels. One of them even takes their bathrobes, which I've always thought was an exquisitely inventive twist, because it forces his victims to get dressed before they raise the alarm. I mean, what woman on earth would invite the night manager and the police into her hotel room wearing only her nightgown? None. At least none over fifty and they're the ones with the best jewelry.

But, actually, it didn't matter who'd stolen the Empresse emerald—I needed to find the person, bring him (or her) to justice, and get my good name out of the papers and off the caper.

And truthfully? If I were into all that Freudian, psychoanalysis business? This was exactly what I needed. It had the brisk, slap-in-your-face effect of whipping my attention off Thomas and giving me something else to think about besides myself and my humiliated heart.

By the time my café au lait was gone, I was completely revitalized.

EIGHT

I returned to the safe in my bathroom and sorted through the various identities I'd created and made a selection: Priscilla Pennington, wealthy widow of an English lord. The fictitious Priscilla lived on a large estate outside of London in Buckinghamshire.

Like me, Priscilla was a woman of a certain age. Elegant, slightly plump, still quite beautiful—easily mistaken for Catherine Deneuve or the late Princess Grace. A little tuck-up work done here and there to keep elements of the neck, chin and eyes gracefully in place.

And the body? Ah, yes, the body. Well, that's what well-tailored clothes and fabulous jewels are for, *n'est-ce pas?*

Shortly after lunch I loaded the few pieces of luggage that would fit into the tiny trunk of my brand-new, black Jaguar XK convertible, tied an Hermès scarf over my head, put on my dark glasses, settled the dog and a handful of her toys in the passenger seat, and hit the road for Paris.

There wasn't much traffic, and while the kilometers whizzed past, I thought about Sir Cramner and the twists and turns my life had taken since that day on Carnaby Street over thirty years ago. And now, just when I thought everything was settled and fine, a big change loomed. Where would it lead?

When I was still a fairly young woman, about twenty-eight or so—I'd been at Ballantine & Company for about ten years—Sir Cramner had come out of his office one afternoon and stopped in front of my desk. He was an imposing man, robust and mustachioed. Always impeccably dressed in a Gieves & Hawkes three-piece suit, a watch fob looped through his vest.

"We've had such a good month, Kick, and Lady Ballantine has gone to Scotland to visit her mother. I think it's time for us to take a little pink champagne holiday." That's what he called our occasional breaks at Claridge's where we'd call room service nonstop for a day or two, "pink champagne holidays."

"Really?" I answered.

"Yes, but I mean a real holiday, a weekend on the French Riviera."

"You don't mean it, sir." We'd never been outside the city limits of London together. In fact, outside of the office, we'd never even been seen in public together. Sir Cramner loved me, but not so much that he would risk a scandal. With the exception of our Claridge's sprees, all our time was spent at my flat on Eaton Terrace, quietly enjoying each other's company.

"I do mean it. We leave tomorrow morning. I've got the tickets. I'll come for you at eight o'clock."

We flew to Marseilles on a BOAC BAC-111—it was my first

ride in an airplane and holding hands in public with Sir Cramner and the in-flight Dom Pérignon calmed any butterflies I
had. A car took us to the Hôtel du Cap in Cap d'Antibes where
we checked into a vast suite that overlooked the gardens and
sparkling bay.

I'll never forget how thrilled I was to be out in the open with
him—even if it was early spring and the glamorous Côte
d'Azur season was weeks away and the hotel's famous gardens
had not yet reached their full bloom. We would be able to walk
on the rocky "plage" and stick our toes in the cold water and
have lunch and visit art galleries and go shopping and dress for
dinner and dance in the moonlight on the terrace over the
Mediterranean. We might even meet other couples. We might
make some friends that would be *our* friends. Our first friends.

I had no expectation that Sir Cramner would divorce his
wife and marry me. He wouldn't. I had accepted that I would
live in the demimonde and I didn't mind, especially now that
the conditions were so very comfortable. But there we were: together in public on the French Riviera. It was as though I were
in a fairy tale. More than I had ever hoped to dream.

"You know what you mean to me, Kick." He cleared his
throat and I suspected he was struggling to control his words,
that what he really wanted to say was, *You know how much I love
and adore you, Kick*. But between the two of us, propriety always ruled, the real words had yet to be spoken. We were
standing on the terrace of our suite where the sun made everything white and blinding and made the sea and boats glitter
like diamonds. "Well, I thought you might like to have this."

He handed me a black velvet box. I opened it. Inside lay a brilliant-cut, white diamond suspended from a thin platinum chain.

"Cramner," I said. "It's magnificent."

"It's the Pasha of St. Petersburg. Thirty-five carats." He removed the necklace from its case and clasped it around my neck. "It came into the house for sale and I grabbed it before you had a chance to see it. You are my good luck charm, Kick, my life preserver. I wish there could be more for us."

"You have made my life more than I ever imagined possible," I told him.

As it turned out, we never, through thirty years together, until the very end, seemed able to say *I love you* to each other. But we meant to. It was implicit. Sir Cramner couldn't say it because he was a Victorian gentleman and they did not go for such admissions of weakness, and as I've already mentioned, he would never risk a scandal. And I couldn't say it because I didn't know what love was. Love, to me at that time, was anonymity, privacy and a meal ticket, and I would do anything to get and keep them. Anything. There was little honesty or honor in my motives. But I loved him as best I could. As the years passed, and I became more financially and personally secure, I believe I came to love him properly.

Since the moment he placed the Pasha around my neck, I have never taken it off. It is permanently nestled among my bosom and feeling the diamond against my skin or grasping it in my fist has kept me grounded on more than one occasion.

"I'm going down to change some money," he said. "Meet me in the bar once you're settled and we'll have lunch."

It's hard to describe how excited I was. I lived a completely cloistered life between home, business and my time with Sir Cramner. My only hobby was stealing a piece of jewelry from the auction house every now and then, making a perfect replica of it in my workroom at home, and watching it go up for auction and sell, undetected, while the original stones and smelted precious metal ingots ended up in my vault in Switzerland. I never looked at other men, although many of them looked at me. I had no practical experience with men anyway. Amazing as it seems, when it came to sex, I had gone from the bench seat of a pickup truck in an Oklahoma oil field to a downy bed in a suite at Claridge's with no experiential stops in between. But the fact was: I didn't need anyone else. I was committed to self-preservation and everyone with half a brain knows that if you want to be in control of your life and protect yourself, the first cardinal rule is, you don't fall in love. At least that's what I thought, until I met Thomas. And frankly, now, as I sped along the A-8 to Paris, I wasn't exactly sure what I thought anymore.

I dressed carefully that day at the Hôtel du Cap. No more colored mascara, minidresses, pink go-go boots, and ratted hair for me. I now wore expensive silk and lace lingerie, designer suits and shoes, and lovely, appropriate jewelry. My blond hair was smoothed into a sleek twist and my makeup was understated and professional. I put on a taupe shantung suit with white piping, cap-toed Chanel sling-back pumps, pearl earrings, and a jagged torsade of uncut and unpolished amber. Brimming with happiness, I went down to the breezy lobby and into the bar.

I saw him immediately. He was sitting with another couple on the terrace. My natural reticence and instincts told me not to join them. I took a small table indoors and ordered a *coupe de champagne*. Shortly he came in.

"This is a disaster," he said. "It's Lady Ballantine's sister and her husband, Lord and Lady Farmington. I'm simply astounded they are here. No one's here this time of year."

"Oh, dear."

"I'm sorry to leave you by yourself for lunch, Kick, but I don't see any immediate solution."

"I'll be fine. I'll see you after lunch. We'll go for a walk." I swallowed my disappointment.

"Don't worry. I'll get rid of them."

Well, after lunch it wasn't any better. They were there for the same amount of time we were—resting up in preparation for the gala summer season ahead—and, since he was alone, they asked him to join them for dinner.

As I've mentioned before, I knew Sir Cramner loved me but would never risk or tolerate a scandal over me. And also, as I've mentioned, up until that time, my only forays into theft—since my release from reform school—had been strictly in-house affairs. But now, I was hurt, and resentful, and I wanted to get even. Not with Sir Cramner. As far as I was concerned, he was as much a victim of his sister-in-law's overbearing hospitality as I was. No. I wanted to get even with Lady Farmington and her sister, Lady Ballantine, for stealing my holiday.

Once Sir Cramner left for dinner—he looked so distinguished in his evening clothes—I broke into a supply closet using my lock-picking sticks and helped myself to a maid's uniform. Then, dressed as help, I broke into Lady Farmington's suite and stole all her jewelry, which was quite good for a stuffy Englishwoman—lovely old art deco family pieces with some excellent stones, mostly diamonds, sapphires, and emeralds. It was silly how easy it was, if one were prepared, which I always was. (Since I turned sixteen, I've always carried a set of lock-picking tools in my purse, along with a jeweler's loupe and jeweler's needle-nose pliers.) By the time Sir Cramner got back that night, the pieces no longer existed. I'd buried the stones deep in my cold cream jar and tossed the settings into the ocean.

The next day, while he was boating with his brother-in-law, I rented a car and drove to St. Rémy and put a down payment on my jewel box of a farm, La Petite Pomme. The minute I saw it, I knew it was home. My secret home.

Sir Cramner and I flew back to London that night, three days early, and never really left town again.

A week later, he presented me with a Van Gogh of a sunflower field in Provence as a consolation. He had no idea how providential the painting was—he never knew about my little farm—and how years later, the painting would lead Thomas to me.

NINE

It was dark by the time I reached Paris.

"*Bonsoir, madame, bienvenue à l'Hôtel Ritz.*" The doorman opened my car door and helped me out.

"Thank you." I was stiff from the drive and stretched my arms over my head.

"Have you driven far?"

"London."

"Oh, my. How lucky you are in this beautiful car."

I smiled at him and tucked Bijou under my arm. "Take good care of it."

"*Bien sûr.*"

"Welcome, Madame Pennington," the young woman at the registration counter said. "Your suite is ready."

I followed her into a tiny elevator directly across from her desk, up to the second floor, and down the quiet corridor to a set of double doors. My suite was blue and green satin damask, with the down cushions on the chairs and sofa plumped into giant marshmallows. A tall crystal vase of pink roses sat on the coffee table and filled the room with their sweet, subtle fragrance. Two sets of double doors opened onto the garden courtyard three floors below, where the cocktail hour was well underway. The sedate popping of corks, tinkling of ice cubes on crystal, and muffled rattle of plates and cutlery drifted up. I knew the garden was full of bankers, businessmen, international tycoons, and famous models, all making deals, arranging assignations, admiring each other, and furtively looking to see who else was there and who was admiring them.

I unpacked, fed Bijou, arranged all my cosmetics and toiletries—which are significant in number—along the glass bathroom shelf (I always put the ones that aren't in pretty bottles inside the cabinet), and then submerged myself in a steaming hot rose-scented bubble bath in a tub that was as big and deep as a swimming pool. I closed my eyes. I thought about Pamela Harriman. She'd been very, very savvy about men and on top of that, she'd had the sublime style and wit to die right here in this hotel, right downstairs in the swimming pool doing laps. What a woman. She'd never been caught with her mouth hanging open by one of her husbands leaving her. She spotted trouble coming and left them first.

What kind of a husband steals his wife's *jewelry*? Have you ever heard of anything so low?

The bath soaked the long drive out of me, and in spite of the fact that I was in Paris on business, not here to enjoy myself, I still had to eat.

I dressed inconspicuously in a black suit and pearls and went down to the bar where I was seated by the door to the garden, perfect for watching people watching themselves.

"Madame?" The waiter placed a starched linen cocktail napkin and small dishes of olives and almonds on my table.

"Chopin vodka, straight up, please. Very cold. Two twists."

"*Bien.*" He made a quick bow.

I always carry a novel with me in my purse—tonight it was a wonderful, ripping adventure about African diamond mining—and once he was gone, I quickly lost myself in the story. I'd only had a couple of sips of my vodka when the temperature in the bar suddenly changed, fizzed up, as though a electrical current had buzzed through and set everyone's skin aglow. The waiters seemed to move more smoothly and the customers seemed to sit up a little straighter. Then, like Cleopatra on a barge, or Elizabeth the First on a progress, she sailed grandly through the door from the lobby, leading her entourage. Marjorie Mead. The movie star. Even I recognized her and I seldom go to the movies. Never, actually.

She was more magnificent in person than in her pictures, which I'd often seen on magazine covers. Maybe five-seven or -eight, glossy black hair cropped straight at her jawline and eyes the color of Burmese sapphires. Her skin was creamy and pink and her full lips shone with red gloss. Marjorie was in her mid thirties and had a filled-in woman's body that she made no effort to conceal. She wore a flippy black chiffon cocktail dress and high-heeled black satin Manolo sandals, a serious diamond necklace encrusted with good-sized stones and matching earrings. A black fox stole hung jauntily over one shoulder. Marjorie was a movie star in the old tradition. She was combustible and it was fun to watch her move through to the garden. She knew she was causing a sensation, even in a bar as jaded as the Ritz's Vendôme—she loved it, and we loved it. And then she was gone. Seated outdoors behind a screen of palms.

After a while, I finished my drink and signed my check. Bijou and I walked through the Jardin des Tuileries and across the river to one of my favorite restaurants, Voltaire, where monsieur took me into the cozy, paneled back room to a corner table and served me a fine dinner of sliced grapefruit and avocado, sautéed scallops, duchesse potatoes, and gratinéed tomatoes, a little cheese plate, and a half bottle of Chevalier Montrachet that was so lovely I was sorry I hadn't ordered a full bottle. The service was formal and unobtrusive and gave me the uninterrupted time to formulate a number of strategies and scenarios for how I could reclaim the Empresse emerald. Of course, the constant fly-in-the-ointment, the brick wall each idea kept running into, was that they all hinged on my ability to identify the burglar. That was the issue and it was a big one. On the positive side, though, the robbery was only slightly more than twenty-four hours old, so things were just starting to shake out. The best possible scenario was that I would go to the museum, spot the thief, follow him or her to his lair, and while he was out, simply reclaim the necklace and leave it at a police station or bank—someplace safe—make an anonymous call about its location, and that would be that. That would be the simplest way, fully recognizing, of course, I had virtually no control over the situation.

Thomas—an inveterate intellectual snob, which was one of the reasons I loved him—claimed that most criminals did not have the intelligence to think their crimes through, or get the global view of their actions, and so ultimately were unable to keep themselves away from the scenes of their crimes. Which I feel obligated to point out was one reason I'd been so successful: I never looked back and except for that one exceptional bracelet—the Queen's Pet, which was so extraordinary it would have been a crime to take it apart—I never held on to my loot. I broke it all down immediately, melting the metal, and selling or banking the stones. But as Thomas had also pointed out: There was no one else like me. But that's neither here nor there, is it.

The point is, I was banking on the fact that he was right, that this new incarnation of Shamrock Burglar was of the common variety and would be unable to resist admiring his achievement and people's reactions to it. In which instance, I would apprehend the person and solve the case. After all, even though it had only been for six months, I'd been married to one of Scotland Yard's most famous detectives and I'd picked up a few pointers along the way. It wasn't going to be that hard.

The waiter brought a plate of tiny, chewy macaroons with my check. Oh, my God. The macaroons alone made the trip worth it. Thomas would love . . . no. I wasn't going to think about what Thomas would or would not love. Thomas was gone.

I would take it from here.

TEN

It rained hard during the night and I slept in. When I woke up at nine-thirty and opened my windows the air was beautiful and clean.

"*Bonjour,* Madame Pennington," the room-service waiter said, handing me the morning paper. "*Votre petit déjeuner.*" He rolled in a table covered by a shell-pink Portault linen cloth with a bouquet of white roses in the center. The table was laden with silver pots and domes, a pink and white Limoges morning breakfast cup as large as a cereal bowl, a carafe of freshly squeezed grapefruit juice buried in a bowl of chipped ice, an empty glass, and a pink napkin as big as an Hermès scarf. So much to-do over a glass of juice, café au lait and toast.

There was only a small follow-up article in the morning paper about the burglary from the Musée Montpensier, stating that the police had a number of leads they were following up, which I assumed meant they had no clue.

I took my time. I'd decided not to get to the museum until after lunch because if security was tight, I wouldn't be able to go and spend the whole day without raising some sort of suspicion and drawing attention to myself, which was the last thing I wanted to do. So, after a leisurely breakfast, I bathed and dressed for the afternoon—lacy lingerie, a peridot Chanel suit with sugary silver-pink braid, several strings of pearls, two old-fashioned jangly charm bracelets, and comfortable pumps, good for walking. Bijou and I left for a brisk constitutional through the Jardin des Tuileries in the sparkling noonday sun.

There is nothing on the earth like springtime in Paris. Nothing. It is heartbreakingly beautiful. If you're a romantic or a sentimentalist, or if your heart isn't broken already, it will be by the beauty of Paris. Paris can fill you with such a powerful longing for love, that if you aren't careful, it will knock you to your knees. It was that kind of day.

I felt no such longing. I'd been down the love road and it was over, thank you very much. I didn't need it. I had experience. Maturity. And my dog. I was relaxed and happy. Really, I was. What was done, was done. I'd take care of my business, clear my name, and move back to my comfortable life on the farm. A life—I reminded myself again—that had been as comfortable without Thomas as with him.

Flowers were everywhere. Everywhere. The rain had washed the city and left everything shining and glistening. As we circled the garden, the ornate gold trim on the Pont Royale glinted in the sunlight and children bounced on the teeter-totters and swung on the swings. I circled the garden twice, ending up at the Place du Carrousel, where I passed through the arched gateway beneath the Louvre out to the Rue de Rivoli.

Rue de Rivoli boasts a unique and disconcerting combination of elements. Great hotels such as the Meurice and the Inter-Continental, exclusive boutiques, unfriendly and dirty little cafés, and lots of junky shops filled with overpriced tourist-related paraphernalia, all the latest things. Today, the sidewalk stands and racks were full of copies of the purloined emerald necklace, Josephine's l'Empresse, in all its possible incarnations: key rings, earrings, full-sized copies, dog collars, and leashes. I couldn't resist. I bought one for Bijou. The diamonds, emeralds, pearls, and giant emerald pendant looked precious on her snow white fur. We all oohed and ahhed over how cute she looked. Frankly, I don't think she was too crazy about the 255-carat fake cabochon pendant that was as large as a good-sized hen's egg and banged her little knees, but she was a good sport about it.

We strolled through Place André Malraux, with its famous splashing dolphin fountains. Theatre patrons milled about, enjoying the sunny intermission of the matinee at the Comédie Française, home of France's classics, mostly Molière. The marquee said *Le Bourgeois Gentilhomme*. It was always either that or *Cyrano de Bergerac*. On the far side of the square, I cut over to Rue de Montpensier, address of the Musée Montpensier.

The museum occupied a classic old palace, its limestone walls and black balustrades in dire need of cleaning and fresh paint. The entrance was an arched carriage gate in an ornate, overly wrought wrought-iron fence that ran along the street. It didn't take a genius to figure out that the robbery was probably the best thing that had ever happened to this obscure little private niche institution. I imagined they'd scarcely had more than fifty visitors a month before the Shamrock Burglar's attack. But this afternoon, a line of people, waiting their turn to see the empty display where l'Empresse had once reigned, snaked back and forth, filling the good-sized, cobblestone courtyard. The atmosphere was that of a cocktail party.

I waited for over an hour before paying my fifteen-euro admission. According to the guidebook at the hotel, it was five euros, but it had tripled overnight. I purchased a small brochure about the collection and filed into the grubby establishment.

Paris, arguably the most beautiful, stylish city in the world, has dozens of private museums celebrating practically every aspect of civilization, from fashion to horses to public health. However, France, being a primarily socialist country, has little cash left over for restoration of its minor public institutions— and the private ones are completely on their own. Philanthropic practices—the solicitation of large and small-scale funds from corporations, individuals, and foundations for restoration, renovation, new construction, acquisition, endowment, and so forth of both private and public institutions—as they exist uniquely in the United States, and now fledglingly in England, are unknown. And with the exception of major institutions with thriving gift-shop operations such as the British Museum, the V & A, the Metropolitan, the Vatican, and the Louvre, to name a few, museums are not moneymakers. Like all the arts, they're typically money-losing propositions. There is no way the admission fees can support operations, much less new acquisitions. If there is not a deep-pocketed patron or two committed to upkeep and maintenance, things fall apart. And I'm speaking just of the building and infrastructure. The collection is an entirely other matter requiring lots of expertise, lots of passion, and lots and lots of cash. Often a museum has been the vision of one person and unless the vision is kept vital, it languishes, wilts, and eventually dies due to lack of interest.

Judging by the condition of the physical plant of the Musée Montpensier, I'd say, prior to the burglary, last rites had been administered and the actual dying breath was imminent. The place was falling apart. The obvious question was: Had a member or associate of the DeBussy family that owned the museum staged the robbery? I know I'm not a detective, but that would certainly be the first place I'd look, and it was a cunning way to get publicity. But not on my hard-earned impeccable reputation, thank you very much.

I decided to keep my mind open but as the line passed the weeping owner, Madame DeBussy—a bedraggled sixtyish Parisienne who must have flunked out of crying class at the Comédie Française Academy because she couldn't resist peeking through her fingers to see if the line was still growing—I saw that she looked the type: canny and shrewd. She grudgingly accepted condolences from sympathetic visitors but became obsequious over their small offers of extra cash. According to a hastily handwritten sign, for an extra fifty euros, she would lead a visitor on a private tour and share unpublicized tidbits about her personal experience of being the one to discover they'd been robbed—not only of their greatest treasure, but also a crucial element in chronicling the entire history of the Empire. The legacy that generations of her family had selflessly worked to protect and preserve was gone. The sign had an annoying, whining sound to it.

The line then passed through the gift shop that offered dusty trinkets and postcards, T-shirts with pictures of a shocked-looking Josephine and the words "I've been robbed!" in several languages, and its own version of the missing necklace. I was pleased to see my copy was better.

Bijou, who was short on patience, put one of her paws on the back of a man's leg and barked. "Oh, excuse me." I yanked on her leash.

He turned. Oh, my God, he was so good-looking, I almost gasped.

He stooped down. "What a precious little dog."

He looked and sounded exactly like Cary Grant.

ELEVEN

I picked her up. "Bijou, you come here. I'm so sorry—she has no manners."

"Bijou? What an apropos name—she's already wearing the latest collar." He turned to one of his friends. "Look at this dog, with the collar!"

I laughed. "Isn't it silly? I couldn't resist."

"She's precious," said one of the ladies. And then that entire group of friends, all well dressed and happily tipsy from lunch, circled round and made a big fuss over Bijou, which she loved.

I recognized one of the women—she looked familiar, not like someone I knew but someone whose picture I'd seen—but I couldn't place her. American. Petite with lots of blond hair, a well-tucked-up face, and a couturier suit, one of those little jeweled butterfly pins—a mêlée of stones and colors—on her shoulder. I realized it was the Texas billionairess, Sissy McNally, and for a moment I was alarmed, afraid she'd recognize me, too. She'd been the houseguest of a wealthy French couple with a country house near Aix and had attended the charity picnic at my farm. But it had been such a crowded, busy occasion, we hadn't even met, and frankly, I imagined she went to two or three parties every day and seldom had a clue whose house she was in. It was the way that jet-setting world worked . . . floating from luncheon to tea to dinner, from one change of costume to another. Her eyes took mine in briefly and moved back to her friend. Not surprisingly, there was no hint of recognition in them.

Finally, the line moved forward and entered a vaulted rotunda, the former main salon of the house, where the Empresse had been on display on a pedestal in the center of the room. The air was close and hot, humid from the rain. The windows were filthy, the walls and doorjambs black with smeared fingerprints.

On the slim chance that I was wrong and it was *not* an inside job—I scanned the crowd for possible suspects. One element that made this robbery unusual was that it exhibited the characteristics of trophy-hunting. No one in his right mind would melt down a piece of the importance of l'Empresse. This thief was a daredevil and a show-off. A hotel-type robber, someone smooth and sophisticated. Good-looking and charming.

I spotted one possibility on the opposite side of the room. A lanky, Latin-looking, sexy man—a slightly older version of Antonio Banderas. Sleek and taut, immaculately dressed and groomed, dark mustache, easy smile, good teeth, intelligent eyes. He was with a woman somewhat older than he who had on a few especially staggering pieces of jewelry, particularly for the afternoon. He whispered to her from behind his hand, making her titter. She swatted at him with her rolled-up guidebook.

I kept looking. Nobody else—male or female—was well groomed or well dressed enough. Except Cary Grant, of course, and his gaggle of tipsy ladies. Successful jewel thieves, at least those who rob significant pieces from people's homes or hotel rooms, are a first-class-looking bunch. We have to be. We have to fit easily into our surroundings, which are by definition first-class, and we're precise about everything. If you were to put an accomplished cat burglar in a bum's clothes, his posture, his stance, haircut, manicure and just the way the clothes hung on him would be a dead giveaway. It would be like putting a quarterback in a tutu. We can't help it—we're insiders. Culture and refinement are our stock-in-trade.

Antonio Banderas put the woman's arm through his and patted her hand. I watched them go outside and circle the sculpture garden and leave.

A large sign, in French, English, German, Japanese, Chinese, and Arabic sat on an easel at the entrance:

Exactly *as things appeared when the museum was opened on Tuesday morning and the audacious affront was discovered by Mme. DeBussy, herself. Shame, shame on you, Shamrock Burglar.*

Which sounded much more expectorating in French: *"Fi donc! Fi donc à vous, Voleur de Trèfle."*

I could almost see the Gallic lips curling, spitting out the words, and then feel their Parisian disdain burn my neck. I could also almost see Mme. DeBussy sitting at her kitchen table, cigarette smoke curling into her eyes, cat sitting on the table watching her, getting herself all worked up with phony indignation, licking her pencil stub, and composing the scathing indictment.

A very poor replica of the necklace now sat on the pedestal on a smooth black velvet-covered bust of neck, shoulders, and upper chest, similar to a jeweler's display. The concentrated spotlights that must have set the real emeralds and diamonds on fire only served to intensify the deadness of these fakes. At the base of the bust was a mockup—"*Exactément* as it was found!" announced the sign. A stiff invitation-sized ecru card, with my alleged handwriting on it, and a small bouquet of wilted shamrocks tied with the golden ribbon completed the picture.

The display had two glaring, telltale errors that only the real Shamrock Burglar—the Voleur de Trèfle—and the London police would know and keep to themselves: I never left an actual calling card, per se, feeling that the bouquet was keepsake enough, and as I've mentioned before, the ribbon was all wrong.

But it didn't matter. Even if the police knew it was a fake, which the most rudimentary amount of police work would have revealed to be the case—all it would have taken was one phone call to London, to New Scotland Yard where possibly my estranged husband himself would answer the phone. But now, even if they said it wasn't the real Shamrock Burglar, no one would believe them.

One last item: The Shamrock Burglar replaced stolen pieces with replicas that were indistinguishable from the originals. My replicas, which I crafted myself in my workroom, were of such high quality, only the most experienced eye could tell they were fake. The Shamrock Burglar stood for quality. I would never, ever leave behind a hunk of junk like the one in this second-rate display.

I was starting to loathe Madame DeBussy.

I leaned toward the necklace and squinted like everyone else, and then moved away. I pulled the brochure out of my pocket and pretended to study it while I examined the room itself.

There were five tall archways, approximately fifteen feet high, surrounding the rotunda: the one by which we'd entered. To its left, one led to the garden; another to a gallery and the other exhibits; one was roped off with an ACCÉS INTERDIT, DO NOT ENTER sign blocking a stairway; and finally one as the exit through what might originally have been a music room. Antiquated video cameras were pointed at the various doorways, and I wondered where the security room was and who monitored the screens. Or even if there were screens at the ends of the cameras. This didn't look to me like an institution that could afford a high-tech security system and if it did have one, why hadn't we been shown the robbery in progress on television news? I was certain they had no real video surveillance but instead counted on the observation talents of one or two daytime guards and a nighttime retiree who played pinochle against himself and drank. I strolled from camera to camera, studying them boldly from all angles. There were no wires attached to them.

There were five ways into this room, and I supposed there were ten times that many ways in and out of the building itself. Based on what I'd seen of the security, no fancy planning or heroic acts would be required to rob the place. Frankly, if I were going to do it, I'd just use the front door.

"Have you been to this museum before?" It was Cary Grant. He had the most elegant international accent—possibly Italian but with a little Hungarian or something mixed in. His black hair had lots of silver and was perfectly barbered. His charcoal suit was elegantly cut and his silvery blue tie matched his silvery hair and his silvery blue eyes. He was just plain gorgeous.

I shook my head. "No."

"I haven't either. To tell you the truth, I'd never heard of it until lunch today—we were just down the street at Le Grand Véfour—and the ladies wanted to come look. The rest of the collection is through there but there isn't much to look at."

"Really." I returned to my pamphlet in the same sort of dismissive way that one does when the passenger seated next to you on the plane wants to talk about your trip, their trip, your life, their life.

"I wonder how he did it. The museum looks very secure to me—all these cameras and bars on the doors." He indicated with his hands.

"I haven't the faintest idea," I said. The barred gates at the doors were a joke. Their binding cement was so old it could be chipped away with a mascara wand. But naturally I didn't point that out.

"You look so familiar to me. Are you certain we haven't met before?"

"Quite certain. Have a nice afternoon." I smiled, picked up my dog, and walked away.

Just because my husband had deserted me didn't mean I was desperate for attention. Besides, I'd never let myself get picked up before and there was no way I was going to start now, especially by some gigolo in a broken-down French museum—no matter how good-looking he was.

I wandered around for another hour, pretending to admire the so-so collection. Many of the pieces were actually very good replicas and I assumed that if the DeBussys had actually ever possessed the real things, they'd sold them long ago to keep the lights on. I studied entrances, exits, security, and patterns. I stayed until closing and saw a handful of other possible perpetrators I would keep an eye on over the next couple of days, but I was fairly certain I would be wasting my time.

TWELVE

Bijou and I dined that evening at a table for two in the hotel garden, a perfect dinner that started with a Chopin martini and ended with a luscious crème brûlée. The entire time, a small voice kept asking me exactly what I intended to do, but the fact was, I didn't know. I needed something more to go on—a further indication. Assuming it was an actual robbery, had it been a one-time thing? A prank? Or had there been other, similar incidents and this was the first time it had been made public? At the moment, there was nothing I could do but wait. If this was a real pro, he would strike again.

I slept like a baby, and when I got to the lobby on my way to La Durée for a little pastry and pot of hot chocolate to start my day, the blue-suited employees at the registration desk and cashier's window, always the epitome of discretion and courtesy, seemed slightly preoccupied, distracted. And more of the hotel's vigilant, low-key security detail, which was the size of a small private army, was evident. Even in the most normal times, there were more guards than guests, and this morning, they outnumbered us two to one.

I went to the cashier's window to get some change. "What's going on?" I asked the young woman.

"Going on, madame?"

"All the security." I handed her a stack of euros.

"Our security is always very tight, madame."

"I know, but I can tell something has happened. I didn't watch the news this morning. Has something happened in the world? Are we at war? Please tell me there haven't been any terrorist attacks in Paris."

"*Non. Non.* Nothing so serious as that, madame." She leaned toward me. "Le Voleur de Trèfle," she whispered. "One of our guests was robbed."

I forced my expression to remain fixed. "Pardon?"

The young woman nodded slightly as she placed my large bills alongside the drawer and withdrew my change. "*C'est vrai.* She put all her jewelry on her bed table and when she woke up this morning, it was gone, replaced by the note and the little bouquet of *trèfles.*"

"You're joking, of course," I said. My face remained composed, although I believe my eyes may have widened a little bit and my voice sounded normal. But inside? My heart fluttered and my knees went slightly weak. I was astonished. I tried not to gape at her.

"No, madame. This is no joke. She should have deposited her jewels down here in the safe because there's nothing we can do to help her replace them and I don't suppose her insurance will cover them since she took no step to protect them. However, they were exceptionally fine pieces, easily identifiable, so perhaps she'll get them back."

"Really," I said, still trying to take it all in. "What were they like?"

"Very unusual—they were white tigers."

"White tigers?"

The woman nodded. "I saw them. She showed them to me last evening when she came to cash a check before she went out. They were magnificent. A brooch, earrings, a necklace and two bracelets, oh, and a ring—all solid diamonds with onyx for the tiger stripes. They were very dramatic. The tigers were big."

I knew the White Tiger Suite well. Cartier had made the pieces especially for an American collector, and when she decided to sell them, we did everything we could to try to attract her to Ballantine & Company. She went to Sotheby's in the end. Her entire collection had been astounding, and the white tigers were the stars. The suite went for a disappointing million dollars—I know they'd been anticipating at least twice that amount. The hotel cashier was right: The tigers were big, three-dimensional, with pear-shaped emerald eyes. The brooch and the bracelet were particularly attention-getting. The brooch was a perfectly formed, five-inch-long tiger in a walking stance, and the slightly smaller version on the bracelet was draped across the wrist as though he'd been commanded to lie down but was ready to leap. Another thing I remembered about the suite were the tigers' faces: They were beautiful. Sweet and inquisitive, begging to be understood. They were eerie.

This was no ordinary heist. It had obviously been planned for some time, and there was no question that the pieces had been taken as trophies. From a jewel thief's point of view, the whole point of stealing jewelry was to take the most versatile, marketable piece possible, break it down, sell the stones, and melt the metal, rendering the lucre unidentifiable and easily concealed. That's how jewel thieves make their living. Steal the stones, sell the stones. Not by stealing one-of-a-kind Cartier pieces that had no particularly important or large gems but were certifiable works of art with impeccable provenances. These had little breakdown value, they were all pavé. Excellent quality to be sure, but pavé nevertheless.

Well, I'll say one thing for whoever this was: He or she had excellent taste, which I was grateful for because I'd hate to have my name associated with anything second-rate.

I don't mean to be a snob, but I was so, so grateful my impersonator wasn't Madame DeBussy. But more than that, I was alarmed and angry. This person was obviously having fun, playing a game, at my expense. With Thomas out there, gone straight, I was the one who would take the fall. I realized I needed to distance myself from the scene as quickly as possible. My mouth had gone dry. I took a breath and licked my lips.

"Goodness," I said. "*Quelle dommage.*"

"*Oui.*" The cashier snapped my crisp new bills into the shape of a fan across the marble counter. "Is there anything else I can do for you, Madame Pennington?"

I paused. "You know," I said casually. "I'm going to do some shopping and then have lunch at the Pompidou before I head back to London. Now that I think about it, I think it will be easier if I go ahead and check out now and take my car."

"As you wish."

THIRTEEN

I said I needed a little something more to go on—but this was much more than I'd bargained for. My mind raced as I drove into the cavernous, anonymous, underground parking garage at the Louvre. This was a serious mess. One robbery by the Shamrock Burglar was one thing and I could prove I'd been at home. But two were inexplicable, and for me, indefensible. I was in the center of the crime. The Ritz kept every square inch of its common areas on film. I didn't know about its upstairs corridors, but if they did make tapes of upstairs traffic, then based on what the thief looked like and his size, I might be able to prove I hadn't stolen the White Tiger Suite. But this person was bold and talented, and whether or not there was a video of him advancing to the doors and breaking in, he would have been camouflaged. Thomas, if I ever heard from him again, would never believe it wasn't me. Worse yet, by now he probably had alerted the French Securité, told them of my identity and whereabouts in Provence.

All my old reflexes began to click smoothly into place, firing off each other like falling dominoes. I grew calm. My life had suddenly changed—but I had more lives and options than anyone could ever imagine.

For starters, I had to get out of Paris. Although I hadn't been registered under my own name at the hotel, it wouldn't take a genius to track down a middle-aged woman in a black Jaguar XK with a little white dog. But now, my future depended on finding my attacker and I would approach it the way I did everything: professionally. This was not a game. Before I left the city, I needed to visit the museum one more time to see if any of yesterday's suspects reappeared. I wasn't concerned about being recognized as a too-frequent, too-curious visitor, or being caught on film by the nonexistent security.

"Antonio Banderas" wasn't there. And neither were "Cary Grant" nor Sissy McNally. Neither, for that matter, was anyone who could have filled the bill, in my opinion.

By eleven-thirty, I'd spent all the time I felt I could. I'd skipped breakfast and I knew if I didn't eat a little something, a little hot chocolate, a little cake or cookie, something, before I started the long drive home, I'd never make it.

I picked up a copy of *Été* magazine from a sidewalk stand, walked up to the Faubourg St. Honoré, and into Jean-Paul Hévin's little treasure of a shop. Hévin is simply the finest chocolatier in the world and I knew he'd have just the right thing for me to eat while I figured out what the hell I was going to do next. I went upstairs to the tearoom. It was just starting to fill up with others who felt hot chocolate and dark chocolate truffles comprised a valid meal.

"Madame?" the waitress asked.

"Un pot de chocolat, s'il vous plaît."

"Oui. Et?"

I had to decide. It was excruciating. "Two truffles please: Amaretto and Grand Marnier."

I settled into my table, trading my dark glasses for readers, and pulled the magazine out of my bag.

The actress, Marjorie Mead, was on the cover of *Été*. She was the guest of honor at this year's Gala di Portofino, a glitzy, jet-set, celebrity-heavy fund-raiser for refugee charities. The gala was always held at Villa Giolitti, ancestral home of Count Giancarlo Giolitti's family since the 1200s and reliquary of the Giolitti collection, one of the finest private art collections in the world.

The article went on to say that DeBeers LV was underwriting the gala and not only would Marjorie Mead be there with many other luminaries, but so would the DeBeers Millennium Star, the largest perfect diamond in the world—203 carats of sheer perfection, to be exact. When it came to trophies, this one would head anyone's list. I'd had the pleasure of seeing it at the Millennium Dome in London before all the major stones at the show had had to be replaced with fakes in order to foil a grand-scale grand robbery attempt. The burglars should have checked with their children—a five-year-old could have told them their harebrained scheme would never work.

Their plan was that in the morning just before the Dome opened to the public for its daily business, they would crash a bulldozer through the wall and drive straight to the jewelry vault where the employees would just be bringing out the Millennium

Star and a collection of twelve very rare blue diamonds to be displayed for the day. They would grab the gems, race to the river's edge, and jump into a waiting speedboat that was equipped with a mounted submachine gun, and make their escape.

There were a number of serious problems with this plan: First of all, when two or more people are in on a secret, it isn't a secret anymore. There were five or six people in on this one, and as a result, somebody told somebody who told somebody who told the police. By the time they made their daring and spectacular smash through the wall of the Millennium Dome and roared to the vault, virtually every single employee in the building—janitors to ticket-takers to precious stones display attendants—was an undercover police officer. All the real diamonds had been replaced by undetectable fakes—synthetic replicas—weeks earlier when the authorities had first gotten wind of the plan. And, just to complete the robbers' humiliation, the police let them run into the giant vault to grab their loot and slammed the door behind them, locking them inside.

If they'd succeeded, it would have been the largest jewel heist in history. Instead, they were all serving at Her Majesty's Pleasure till Kingdom Come.

Understandably, DeBeers LV got a little edgy about showing off its crown jewel and the Millennium Star was not seen again until the firm underwrote the Oxfam gala at the Cannes Film Festival in 2002. Their official spokeswoman, the well-known model, Iman, wore a dress especially designed for the occasion with the Star hanging as a pendant from her necklace. The upcoming gala in Portofino would be its next public appearance.

If the new Shamrock Burglar was taking his métier seriously, which he appeared to be, a successful grab of the Millennium Star would be a crowning achievement to anyone's career.

I finished the truffles and ordered one of the little chocolate cakes, similar to the bagatelles I'd made at home, just to see how his were different from mine. Jean-Paul's had a whisper of something, maybe Grand Marnier. And mine were wrapped in silver-leaf. Other than that, they were identically delicious.

By the time I left the tearoom, my plan was set.

FOURTEEN

Strange as it may sound, taking the Ritz robbery into account, I left Paris feeling back to normal, back to my calm, controlled self. I had a sense of focus and security. The trip had been worthwhile because it gave me a glimpse into my nemesis's modus operandi. This person was stealing for the thrill of it— getting high on the tantalizing danger of audacious theft. And I was right there with him, back in familiar territory, planning what would become the most sensational jewel robbery of all time, if it came off: the theft of the DeBeers Millennium Star. Let me be clear, I wasn't planning to actually *steal* the Star myself, but I needed to think that way, and going to Portofino was the only thing I could think of to do. It would be the biggest gamble of my career, and gambling is something I have never taken to. However, it was time to get creative.

I put the top up on my car, and as soon as I was outside the City, I put my foot on the accelerator and tore into the country-side. I love to drive. And today, I particularly appreciated the power of my Jag and the concentration it required at high speed so I wouldn't think about my husband. I couldn't afford to. What I had to do was *out*-think him.

What was wrong with him anyway?

I wondered if he'd come home while I was gone. Two days ago, I wanted him to, now I prayed he hadn't. I couldn't predict what he would do, I could only assume he would arrest me. If he was there in the house, I'd make an immediate left turn to Plan B, and head for Switzerland where I'd stashed the majority of my assets.

Just south of Lyon, I exited off the A-7, the famous high-speed Auto Route du Soleil, and got on the old highway, Route 86, which wound down the opposite side of the river through local traffic that crept along at a one-horse, hay-wagon pace.

I reached over and patted my sleeping Bijou. "Don't worry, darling girl. It will all be fine." Of course, for her, everything was always fine, as long as her meals were served on time. I knew I was talking to myself.

I kept to the back roads from Avignon to Éygalières to avoid detection by the local gendarmes in case they happened to be looking for me, which I assumed they were. Evening shadows reached deep across the valley as I approached the farm, and I saw the blue of police lights flashing through the trees behind me. I switched off my headlights and darted onto the road opposite my entrance and watched, horrified, as two police cars turned into La Petite Pomme.

Once they were out of sight, I checked carefully, saw no other traffic, and gunned the engine. The Jag leapt across the road like a rocket and shot straight into a small thicket of trees and bushes, where it was invisible. I tried not to think about scratches on the dozens of coats of its hand-rubbed paint. I got out and skirted the edge of the field along the cypress trees, and watched through the orchard where just four days ago Thomas and I had been sipping a special bottle of wine, eating lemon meringue pie and celebrating our anniversary.

More police cars arrived—there were six all together. All the lights in the house were turned on and I could see figures moving around, searching it.

"Oh, Thomas. How could you?" I muttered under my breath.

It made me sick. Not just that they were handling my things but because I knew he had betrayed me.

After an hour, they left and I drove home in the dark.

FIFTEEN

I loved my life. I didn't want to start over somewhere else. This was where I wanted to stop. I looked around my perfect little house, everything just as I had collected and placed it with love and thought over the years. I didn't like to travel. I liked the humdrum repetitions of my daily life—waking up in my bed and looking out my window to the mountains across the valley. And now I had to leave. What choice did I have? None. Unless I wanted to turn myself in and go to jail. I was a wanted woman. And now I was about to be a woman on the run. I was too old for this.

There was an official-looking note taped to my front door: "Mme. Keswick, please call the St. Rémy police department immediately. It is urgent. Chief Bernard."

Dans votre rêves, monsieur.

In your dreams.

Inside there was little evidence they'd been there, except the cookie jar and candy dish were empty, and all my little bagatelles were gone, which upset me further because I'd looked forward to finishing them myself. I was relieved to see it didn't look as though they'd been pawing through my drawers or my closets or my bath and dressing room. They also hadn't appeared to have found the wall safe in the living room, which would have been fine with me—it was empty. And unless they were highly skilled detectives, which they weren't, they never would have been able to find any of the other vaults and hiding places.

There were messages on my answering machine from the police to the same effect as the note—call immediately—a couple of calls from Flaminia and dinner invitations from friends. Several hangups from unidentifiable numbers. My cell phone had a number of unidentified calls as well, probably all from Thomas, and one message from him: "Kick, whatever you do, don't run."

Don't run? Are you insane? *Dans votre rêvès, monsieur.* If you think I'm going to sit around the house and wait for your colleagues to come and arrest me, you're out of your mind.

I closed the shutters, put on some Schumann, fixed myself a large scotch and a plate of cheese and crackers, gave the dog a bath, and went to my closet and started pulling out all my best spring and summertime lingerie and clothes—daytime ensembles to evening gowns. I hung them throughout my dressing room and when all the hooks in there were taken, I laid them all over my bed. Then I began to accessorize. First shoes, then handbags, then scarves, then sun hats. Then jewelry.

My house is a giant vault, nothing is what it appears to be. Floors, walls, flower beds. It's as byzantine as I once was and as I now needed to become again. Like an onion, or one of those Russian dolls that when you pull the head off one, there's another smaller one inside until they get so tiny you almost can't even see them.

The safe of which I'm most proud because I designed it myself—and I must admit, it's ingenious—is the pantry cabinet. The main pantry door opens to top-to-bottom spice racks. Behind it are two more double-sided doors that close over each other like folds in a letter and hold baking and canned goods. When these are fully opened there is a wall of shelves for seldom-required, specialized pots and pans and appliances, such as malted milk machines, pressure cookers, and spare champagne buckets. Concealed behind the appliances, the ice cream maker to be specific, are a secret latch and a hidden combination lock to a secret door. When opened, the door glides silently aside on hard rubber rollers and it is like looking into Ali Baba's cave. There is a fireproof wall of velvet-lined cubbyholes of jewelry behind a thick protective sheet of tempered, fireproof glass, and when the lights hit them, it's like Christmas or New Year's or a blazing French birthday cake exploding with sparklers. My pantry wall is a glass-fronted vending machine of jewelry. It's the Automat of Jewelry. All of which—I feel compelled to point out right now—was purchased legitimately. I have a receipt for every single piece.

I took two more hours to select just the right items to go with my wardrobe and packed them into two traveling jewelry cases. Finally, I retrieved a few high-priced, high-tech tricks of my former trade from the bathroom floor safe, including a high-speed digital scanner, night vision goggles, and an electronic/digital jammer. Old friends I thought I'd never see again. They felt as familiar in my hands as my car keys. At the last minute, I tucked three cans of temporary hair color into my kit.

Well before dawn, headlights off, Bijou and I pulled out of the farm in my small Mercedes wagon. I hated to leave my Jag behind but the wagon was much more anonymous and I needed to disappear with as little smoke as possible.

I didn't look in the rearview mirror. I'd left everything in perfect order, just as I always had for years and years when I'd had to leave Provence and be in London for months at a time. It would all be there when I got back—I would walk in and find everything exactly where I'd left it. And there would be a note on the counter from Pierre saying fresh milk, butter, and eggs were in the refrigerator. A fresh baguette would be on the counter. He carried out his duties religiously, sometimes fruitlessly for months at a time. I gave no energy to the possibility that I wouldn't be back. The assurance that things were always normal in Éygalières had carried me through many dark days and occasional lapses of confidence. I could count on Pierre and La Petite Pomme never to let me down.

I drove to the Marseilles airport and parked in the long-term lot, figuring if the police found my car, they'd conclude I'd left by commercial air. I loaded all my luggage onto a cart and went to the Hertz counter where I rented a silver Mercedes SL500, with a less interesting engine than my supercharged Jaguar XK, but still a very beautiful machine.

Bijou and I stopped for breakfast in a little café in St. Raphäel and by the time I pulled back onto the A-8—La Provencale—

the sun had crested the horizon and burned off the morning mist on the Mediterranean. I zoomed along, top down, with totally impractical, hard-sided Louis Vuitton suitcases sticking out of the backseat like giant brown-and-gold shoe boxes. I smiled as I passed the exit for Juan-les-Pins and Cap d'Antibes on my way around the Corniche to Portofino, the crowning jewel of the Italian Riviera. The last time I'd been on the French Riviera, the highway was a two-lane road and I was a girl. Sometimes I couldn't believe how much time had passed between then and now.

The French and Italian Rivieras are dotted with some of the finest hotels in the world, and one of the best of the best is in Portofino. With the gala coming up in a couple of weeks, I knew my double and every other jewel thief worth his salt had it on their itinerary. Some of the most stunning jewelry in the world would be arriving there shortly. My plan, such as it was, was to craft a scheme to steal the Millennium Star—I was, after all, the preeminent extant jewel thief in the world, and the Star, the preeminent jewel. But beyond that preliminary vision, the rest was hazy and would remain that way until I got to Portofino and got the lay of the land.

There were only a couple of initial, preparatory steps I could take, but they were key.

I called from the car.

"*Pronto?*" a woman's voice answered.

"*Buon giorno,*" I said. "This is Lady Pennington calling."

"*Sì,* Lady Pennington. How may we help you?"

I explained that I'd just lost my husband (which was true)

and that, as she knew (which she didn't, but she pretended as though she did because she was in the business of being gracious and hospitable), Portofino had always been one of our favorite spots and did they have a large one-bedroom suite available for three weeks—I needed to rest. They did have room, except for the three nights around the gala. "But we will make every effort to accommodate you during that time—we often have a last-minute cancellation for the festivities."

"I'm sure it will be fine. I'll see you in time for lunch."

"We look forward to seeing you again, Lady Pennington."

"*Arrivedérci.*"

My next call was to an old friend in Zurich—the finest synthetic stone fabricator in the world. I ordered a duplicate of the Millennium Star. The cost was $250,000 and the synthetic replica would be delivered to me at the hotel in seventy-two hours.

Next, I called my contact at EKM Elektronika, also in Zurich, and ordered a number of the latest gizmos, each of which had a legitimate and an illegitimate use. For instance, the garage-door opener could be used to open a garage door or unscramble the electronic code of the most sophisticated security door or gate. The TV remote control could be programmed to change channels or short out the electricity to a single house or an entire neighborhood. A tube of lipstick could deliver a painless dart tipped with a powerful, fast-acting amnesiac in the blink of an eye. I covered every base I could.

SIXTEEN

ONE WEEK LATER

The waiter arranged breakfast on the terrace of my suite that overlooked the little island and the sea. A crisp white Pratesi linen cloth appliquéd with a nautical blue binding covered the glass-topped table. He then placed a small vase of yellow and white freesia; laid out a service of spotless Buccelatti silver flatware, including a bone-handled fruit knife that he placed carefully along the edge of a plate of peaches; a dish of butter and bowls of raspberry preserves and orange marmalade. And, finally, a basket heaped with warm crusty rolls and sugary muffins wrapped like a present in a linen napkin and tied with a sunflower-yellow grosgrain ribbon. I enjoyed watching him work, appreciated his attention to detail, appreciated whoever did all this exquisite ironing. The starched piqué towel draped over his forearm never moved an inch.

The air was perfumed and soft. It was so quiet and beautiful and peaceful in Portofino. If I had to, this would not be a bad place to start a new life. Perhaps it was time for me to make a big change. Every now and then, I'd had to remind myself that the reason I was there was to get invited to the Gala di Portofino, keep the Millennium Star from disappearing out the back door with my name on it, and identify my impersonator.

I was no closer than I'd been a week ago to getting myself invited to the Gala. As a matter of fact, I hadn't even heard anyone mention it.

"*Café, signora?*"

"*Sì, grazie.*" I sat down and tightened my robe around me.

He poured a small cup of breakfast coffee—so thick and rich and strong, it's ridiculous. I love it but I have to add a large dollop of thick cream—more than a dollop actually—and two sugar cubes before I can drink it. He poured freshly squeezed grapefruit juice from a glass pitcher into a tall glass and then removed the silver dome from a plate of eggs scrambled with cheese and chopped spicy hot sausages and a huge bouquet of watercress as a garnish.

"*Grazie,*" I said again and reached for the morning *Tribune*. "Oh, my goodness," I gasped.

THE SHAMROCK BURGLAR STRIKES AGAIN! The story was on page one. The headline was huge.

"*Sì,*" the waiter said. "Very exciting. But Ladro Trifoglio here in Portofino?" He wagged his finger. "No. No."

He made it sound so refreshing—like a cool drink on a hot day. The Shamrock Burglar: Ladro Trifoglio.

"*Sì,*" I agreed. "Ladro Trifoglio. Very exciting."

"Will there be anything else, signora?"

"No, *grazie.*"

"*Prego.*"

I read the story. This person was on a vigorous bender—two robberies at two Riviera hotels on the same day! The secluded Villa Rose on the Gulf of Saint-Tropez, and the better-known classic, Le Palais de Beaulieu—both secure, elegant, old-fashioned destinations for ladies of means traveling alone. This was a story as old as time. Sometimes these solitary ladies were widows and divorcées actively on the hunt for well-off widowers and divorcés, sometimes they were simply looking for a lovely intermezzo with a man who was well mannered and could dance and would let a lonely woman treat him to a drink and dinner without making her feel cheap or humiliated. There was no shortage of such available men, playboys and gigolos, on the Riviera.

Each of these particular hotels had a formal dining room where it was considered de rigueur to dress for dinner, which of course—as I'd rediscovered in my new state of alone-, but not loneliness—is a significant part of the regime when you're traveling unaccompanied: not only the anticipation of getting done up, but also the act of getting done up itself.

My newly single state was like a refresher course, reminding me that even if there's no one with whom you can share a dressing drink or review the day, there is still the pleasure of a long toilette, a sweet-smelling bubble bath, a revitalizing masque, a silky new almond body lotion, a leisurely maquillage, possibly with the added fun of a new shade of lipstick or blusher purchased that afternoon at one of those glittering little parfumeries on the promenade, and a flute of fizzy, sparkling Mumm's Cordon Rouge, with the distinctive red ribbon on its label.

And as any woman knows, the bath, the makeup, the champagne, and the jewelry, when combined with the anticipation that some dashing gentleman may invite you to dance after dinner, are often much more fun than the evening.

The *Tribune* article said hotels along the Côte d'Azur had begun reminding their unescorted female guests to deposit their jewelry in the hotel safety deposit boxes at the end of the evening. But really, ladies, let's be honest: Everyone knows that when passion strikes, nothing could kill it quite so effectively as excusing yourself to stop off at the front desk to match up your safe-deposit box key with the night clerk's and disappearing for a minute or two into a tiny, airless, private room to strip off all your twinkles before you join your new friend for the elevator ride upstairs. It really annihilates the spontaneity of the moment. And believe me when I say, there's nothing more deadening to the twinkle in a middle-aged woman's eyes than the removal of her sparkles, whether they're real or not.

Anyhow, the sad reality is that usually by the time you wrap-up in the safety-deposit room and get back to your new friend, he's gone. He's back in the bar chatting up some other lonely lady who's still wearing all her jewelry and had the wit to freshen her makeup while he was in the lobby twiddling his thumbs and growing impatient waiting for you. This is why it's always important to have a good book along. Gigolos are very fickle.

And let's be *really* truthful about this: When you get right down to it, it's probably the end of a long day and you're probably tired anyhow, and up to here with fixing your lipstick every five minutes, and all you are really starting to want is an uninterrupted good night's sleep.

SEVENTEEN

The most remarkable thing about these hotel jewelry robberies
was that there was still not a clear physical description of the
ersatz Shamrock Burglar, at least not in the newspaper where it
could do the most good. Each victim vehemently denied she'd
spent the evening with anyone in particular or invited anyone
to her room. It didn't make sense. I know that none of these
ladies wanted to admit she'd been desperate or duped or
robbed, but now that there was a string of robberies all committed by the same person, it seemed to me this would be the
time to take a deep breath, swallow the embarrassment, band
together, and help the police. The ladies didn't have to let their
names be released and no one would publicize their pictures or
put them on television. But it was time to get the word out
about whatever this person was doing, just so other women
could be alert. Whatever his modus operandi was, it was very
persuasive. Had he threatened them? Did he tell them that if
they gave a physical description, he would come back and kill
them? I couldn't think of anything else that would make them
keep their mouths shut so tightly.

Or was it something too embarrassing to make public, even
to the police? Did they lead secret lives and would rather die

than let it get out? Or was it a couple of people? Some sort of sexual ménage? Making the loss of the jewels easier to tolerate than the risk of such a tawdry scandal? Had they been drugged and really couldn't remember anything? Or, and I knew this was also a very strong possibility: Were they in on the thefts because they'd had to sell the real pieces a while ago and these were all fakes that they'd collaborated to have stolen to collect the insurance?

At Ballantine's, it was not at all uncommon to have heirs arrive with their late mother's or grandmother's or Aunt Tillie's collection of jewelry wishing to have them auctioned—the Property of a Lady—only to be informed by our jewelry experts that all the stones were glass or synthetics and the metal was not platinum as they believed but rather silver-plated fourteen-carat gold. Aunt Tillie had sold the stones ages ago, probably to pay for her face-lift or that moth-eaten old mink she'd left behind and that they'd just given to the jumble.

My exquisite now-missing bracelet, the Queen's Pet, was just such an example of a real piece turning up in an unexpected place, while what's believed to be the real thing is actually a fake. I'd stolen the Queen's Pet from the late romance author, Lady Melody Carstairs, who, according to my yardstick of ethics, deserved to be robbed. She'd made her fortune on her virgin image until one day a young woman turned up claiming—with very good evidence—to be her daughter. Lady Melody's lawyers savaged the woman in court and she ended

up committing suicide. A perfect example of the powerful de-
stroying the weak and defenseless. Of course, at the time of the
robbery I had no idea that her Queen's Pet was the real thing
and had originally been the property of Queen Victoria and
later part of the Queen Mother's collection. It was only after
close examination that I realized what I had, a piece of uncommon beauty, value, and structure. I surmised the Queen
Mother—who was as notorious for her gambling debts as she
was for her love of gin—had sold the original to Lady Melody
for an enormous amount of cash. It is truly priceless, a two-
inch wide cuff made up of five rows of wonderfully matched,
five-carat, old mine diamonds culminating in an oval, diamond-
encrusted clasp that hides a secret locket with a miniature Winterhalter portrait of Prince Albert.

It had fascinated me to think that I had had the original in
my possession while the royal family innocently held the
replica. Just as it now fascinated me to try to fathom why
Thomas had taken it.

Was there a Shamrock Burglar for hire who was known only by
word-of-mouth among a certain world of ladies who lived in
the exclusive stratosphere of the very rich? Maybe these 'victims' weren't victims at all—maybe they were part of a crime
ring! The concept of a merry band of heiresses stealing their
own and their friends' jewelry was as delightful as it was intriguing.

I poured myself a second cup of coffee. It could be any or all of these scenarios. There must be a great deal of information the police were unwilling to make public. Some relationship, some common element that linked these women.

I put down the paper, spread a fat swath of butter on a triangle of crunchy nut toast, added a big plop of marmalade, and turned on the television. It wasn't long before the story came on. It was a juicy, gossipy story—a summertime scandal made in heaven for the media.

The SkyWord reporter, Giovanna McDougal, a trim, pretty young woman with cropped blond hair, a white T-shirt, and print cotton skirt, stood on the terrace of the hotel in Beaulieu with flower boxes of sizzling red geraniums and the shining Mediterranean as her backdrop.

"It was here in this fairy-tale setting," she explained, "in the heart of the Côte d'Azur, playground of the rich and famous, that the ubiquitous Shamrock Burglar struck again. Two more robberies last night at two more of the world's most exclusive resorts. Here in Beaulieu, over half a million dollars in diamonds were stolen from an unidentified guest's dressing table as she slept, replaced by the now-famous bouquet of shamrocks and their elegant gold satin ribbon. A second robbery occurred at another beautiful watering hole not far down the road. This makes four robberies in just ten days by the elusive Shamrock."

I was completely captivated and sat at my breakfast table watching with bewildered fascination along with everyone else on the Rivieras. I felt detached from the whole affair and started not to take it so personally. At least, if I had to, I could prove I'd been here for the last week, not in Cap Ferrat or Beaulieu.

Giovanna McDougal continued. "We're fortunate to have joining us Commander Thomas Curtis. Commander Curtis retired recently as one of Scotland Yard's most respected investigators. He is now head of the international task force assigned to apprehend the Shamrock Burglar. Welcome to SkyWord Commander Curtis."

WHAT?! I almost fell out of my chair. There he was, talking to Giovanna McDougal on a terrace in Beaulieu. It was surreal. He looked wonderful. The sun gleamed off his white hair, and his piercing blue eyes were as beautiful as ever as he squinted slightly in the morning sun. Never a clotheshorse, he had on a badly wrinkled linen suit and regimental tie—that was so Thomas, a regimental tie with a linen suit. At least his shirt was ironed and I was grateful for that. And I knew his shoes were shined. I wanted to pick up the phone and say, "Thomas, I'm just down the road from you. Please get over here and let's get this whole thing straightened out. *It's not me—I'm not the Shamrock Burglar anymore.*"

I wanted to kiss him and put my arms around him and smell his Trumper's lime cologne. I wanted him to put his arms around me. I couldn't seem to get my mind around the fact that we were on opposite sides of the game now. That he was publicly and officially in charge of tracking me down. I watched, completely mesmerized.

"You had quite a lot of experience with the Shamrock Burglar in London, didn't you, Commander?" Ms. Giovanna McDougal asked.

"I did. Although it was never my assignment—I focused primarily on homicides—I'm well familiar with the case and its intricacies."

"In spite of the hours New Scotland Yard has spent on the case, it's never even had what could be categorized as a strong lead on the elusive Shamrock."

"No. Quite right." Thomas clearly didn't care much for the question, but he answered it.

Giovanna just seemed to float along, not particularly interested in Thomas's responses so much as in her questions. "And now the Shamrock has gone international. Are you convinced this is the real thing?"

He nodded. "Yes. We are. It has all the earmarks of the original."

I'm getting to hate you, Thomas Curtis.

"What's next?" Giovanna asked.

"We're closer to the Shamrock now than ever before. I expect we'll have an arrest in the next few days."

Really? That's what you think. You couldn't catch me then and you can't catch me now.

I went inside and dug out my Michelin maps and red book and studied the coastline between Beaulieu and Portofino and tried to put myself in Thomas's position, just as I knew he was trying to put himself in mine. I felt confident my impostor would show up in Portofino very soon. But I was also quite sure Thomas hadn't connected the dots to the DeBeers Millennium Star and the Gala di Portofino. Yet. Which property would I think would be hit next if I were him? There were a number of excellent choices between here and there. Even the most bumbling, inept burglar could make a fantastic living robbing hotels and villas in Monte Carlo alone. I couldn't decide. Thomas and I were in the same boat—we'd just have to wait and see. In fact, as far as I was concerned, it didn't make much difference what the burglar did until the gala. I had made my plan, staked out my territory, and now was not the time for me to start moving around.

I finished my breakfast and decided to get in the shower and put myself together before I planned the rest of my day.

If I looked over the side of my terrace, the front edge of the main dining room and bar terrace two floors below were visible. I had a perfect vantage point. I checked for familiar or suspicious faces several times a day from my perch but so far no one familiar had appeared. Until now.

It was the man who looked like Antonio Banderas. The same man I'd seen in the Musée Montpensier in Paris.

I watched the captain hold a chair for him. He was dressed in tennis whites, a sweater tied jauntily around his shoulders. He was the tannest person I'd ever seen.

Every now and then his eyes would roam the terrace, but he knew as well as I did that no woman worth robbing was going to show up for breakfast in public.

We were all still upstairs with our faces packed in ice.

EIGHTEEN

Since arriving in Portofino, Bijou and I had spent our afternoons hiking along the rocky, steep hillsides above the port, climbing precipitous, endless stone stairways, and ducking through narrow passages that smelled of mulch and antiquity and led like secret tunnels to the villas dotting the hills. It was easy to understand why Portofino's real estate was among the most sought after and costly in the world. The air is fresh and balmy, easy to breathe. The vistas are soothing, nothing jars the eye because everything is in its perfect place, as though arranged for a picture postcard. The sky is always cerulean blue with a few puffy clouds floating about; the yachts bobbing in the harbor are big and white; flowers billow from every window box and cascade down stone walls that have disappeared under thick blankets of ivy and jasmine. It is a perfectly cared-for town for the super rich. Privacy and anonymity are available and respected. It is heavenly.

It was still fairly early in the season and a handful of the villas that had been closed for the winter were just concluding their spring cleanings—windows thrown open with dustcovers being shaken and snapped in the fresh ocean air. Most were spectacularly well looked after—painted in the rich ochre, pink, and terra-cotta colors and trompe l'oeil style that Portofino is known for. A few of the villas were run-down and overgrown, in need of repair—their owners out of town or out of money.

I had succumbed to the charms of this ancient town and purchased a small house as an investment, as well as a hedge against a plan gone awry. It was a charming, little pink-stucco *borgo*, snuggled into the hillside—too small to be of interest to anyone but a single woman and her dog. The garden was overgrown and the house needed a great deal of work but was livable. If I were going to end up changing my life, it would be on my terms. I wanted to be ready.

Every day, at some point on my circuit, I passed the walls of Villa Giolitti, a gigantic yellow and white, three-story affair with pink shutters on its dozens of windows and doors. It sat on several private acres on the top of the hill and was in glorious condition. Legions of gardeners worked the grounds and there was a constant stream of traffic in and out of its main gate, which was formidable, not a fancy wrought-iron affair, but rather greenish sheets of solid steel that when closed barred even a small ray of sunlight from escaping. A couple of times, warned by the squeal of tires and the roar of a fast-approaching big engine, I'd had to pick up the dog and step off the road to get out of the way as a red Ferrari convertible with a woman behind the wheel screamed around the corner. Another time it was a black Lamborghini, but I couldn't see who was driving behind the tinted windows. Villa Giolitti was the residence of Count Giancarlo Giolitti—one of Portofino's leading patrons. The Gala of Portofino was held at this villa.

I'd thoroughly scoped out its perimeter, looking for openings I could breech in case I didn't get invited to the party and had to crash it. Scaling the wall was out of the question, and I found only one gate that, as far as I could tell, didn't have cameras. It was another large steel affair, as high as the villa wall, approximately ten feet, and looked to be seldom used. I assumed it was just for major landscaping undertakings because there was a regular service entrance that accommodated the staff and service trucks. One afternoon, the gate was open and I saw that it was controlled by an electronic keypad on a drive-by post, which presented no problem to my garage door opener/digital electronic scanner. While I'd been able to assess the security outside the villa walls, I could only guess at what steps had been taken inside and I assumed they were significant. If I had to, I supposed I could make it up to the big green gate in my ball gown. I'd rather not, of course. I'd rather receive a proper invitation.

As I walked, I constantly worked two smooth stones in my hands. One was approximately the size of the Millennium Star—the perfect copy of which had arrived, on schedule, from Zurich and was now in the hotel's vault—and the other a little larger, about the size of the Empresse de Josephine emerald.

My route was the same every day. Bijou and I were getting to be known by the locals, the gardeners, and the household help—which was part of the plan, because if I should come under any suspicion, I'd want locals to be able to say, *Oh yes, we see her every day. She and her little dog on their walk. She lives somewhere nearby.*

Today, I hiked over the hill and stopped for lunch at a trattoria on the square in Paraggi, a sleepy little cliff-top town. I ordered mussels that arrived with garlic and olive oil in a skillet so hot and sputtering it was impossible to touch, a fresh loaf of bread, an arugula salad with garden tomatoes, and drank glasses of red wine from a pitcher the owner refilled out in the garden from a giant cask. The air smelled of pepper and spice and the little Bay of Paraggi sparkled at the bottom of the cliff as though it were covered with diamonds.

I was so happy. In fact, if I kept my mind off the real world, I was actually as happy as I'd ever been in my life.

I never take anything for granted, and it didn't escape me for a second how fortunate I was to be able to be in such a beautiful spot and how eternally grateful I was I'd chosen precious gems as my métier, not insurance or accounting or something that didn't involve beauty, and romance, intrigue, and danger. I was also starting to enjoy this plotting and planning, to remember why I'd loved my business so much. Who knew? Maybe I actually would steal the Millennium Star and keep it for myself.

I read my book during lunch and then, over a hazelnut gelato, flaky sugar cookie, and espresso, I thought about "Antonio." Was he the one? Or just a run-of-the-mill second-story man? Or just a coincidence—a good-looking, nicely decked-out fellow who'd been in Paris and was now in Portofino for the gala? I'd exhausted myself trying to figure out how I was going to go about getting invited to the party. I knew some opportunity would present itself. They always do if you give them a chance, but when would people start showing up? Showing a little interest? The hotel manager had sent me a note saying that they would be able to accommodate me during the gala days after all, and I wouldn't need to leave the hotel or change rooms. Was this a good sign or bad? Did it mean people were canceling? When would things start happening?

I ordered a little limoncello and it made me feel much better.

It was midafternoon when I got back, and the hotel's typically quiet parking area was jammed with Ferraris, Lamborghinis, limousines, and Porsche Turbo convertibles. The lobby buzzed with famous and important-looking new arrivals and mountains of expensive luggage.

"What's happening?" I asked as the man at the front desk handed me my key.

"Gala di Portofino," he said, beaming.

My heart skipped a beat. "Tonight?"

"No. No, Signora Pennington. Three days. But many parties happen around it. Very fancy. Very fun. It will get even busier."

Finally.

It was fun. Fun to watch. Everyone seemed excited to be here. No one was having a tantrum. No one was showing off how important he or she was because they were all important. We all knew the trouble would start when they began to arrive at their suites and rooms and then some would be obviously much more equal than others. Everyone simply cannot have an ocean view.

I wouldn't want to run a hotel for anything.

Antonio was at the concierge's desk, his back to me. I leaned toward the front desk man. "Tell me, signor," I said under my breath. "What is that man's name? I think he's an associate of my late husband's."

The clerk glanced over and then leaned in conspiratorially. "That's Count Alesandro de Camarque," he said. "From Rio de Janeiro."

"Rio. Right." I breathed a sigh of relief. "Alesandro de Camarque. Thank you so much."

I retrieved my jewelry cases from the hotel safe and got upstairs quickly before the new arrivals began to get to their rooms, and the joy in the lobby began to unravel.

NINETEEN

Several hours later, after a manicure, a pedicure, a massage, a nap, and a long bath, I sipped a glass of Cordon Rouge while I dressed. I'd gotten a flattering bit of color in my face from all my hiking, so I selected a white wool crepe evening pants suit that would complement my tan. I stepped into high-heeled sandals, and added a necklace of pure white, sixteen-millimeter pearls that rose and fell across my *belle poitrine*—as Sir Cramner liked to call it—as though they were a string of miniature Ping-Pong balls lolling on the sea.

I opened another jewelry case and after some consideration decided on a twelve-carat, emerald-cut diamond engagement ring that went perfectly with my own pavé diamond wedding band that I refused to take off no matter how much of a bastard Thomas was being—he knew it wasn't me. He knew it and all he needed to say was, "No, there are distinct differences between London's original Shamrock Burglar and this one. This is clearly a counterfeit. A copycat." But, no. He said, "Yes it all seems identical." Or something like that. You bastard. You *bastard*. Well, this story wasn't over and I was going to win this argument, and I would keep my wedding ring on until I saw him in person—probably in court at our divorce proceedings—and

I would throw the damned thing right in his face and say, "I never gave up on you. I never turned you in, you . . . , you . . . , excuse-my-French . . . , you *shithead*."

We'd made promises to each other, and a promise was a promise.

I added a spectacular diamond and Persian turquoise suite that, because it was set in gold, made the pieces more casual, more appropriate for summertime. They weren't quite in the trophy category but they were exquisite. The brooch, bracelet, and earrings were Cartier estate pieces from the thirties. They looked like comets or shooting stars. The fact that the diamonds were set in platinum before being placed on the gold made them sparkle as though they actually were stars, shining in a creamy, azure sky.

I dabbed a little Bal à Versailles behind my ears and took a last look in the mirror before I went down. I looked wonderful—healthy, tanned, well rested. Rich. I looked like someone it would be fun to be with and easy to rob and the fact was, I was.

"*Buona sera,* Signora Pennington, will you be dining with us this evening?"

The last of the sun, setting over the sea, had turned everything gold and set my jewelry ablaze. Evening had brought the jasmine to life and the air was practically dizzying with its rich, erotic scent.

"I will."

He guided me to a cocktail table along the railing. The terrace was about three-quarters full with dressy guests—some couples but also a number of larger groups of famous movie stars and jet setters.

Bijou jumped onto the chair next to mine, and looked about expectantly. She still wore the faux diamond and emerald collar I'd bought on the Rue de Rivoli. I'd disconnected the emerald pendant—the copy of the purloined Empresse de Josephine.

Alesandro de Camarque was there, facing me, just one empty table away. He was alone, smoking a cigarette, sipping what looked like scotch or bourbon on the rocks, wearing his dark glasses. He wore a crisply pressed natural linen suit and an open-necked shirt. He kept his face on the ocean as I was seated, but I could feel his eyes on me. The fact that he was known by name at the hotel, and an aristocrat at that, meant nothing. There is no titled aristocracy in Brazil and he looked too Spanish to be Brazilian.

However, Brazil is home to many nefarious and notorious individuals living outside the law. So is Colombia. The most accomplished jewel thieves in the world today come from Colombia, with Russia and Uzbekistan not far behind. The Colombians work in high-speed rings—pieces disappear so fast, sometimes the victims aren't sure if they'd even been there at all. That's an exaggeration, of course, but the Colombians' ability to coordinate the theft and passing-off of a piece of jewelry in one smooth movement is a technique that requires split-second timing, talented acting, and seamless choreography—not to mention hands with the sensitivity and dexterity of a surgeon's. Alesandro was neither Russian nor Uzbekistani but he could certainly be Colombian. And, I couldn't help but notice, he was handsome and fit enough to be able to entice and rob two ladies in one night.

I wondered who he was taking to the gala—it would not be his accomplice, if he had one. It would be a foil, a legitimate consort, such as I. His accomplice would be there in a different guise altogether.

"May I bring your regular vodka martini or would you like to try something new?" the waiter asked.

"Something new? Well, I'm not sure." I spoke just loudly enough for Alesandro to hear me. "I haven't tried anything new for decades. What do you recommend?"

"You might like to try a limoncello martini. Very tart."

"Very powerful," I said. "I had a limoncello after lunch."

He shrugged slightly. "You're among friends and you won't be driving, will you?"

I laughed and shook my head. "I'd love to try it."

"And for our friend?" He indicated the dog. "A little Pellegrino water and biscotti?"

"*Grazie.*"

Once he was gone, Alesandro looked over at me and took off his dark glasses. He really was unbelievably handsome—not pretty, but masculine and weather-beaten. His eyes were lively, black as coal, shining with intelligence and humor above his dark mustache. "What is your dog's name?"

"Bijou." I fed her a little piece of cashew.

He nodded. "Seems an excellent choice." His voice was smooth and deep, his accent lyrical and Latin. He exuded a powerful, raw sexuality that could seduce from a distance. He was a perfect model of a playboy, gigolo, jewel thief. It would be easy to be attracted to him. Even for a professional like me, Alesandro was Trouble with a Capital T.

"Oh." I self-consciously touched my brooch with the hand with the large diamond ring and smiled. "One of my weaknesses."

The waiter returned with my cocktail. "Limoncello martini, *signora*. A gift from our barman. If you don't like it, I'll exchange it immediately."

I took a small sip. It was so lemony it made my eyes water. "Wow."

"You like?"

"Very much. *Grazie.*"

"*Prego. Y per piccolo Bijou.*" He placed a small dish of water on the terrace and laid three tiny dog biscotti on the table.

I pulled out my book and began to read.

My drink was so good, and so strong, I had to force myself to go slowly. Limoncello is a very fast drunk. It is a dangerously and deceptively powerful distillation of Sorrento lemons soaked in grain alcohol for ninety days at which point a little shot of sugar syrup is added. It is a lemonade-for-grown-ups that makes you drunk in about thirty seconds. If I weren't careful, I could become a limoncello addict, I liked it so much.

The waiter brought Alesandro his second cocktail and just as he was about ready to make a move in my direction, a party of four was shown to the table that separated us. It was obviously an important group because they had stopped at every table along the way to visit. Then one of the women turned and looked right at me—it was Marjorie Mead. The gala's guest of honor. She had a wonderful, genuine smile on her face. She was with a famous director whose name completely left my mind when I recognized the man who was obviously their host, dashing and well known to everyone on the terrace, guests and staff alike. It was the man I met in the Paris museum. The man who looked like Cary Grant.

He looked at me and I saw the recognition in his eyes, too, and after his party was seated, he came over and took my hand and kissed it. "Signora," he said. "Lovely to see you again. Now I can say, 'Haven't we met somewhere before?'" He laughed. "Would you care to join us?"

My plan began to coalesce. I had two credible suspects, two solid links in the chain. Both men—this gentleman and Alesandro de Camarque—had been at the museum and now both were in Portofino.

I glanced at Alesandro. I would play hard-to-get. It would do him good.

"Yes, thank you. I'd love to," I said.

TWENTY

"Let me introduce you to my good friends," he said. "Marjorie Mead—our glorious guest of honor."

"Good evening," I said as we shook hands. She had a good, firm grip and a straight, level gaze. "And congratulations."

"Thank you. It's great fun."

". . . and Mickael and Katrine Forcescou. Mickael directed Marjorie in *La Femme*."

"Good evening," I said to each. *"Buona sera."*

"And now, signora, forgive me. I know your dog is Bijou, but I don't know your name."

I smiled at him. "I don't mean to be difficult, but I really think you ought to tell me yours first."

"Oh! *Dio*." He clapped his hands on his chest and laughed. "Forgive me, again. My ego is so insufferable I sometimes forget there are still some poor souls on this planet who don't know me! I am Giancarlo Giolitti, at your service."

"Priscilla Pennington," I answered.

"Bella," he said as he sat down next to me.

So this was the famous Count Giancarlo Giolitti, Portofino's greatest patron. Not a gigolo after all.

"See, Giancarlo?" Marjorie said. "Now aren't you glad Consuelo couldn't make it? I'm sorry to say so, but she's really not very much fun. Actually, she's not any fun at all."

I didn't know who Consuelo was, but I was delighted she couldn't make it. And when it came to fun? Well, if I put my mind to it, "fun" might as well be my middle name.

Marjorie turned to me. "Consuelo is a dreary, dour woman that Giancarlo always trots out for these affairs because he knows if he takes one of the stars to a public function—" then she whispered sotto voce behind her hand "—actually he's partial to star-*lets*, his daughter will not speak to him."

Giancarlo laughed. "Marjorie, you're going to give Signora Pennington the wrong impression." He turned to me and put his hand on his heart as though he were taking a pledge. His nails were manicured and buffed and he wore a gold family crest ring on his left pinky finger. "I swear every word she says is a lie. She is an *actress*! Ignore her!"

"Look out or he'll start chasing you around the table," Marjorie joked.

"I think I can handle him."

Clearly Giancarlo and Marjorie were old, close friends and I learned that she and Giancarlo's daughter, Lucia, had been best friends since they'd gone to school together in Switzerland. As to the other couple at the table: The movie director, Mickael Forcescou, was intense and fascinating. He had a dark cutting humor. His wife, Katrine, was either bored or on some sort of medication.

————

The evening was magic. I joined them for dinner. We had course after course—antipasti, appetizers, *insalata, primi piatti, segundi piatti,* each one better than the one before. The Italian wines from the owner's private cave were among the finest wines I'd ever had, which is saying a lot from a wine snob such as I who generally sticks to French Bordeaux and Burgundies. After dinner, the five of us went into the bar and drank grappa and danced and laughed until after two in the morning.

I'm embarrassed to say I completely lost track of Alesandro.

Giancarlo was possibly the most charming, sophisticated, well educated, urbane man I'd ever met in my life. He was so powerfully seductive, it was easy to understand why Italians had invented the word *animale.* He was also a total gentleman all evening and when he escorted me to the elevator, I wasn't sure what I would do if he suggested coming to my room for a nightcap. I wondered if I'd say yes.

He kissed my hand at the elevator door. "Perhaps you would join me for lunch tomorrow, Bella."

I loved being called "Bella." Thankfully, a sober voice somewhere in the back of my muddled brain shouted at me through all the booze and said, *Keep your eye on the target. You're here to get invited to the party at this man's house. Say no!*

"I'm sorry Giancarlo, but I have plans."

"I understand. We'll see each other again. If you need anything at all, I live just up the hill."

I wanted to say, I know, I walk past your villa every day and it's only the most beautiful place I've ever seen in my life. I swallowed.

"Thank you," I said, instead. "It was lovely meeting you."

"*Buona notte.*"

TWENTY-ONE

The next morning, in spite of an absolutely crushing headache, I bubbled with thoughts of Giancarlo. Certainly much more fun than thinking about Thomas, who—no matter how much I loved him, or used to love him, or whatever—just had the effect of making me angry. Giancarlo was so charming. So fun. So sophisticated. So unbelievably sexy. I realized I had a crush!

Alesandro had spent the whole day on the tennis court yesterday. So, against my better judgment, I decided to take a tennis lesson. I'm not really much into physical fitness. I do the best I can but it's not really very good. I do try to walk regularly, and I enjoy it. I've been enjoying my hikes here in Portofino but I haven't really pushed myself to anything close to what anyone could call an actual limit. I've certainly never done anything that's made me perspire. But I decided tennis would be a good thing to try since it didn't appear to require too much strain or skill. From my observations, it seemed that if one were to use one's head, one could simply reach out in one direction or the other and whack the ball. More to the point: I needed to be visible and this was the only thing I could think of to do.

Of course, the proper clothes were the first order of business.

After breakfast—which I'll admit included a Bloody Mary and several aspirin—I followed the trail down to town to what was without question the world's most expensive sports boutique, and purchased the full ensemble—short-sleeved white piqué blouse, very lightweight white gabardine trousers, a snappy navy and red belt, tennis shoes, tennis socks, a sun visor, and a racket that had a face as big as a butterfly net. I know that dresses and shorts are customary for ladies on the tennis court, but no stranger has seen my legs this far in my life and as far as I was concerned, there was no reason to start flashing them around now, even though they are quite lovely. Also, I didn't expect I'd be dashing around so much the slacks would encumber me in any way.

I sprayed on Hermès Orange Verte, a crisp and invigorating scent that I think is also very sporty; added a gold and diamond Rolex on one wrist and a diamond "tennis" bracelet on the other along with three diamond-studded golden bangles, a thin chain of intermittent pea-sized diamonds around my neck, and diamond studs in each ear that were much too large to be worn, tastefully, in the daytime. Compared to the classic, low-key style I preferred, I felt like a Las Vegas billboard, but the smattering of diamonds was just right to attract attention to myself, and distract attention from my tennis game.

If Alesandro were the thief, he would already have catalogued my jewelry from last night—the flash of my twelve-carat diamond ring, the opalescent glow of the rare pearls, and the uniqueness of my brooch and earrings. If he showed up at the tennis court, he would see that I had more money than athleticism. I was a puffball, an easy target.

"My name is Guilberto." The young man extended his hand. "I am the pro."

"Lovely to meet you, Guilberto. Priscilla Pennington."

I believe he was ten years old and his mother had to drive him to work every day. But he was cute and charming and obviously accustomed to teaching complete beginners, otherwise he wouldn't be at such a resort.

"Have you played much tennis, signora?"

"Never in my life."

"Never?"

I could tell he couldn't believe it. I was as old as his mother and surely in the five hundred years I'd been alive I'd picked up a tennis racket somewhere along the way. "Never."

"*Bene.*" His smile was broad. "That means you won't have any bad habits we need to correct."

See what I mean? He was absolutely precious.

After we got past the first ten minutes of him showing me how to hold the racket—he did this by standing behind me and helping me swing—it was time to introduce the actual ball.

Guilberto moved to the opposite side of the net, a large basket of bright yellow tennis balls next to him, and began to lob them gently in my direction. I'd been mistaken. There was much more to tennis than holding my racket out and thinking they would automatically hit it. I had to move and reach. Bend and dash. I connected with approximately one out of every eight or ten.

"This is much harder than it looks," I said to Guilberto.

"Don't worry, signora, you'll catch on."

"I'm not so sure."

Alesandro materialized courtside with his professional-looking stack of rackets and tennis paraphernalia and took a seat and watched my lesson. He made me nervous and—hard to imagine as it may be—I played even worse.

At the end of the hour, I was completely exhausted but also exhilarated and determined. I had actually engaged in a sport. It was thrilling.

"Domani?" I asked Guilberto.

"Sì, signora. À domani."

He really was absolutely darling.

TWENTY-TWO

Alesandro got to his feet, offered me a towel, and poured a glass of water from one of the iced pitchers that sat on a court-side table.

"Thank you." I looked at him shyly.

"You were doing quite well."

How he could keep a straight face and say such a thing escaped me. I wanted to compliment him: He was a credit to his profession.

"You must be either blind," I said, "or desperate for company."

"Neither. May I get you a Campari?" he offered. "It's the perfect, how do you say . . . 'quencher'? . . . after a round of tennis."

"Thank you. That would be lovely."

"*Due* Campari," he said to the waiter.

"Do we know each other?" I asked as I pressed the towel to my cheek, just like a regular athlete, although my cheek was scarcely damp.

"No, but we should. I'll be right with you, Guilberto," he called to the pro who'd begun practicing his serve. He hit the ball so hard it lifted his little feet right off the ground.

We moved to a table along the wall of cypress trees. They swayed slightly in the ocean breeze.

"I am Alesandro de Camarque," he said.

"Priscilla Pennington." I raised my arm and blotted my neck with the towel, purposely drawing the thirty-five-carat Pasha of St. Petersburg diamond from its hiding place inside my blouse long enough for it to catch the sun for a split second. Long enough for him to see it and see that it was a stone of consequence. I was amazed at how detached I was from my brashness. It was the complete opposite from last night with Giancarlo, when I'd been my normal, restrained, reserved self. Just thinking of Giancarlo suddenly made me feel giddy, like bursting out laughing for no reason. I cleared my throat and sat up straighter.

The waiter brought two highball glasses of spicy, cranberry-red Campari. A lemon slice was wedged on the rim of each glass like a yellow pinwheel. He splashed in a bubbly dash of Pellegrino and then set the drinks on the table.

"Have you been in Portofino for long?" Alesandro asked.

I shrugged. "Not too long. A week or so. When did you arrive?"

"Just yesterday."

"Oh? From where?" Possibly, I thought, he might give something away, open some small door that I could chip my way into—some avenue to Colombia.

"I've been with friends on their yacht in Sardinia."

Well, that didn't work.

"How relaxing," I said.

"Are you here for the gala?" he asked.

"Yes." I twisted the lemon into my drink. "I've been invited at any rate, I'm not sure I'll go. I lost my husband not long ago and I'm not sure if I'm ready to start back into the gala life."

He blinked, and for a second an expression flashed across his face. I'm not a mindreader but it seemed to me like a quickening of interest, or a judgment call of some sort in regard to what to do about me. "I'm sorry about your loss. I understand how hard that can be." He sipped his drink and almost smiled, as though at a private joke. "And when you get right down to it, there are so many galas, aren't there. They all just blend together after a while. So"— he shrugged and pursed his full lips—"if you miss this one, there's always the next one. It's all the same people, anyway."

"Are you going?"

"Naturally. I never miss it. It's truly the party of the year," he answered. "So many say the Red Cross Ball in Venice is the best, but this one really is. It's smaller, more fun, and early in the season before everything gets too crowded and crazy. I hope you decide to go."

"I probably will. It sounds as though it will be particularly special this year," I said.

"It does? Why?"

"I'm sure this will sound silly, Alesandro, but I love jewelry. Especially important jewelry. I missed seeing the Millennium Star diamond in London because of the attempted robbery, and I understand Marjorie Mead is going to be wearing it."

He grinned at me, a genuine grin, as though he were

charmed by my candor. He was extremely easy and relaxing to be around. "The gala will definitely be the place to see some very grand jewelry. But if you can get within a hundred yards of Marjorie, and the Star, good luck. I've heard the security is going to be more extensive than ever."

"I'm not planning to steal it, Alesandro. I just want to see it."

"Even so. I'm sure they'll require that she keep her distance, especially with all these robberies happening. Of course, the really wonderful party is the one tonight, the VIP party."

"Oh?"

"Only the celebrities and patrons of the gala are invited. It's very exclusive, small enough that you can really have a conversation."

"Are you going?"

Alesandro laughed and shook his head. "No, no. I'm in favor of supporting the International Refugee Foundation, and I do—the tickets to the gala are expensive enough. But VIP patrons have to give at least a million dollars. Some have given much more, some as much as five million. As I said, this is a very exclusive group." He smiled. "And thank God for them—without them, the party and the charity would probably disappear."

"You're right. Well"— I finished my drink —"I'd better be on my way. Thank you for the Campari, Alesandro. It was just the right thing." I got up to go.

"My pleasure." He stood and we shook hands. "I'll see you again, I hope."

"I'm sure our paths will cross. *Ciao.*"

"Ciao."

I twirled my racket around like a baton as I walked through the forested grounds back to the hotel lobby. There was no question but that Alesandro was a thief. If he wasn't, he would've have been more interested in talking about the burglaries. As it was, he just skipped the whole subject. But: Was he *the* thief?

"Signora Pennington," the front desk man said as I passed through. "This arrived for you." He handed me a heavy ecru envelope. I opened it on the elevator. A thick card with a coat of arms blind embossed at the top and the name Giolitti just beneath.

"Sra. Pennington," it read. "Please join us for dinner this evening at the villa—a salute to Marjorie and our special patrons. I'll call for you at seven. Regards, Giancarlo Giolitti."

I leaned against the elevator wall and looked at the invitation. Relief flooded me. Evidently, Consuelo, his dour and dreary companion who'd not shown up last night due to illness in her family, was still unavailable. I'd be lying if I said it didn't thrill me. For the time being, it would let me stay with my Plan A (Plan B being the one where I made my way up the hill in my evening gown and attempted to breech the villa's security) and put me in the direct vicinity of the Millennium Star and, hopefully, its thief, who might very well be Giancarlo himself. He had all the right qualities for a master jewel thief, and I'll admit, taking my schoolgirl infatuation into account; I was excited and flattered that out of all the ladies he could have invited to the party tonight, he'd invited me.

The camel's nose was under the tent.

I took a quick shower, put on loose silk trousers, a sweater set, an inordinate amount of gold jewelry, grabbed my book, and left for lunch in town. I'd reserved a table on the terrace at Splendido Mare so I could watch the mega-yachts come and go. I wondered if Alesandro would show up. I could tell he was interested in me as a target. But what self-respecting jewel thief wouldn't be interested in someone who'd been doing all the drinking and wearing all the jewelry I had? And I was just getting warmed up.

As it turned out, Alesandro, and a young, quite ordinary-looking woman ended up sitting at the table next to me. I assumed she was one of his accomplices. They were so locked into their conversation, he scarcely acknowledged that we'd even met.

TWENTY-THREE

The Gala di Portofino is known for its exclusivity, which is why it attracts many of the world's top industrialists and financiers. Many people think these VIPs come to the party because they want to rub elbows with major movie stars and celebrities, but the fact is, they want to rub elbows with each other in a neutral, nonbusiness setting. Check each other out. Have "casual" conversations, some of which have been in the planning stages for months. Many deals and mergers are consummated, born, delivered, or die at the gala, which was started in 1945 by Giancarlo's mother, Principessa Giolitti, to assist World War II refugees and displaced persons. It had grown into a powerful international organization that not only assisted refugees worldwide, but also helped governments develop humanitarian policies to deal with an influx of unexpected and unwanted visitors in their countries.

The cost to attend the gala was prohibitive to all but the super rich, or to superdetermined social climbers. The party was limited to two hundred and fifty guests for dinner. Another two hundred and fifty tickets were sold to attend the live auction and dance after dinner. Dancing and Auction Only tickets cost ten thousand dollars each. Tickets for cocktails, dinner, and dancing started at twenty-five thousand, and that was for the honor of sitting in Siberia. Anyone who wanted to get noticed, needed to make a minimum gift of a quarter of a million dollars. This was special event fund-raising at the highest level and every year it raised about fifty million dollars for the International Refugee Foundation. Fifty million dollars can buy a lot of influence in any language and on any number of different levels.

As with all major international events such as this, the celebrities and their hangers-on come for free. That doesn't matter to the paying guests who vie for the privilege of flying a movie star, and her or his entourage, to Genoa in their private aircraft. Or bringing them to town on their yachts. The celebrities' contribution is their time.

As Alesandro had said, while the ball itself would include all the patrons and guests, the party tonight was restricted to the seven-figure donors—the elite of the elite. The normally inaccessible celebrities would circle around them like stars around the sun and make them feel good.

I seldom have trouble deciding what to wear. I know myself well, which is one reason why, in order to accomplish my goals, I'm able to assume different identities and not get lost in them the way an actor does in a role, and also why I've never participated in costume parties. I've never wanted to be anyone but myself. I also have a few rules for living, some may call them bromides and simplistic, but they work for me. One of them is: You never get a second chance to make a first impression. A lot depended on how I presented and handled myself this evening, it would be the crucible for how the next steps unfolded.

Tonight was a little more casual than the actual ball, which was day after tomorrow. So, after two glasses of champagne and a few false starts—some too dressy, some not dressy enough—I finally settled on a monochromatic Chanel ensemble: an iridescent taupe taffeta skirt with a matching quilted-silk jacket and sensational art deco, Cartier estate, diamond-and-topaz jewelry—necklace, earrings, and bracelet. I looked at myself in the mirror. It wasn't working, I was too monochromatic. Just as the phone rang letting me know Giancarlo was waiting in the lobby, I grabbed a stunning Van Cleef brooch and pinned it to my jacket: a four-inch-tall parrot made with vibrant mêlées of sapphires, rubies, emeralds, and intense goldenrod-yellow diamonds.

I looked in the mirror again. Just right. Regal and elegant. I looked like a queen who, because of the brooch, just might have a sense of humor.

"*Buona sera,* Bella," Giancarlo exclaimed when I got off the elevator. He was perfectly put together in his evening clothes. "You look *magnifica.*"

"Thank you, Giancarlo. So do you."

He kissed my hand and guided me through the front door to his Mercedes limousine. Everybody in the lobby watched us. I felt like Cinderella going to the ball.

The drive from the hotel to the villa, such an arduous hike for me, took less than two minutes, and when we passed through the gates, I saw there was serious security in place: Two friendly men in blue suits, white shirts, and ties waited inside the gate, one with a checklist, the other with a walkie-talkie. On the other side of the gate, blending in with the greenery, was a chap in fatigues with a beret, a dog and a gun.

Giancarlo helped me out at the front steps. "Be careful, Bella." He took my arm. "The floors have just been polished and they can be a little slippery."

We entered a high-ceilinged reception hall that was as massive as the lobby of the George V in Paris. Opposite were several sets of Palladian double doors thrown open spectacularly to the sea. The floor was pure white marble with the Giolitti coat of arms inlaid in brass-rimmed amber marble just inside the front door, framed on either side by white marble, single-pedestal tables. In the center of each table sat a potted palm in a gigantic blue and white Chinese brazier. The room was vast and uncluttered, punctuated only by spare seating arrangements of armchairs and ottomans, upholstered in a flaming orange-red duck. Small, square, black-iron occasional tables sat next to the chairs.

Beyond, outside on the flower-banked terrace, a gathering of about seventy-five guests was already sipping cocktails and enjoying the setting sun.

It was extraordinary. Everyone was famous, or at least recognizable—movie stars, royals, tycoons, fashion designers, consorts, and captains of industry. And while everyone might not have been beautiful or handsome, the power and influence this group wielded made up for any shortcomings in physical appearance. They all milled around, chatting happily.

Except for at auctions, I'd never seen so much important jewelry in one place. I knew that a number of the world's major jewelers—Harry Winston, Graff, Raymond Yard, and Van Cleef & Arpels, to name a few—had eagerly loaned pieces to the celebrities. And if these were the pieces they were wearing to the private party, I couldn't imagine what they would put on for the more public gala when the media would be out in force. Tonight there seemed to be only one videographer floating silently about while a handful of photographers snapped away unobtrusively. There were also four security men standing away from the gathering, two at either end of the terrace, not even attempting to blend in. Former soldiers, they all stood "at ease," their feet slightly spread and their hands clasped in front, their eyes taking in every new arrival and scanning the perimeter.

"*Vené*, Priscilla." Giancarlo escorted me through the dazzling crowd. "Let me introduce you. Although you probably have a number of friends here already."

I seriously doubted that. I simply smiled.

TWENTY-FOUR

"Sissy," Giancarlo said. "Please meet my friend Priscilla Pennington."

I wasn't a bit surprised to see Sissy McNally, the Texas socialite-billionairess, at this party—from all I'd read about her, she attended two or three parties every day, including the charity picnic at our farm. And just as at the museum in Paris, she had no inkling, not even the most fleeting, of having met me before.

Up close, Sissy looked to be in her midthirties, but wasn't. She had on a cream silk cocktail dress and a superb replica of l'Empresse de Josephine. So superb it could have been the real thing. The diamonds, emeralds, and pearls in the collar burned with energy, and the dark green Empresse cabochon emerald itself was hypnotic and mysterious against the cream silk of her dress.

She held out her hand. "I'm delighted to meet you. What a gorgeous pin. Where did you get it? Van Cleef?"

I nodded. "Thank you," I said. "I was just admiring your necklace. It's extraordinary. I think that's the largest emerald I've ever seen."

"Oh!" She laughed. "Isn't it a kick? I had to have it. I picked it up in Paris the other day at Fred's. It's a copy of the one that was stolen from the museum. But actually, if you want the lowdown—this emerald is much better than the missing one. I think it's kind of fun." She wrinkled her nose and squeezed her eyes shut in an annoying, ingénue sort of way she was much too old to affect.

Anyone who picks up necklaces at Fred's for "fun"—Fred's is one of the most expensive, and thereby exclusive, jewelers in the world—is living on a planet that has basically nothing to do with this one.

I studied Sissy as closely as I could without being rude—she looked almost exactly like her pictures that appeared regularly in *W, Town & Country*, and *Été*—very petite with meticulously coiffed Texas-sized blond hair and a bright, effervescent, lively face and smile. In person, though, signs of strain showed around her mouth, and there was a blue tinge to the skin around her eyes, as though she might have some sort of slight substance abuse problem. Or else she traveled through too many time zones, too often, to attend too many parties, and took too many sleeping pills. In spite of fresh plastic surgery scars behind her ears, the excesses of her lifestyle were beginning to take their toll.

"I'm so glad to meet you," she drawled in her distinctive Texas accent. "I hope once Giancarlo is through showing you off, we'll have a chance to visit."

"I agree."

"Come, Bella." Giancarlo took my arm.

"Marjorie," he interrupted the guest of honor. "You remember Priscilla from last evening."

"How could I forget?" She smiled warmly and we kissed

each other's cheeks. She was covered in diamonds and looked absolutely sensational in a gauzy, low-cut, red chiffon evening gown. "How did you feel this morning? I've never been so hungover in my life."

"I didn't feel fabulous," I said. "But you look as though you've fully bounced back."

"It's my job," Marjorie confided. "Looking good is all I'm required to do for this occasion. Good heavens—who loaned you that necklace? Cartier?"

"No one. It's mine. But it is from Cartier."

"You're joking? You own it?"

I nodded. "Of course I own it."

"Well, that's the difference between your world and mine: Yours is real. Mine's all make-believe. I'd better get back to work. See you at dinner." She turned to be greeted by another well-wisher.

Giancarlo got me a scotch, introduced me to a couple of other people whose names I didn't catch, and then excused himself to tend to his duties as host. I put up with being ignored for a couple of minutes and then stepped to another group and, when I saw an opening, introduced myself. No reaction. This was a crowd that obviously didn't want or need any new friends.

I tried a *"Buona sera"* to Katrine Forcescou, the Rumanian movie director's wife, but her expression was as out of touch as it had been the night before.

So concluded my attempts at being social. The fact is: I don't want or need any new friends either.

I stepped over to the balcony rail and looked out at the fabled port with its brightly painted buildings and snow-white yachts. From this vantage point, the inside looking out, the gardens of Villa Giolitti were magnificent. Flower-filled terraces descended to a thick grove of olive trees that arced along the stone-walled perimeter. Naturally, I studied the grounds with my thief's eye to see if I could pick out other possible entrances I could use if needed to break in or break out. From inside, it looked like an even greater challenge than I'd surmised from my reconnaissance. Not insurmountable if you had the right equipment and expertise, not to mention youthful agility, but not a cakewalk by any means.

Every square inch of the property was under video surveillance and I assumed there were trip wires and pressure pads out among the flower beds as well. I didn't see any evidence of dogs, but they probably weren't let out until after dark. I turned to study the villa itself and saw that each window and door had two little dice-sized motion detectors whose beams crisscrossed from corner to corner and side to side, very effectively covering the full area of the opening. This was a world-class system. I was impressed. In a town so sleepy and charming, especially an *Italian* town, who would imagine that the twenty-first century's most advanced security technology lay beneath its serene surface.

There was no question but that any move on the Millennium Star would have to be an inside job.

I scrutinized the guests—any number of them could be the burglar. I could only legitimately add one suspect to my list: Sissy McNally. But I added two. Marjorie.

I felt a hand at my elbow. "Let me show you around—no one will even notice we're gone." It was Giancarlo.

TWENTY-FIVE

Villa Giolitti was a sumptuous palazzo of the old order, large as a good-sized hotel, with high ceilings and grand rooms on the main floor, probably a dozen suites upstairs, and staff quarters on the third floor.

"It's been in my family for centuries." Giancarlo guided me down the colonnade with his hand placed gently on the small of my back—it was a warm, intimate gesture that made me feel welcome and desirable. "There used to be so many of us and the whole family would gather here for the entire summer. It was very fun, noisy, busy with all the cousins running all over. But times have changed. I have no brothers or sisters and my cousins are all settled in their own villas with their own families. Now, it's just my daughter, Lucia, and me."

I didn't ask Giancarlo about Mrs. Giolitti. I didn't want to know him that well, especially because, I reminded myself, I was there under false pretenses—phony name, phony interest. Depending on how things worked out, perhaps one day I'd introduce him to the real Kick Keswick.

We meandered through a series of reception rooms, each richly decorated, very formal, very Italian, completely unlike the spare, more public entry hall. Great works of art and family portraits in thickly carved gold frames covered every square inch of the walls. He'd point out one here and there, "That's my ancestor who became pope. We have five cardinals." He named them all. "This Titian shows St. Peter welcoming the pope to heaven with Cardinale Giancarlo Giolitti Primo looking on."

On and on it went.

"What an extraordinary collection," I said. "And it looks as though it's in perfect condition."

He nodded. "Since Heini Bournemiza died and his collection was broken up and taken to Spain of all places, ours is the largest privately owned collection on the Continent. We have two full-time curators and a staff of six restorers. This climate is very hard on paintings. Lucia supervises it all. Fortunately, she is very passionate about the subject and appreciates what we have."

As if on cue, a tall, slim figure approached from the far end of the gallery. She walked toward us purposefully. She had broad, bony shoulders and wore a black bustier, a black organza skirt and sandals.

"Ah, here comes my Principessa Lucia," Giancarlo said. "Let me introduce you to Signora Pennington."

We all know what an Italian *principessa* looks like. Is there any answer other than Audrey Hepburn in *Roman Holiday*? I'm not sure if she was even supposed to be Italian in that film, but she set the standard.

Lucia set a new one. She was the real thing. A swan. Her low-key appearance and demeanor were in direct contradiction to her father's glamorous world of movie stars. She wasn't hard on the eye, far from it. She lacked his perfect features and easy manner but she had an assurance and elegance that could only come from generations of entitlement. Her short black hair was cut with long, squared-off bangs that fell to her eyebrows. Scholarly, black-rimmed glasses with thick lenses framed her dark, wide-set eyes. She wore little makeup, except for a slash of red lipstick. She had crooked teeth and a genuine smile; a wonderful, long neck and strong jaw. Around her neck was a twisted black satin cord from which hung a very, very large cabochon emerald, suspended like a big green drop of water that had fallen from a tree in the jungle. The stone was exotic and dangerous, like the gleaming eye of the tiger.

"Welcome to Villa Giolitti, Signora Pennington." She took my hand.

TWENTY-SIX

"Your father was giving me a quick tour," I said. "I've never seen a private collection like this."

She nodded and turned to look down the arcade of doorways, each one topped by a coat of arms or crossed standards. "Sì. It's a big job. Between the paintings and the villa itself, the work is never-ending." Her words were heavily accented. "We are blessed to have such an important responsibility."

"I wish I could spend the entire evening looking at it." I turned to Giancarlo. "Forgive me, that wasn't very polite, was it? I'm looking forward to whatever the evening holds."

Giancarlo smiled. "Believe me, I agree with you completely. Let's take a moment and have a drink before we go back to the insanity." He pressed a small, old-fashioned button on the paneled wall and a manservant, wearing a starched white jacket emblazoned with the Giolitti crest, appeared out of nowhere. Giancarlo gave him a cocktail order.

We were in a library, no doubt one of many in the villa, and all the books in this room were oversized, some were two or three feet long, and bound in red linen—some were faded, others were crimson.

Giancarlo indicated a cluster of high-backed armchairs that

circled a cocktail table heaped with more of the red-bound volumes. I couldn't help but notice that the fabric on the chairs, while not exactly threadbare, was worn and slightly frayed around the edges.

"That's a magnificent emerald," I said to Lucia once we were seated. "It looks just like the one that was stolen in Paris, doesn't it, Giancarlo?" I smiled at him. "That's where your father and I met—in that funny little museum."

Lucia smiled and laughed. Her hand clasped the stone protectively. "It's not stolen, though. It's mine. It was a gift."

"It's lovely. Large stones have always been my favorite sort of gift." Our eyes connected. "I'd hold on to whoever gave it to you."

An uncomfortable silence followed. Lucia nodded—her expression betrayed no emotion. She glanced at her father who seemed to force a smile in return. As a first impression, there appeared to be little warmth between father and daughter. But perhaps it was just their way, a natural reticence in front of strangers.

Or perhaps her father had stolen it and given it to her as a peace offering for some real or imagined wrong.

"What are the books in this room?" I asked.

"These are all journals and workbooks that contain the history of the villa," Lucia explained. She sat forward, on the edge of her chair, and crossed her long legs. Her posture was divine. "Not the family history, but the history of the building and grounds. These are all notebooks, so the history is continual from the time the villa was built." She turned one of the large

books in my direction—its cover had faded to soft tangerine—
and hefted it open. "Let me see. Ah, this volume shows how the
kitchen garden developed during the 1600s. You see how the
wall was replaced over and over again." She turned the ancient
pages of drawings, some professional, some hastily sketched.
"They understood about drainage at that time, but not so much
about how to prevent erosion. As you can see, by the end of the
century, the problem was solved by digging down and building
the stone wall deep into the ground with proper drains. Sections
of this wall are still standing, doing their job. Several of the notebooks we use today are the originals, such as this one about the
master bedroom. Each room has its own book. Isn't it wonderful? This one's my sitting room."

She opened the journal and flipped through a few pages
showing the progression of a large corner room with sets of
doors on two walls and a fireplace whose mantel had evolved
through a dozen iterations from plain limestone to rococo to
today's white marble.

Speaking of the villa transformed Lucia's face, replacing the
hard planes with energy and light.

"It's fabulous," I said.

"Perhaps you'd like to come for a tour tomorrow?" she
asked.

"I'd love to."

"Would you join us for lunch?" Her face brightened further.

"Yes. Absolutely."

"Wonderful. Come at one."

A dinner chime rang far in the distance.

"Ladies," Giancarlo said. "Shall we?"

I felt more comfortable in the Giolittis' presence than I had in—how many days had it been since this odyssey began? Two weeks? Was that possible? Giancarlo was relaxed and outgoing. And Lucia's reserved demeanor made me sympathetic toward her. I felt a connection, as I would to a daughter.

"I will apologize in advance, Priscilla." Giancarlo had put my arm through his and turned slightly to talk to me. His breath smelled of scotch and peppermint. "I had nothing to do with the meal this evening. The organizers brought in a famous chef from France, if you can imagine, a French chef at Villa Giolitti—I'm so glad my mother never lived to see such a thing! And he selected the wines. So I can make no promises about what will be on your plate. Or in your glass. Tonight, I am a guest in my own house—at the mercy of Melissa Carrington."

"Melissa Carrington?"

"She's director of public relations for the International Refugee Foundation and in charge of the whole affair—tonight and the gala. Very talented but a dragon. She reminds me of a schoolteacher—very stubborn and cold."

"She is not cold, Father," Lucia said. "She is professional." She turned to me. "My father still struggles with women in the working world. He's just too Italian."

"The evening will be fabulous." I chose to change subjects. "Besides, no one comes to these parties for the food. It's the company and conversation and this is definitely a group that won't run out of things to talk about."

Just before we entered the grand foyer, we passed a closed

door outside of which stood an armed guard. He and Giancarlo nodded to each other.

"What's in there?" I whispered to Giancarlo.

"Oh. All the shops that are providing jewelry for the ladies
to wear to the festivities want to keep it in one place. So the
ladies put it on in there when they arrive and then return it before they go home to their hotels or yachts. It's a new security
measure."

"Good idea," I said.

He nodded, bored with the subject. "I suppose."

"Is the Millennium Star here?"

He shook his head. "*Domani.*"

"Ah." Tomorrow.

At the door of the dining room we were greeted by a handsome, blond woman in a chic black Chanel suit, exactly the
sort of suit I used to wear to work every day at the auction
house. "*Buona sera,* Count Giolitti," she said over her reading
glasses. "*Principessa,* you look so beautiful."

"*Grazie.*"

The woman escorted us into the dining room, which was
reminiscent of St. George's banquet hall at Windsor Castle that
can seat more than two hundred people at one table. There were
only eighty guests at this particular dinner but even so, you
seldom see a single table set for eighty. It was breathtaking.
The room's glazed walls glowed with rich, dense, light. Baroque,
sterling silver, six-candle candelabras were placed the length of

the table—it looked as though there were more than a dozen of them—and between each one was a long, low arrangement of orange-red roses. Candlelight from the tapers and dozens of votives scattered around the table flickered off a battery of crystal wineglasses and off the beveled mirror place mats. In the center of each place mat, folded into a cone shape, sat a starched white linen napkin, monogrammed with the Giolitti coat of arms. Each piece of Baroque sterling flatware bore the monogram, as well.

The guests had paid dearly for an inside look at a royal dinner, and they were getting their money's worth. Every person who entered the dining room, even the most jaded, even those who'd attended the dinner in previous years, made an exclamation of some sort. The impact of the beauty was in its simplicity— nothing was overdone. There weren't ribbons wrapped through the flowers, or gold fish swimming in the flower vases, or baskets of favors from the underwriters, or gold lamé draped over the chairs. The beauty was in the fact that every candelabra, place setting, wineglass, piece of linen, and the table and chairs were family-owned, well-used by generations of Giolittis, and classic in their style, shape, and presentation.

"Melissa Carrington," Giancarlo muttered to me as we followed the woman up the length of the table to the end closest to the unlit fireplace, above which hung a Renaissance-era painting of a bacchanal.

"Here you are." She smiled easily. "At the head of the table, of course. Signora Pennington, we put you two down because

the count needs to have Marjorie on one side and the chair of
our board on the other. I hope you understand."

"Of course, I do. This is perfect."

"Count, please let me know if you need anything at all."

"*Grazie,*" Giancarlo said.

"I think she's very nice," I said once she was out of earshot.

Giancarlo shrugged. "I like women who are women. She is a
machine."

While the rest of the dinner patrons wandered in, I wondered how much Giancarlo charged the Gala di Portofino organizers to use his villa. Tons, I imagined. It must cost a fortune
to keep this place going.

TWENTY-SEVEN

I was seated between two tycoons who, once they had introduced themselves to me—Where are you from? Outside of London. Oh.—spent the entire dinner talking to each other around me, which was fine. That was the way the evening was meant to work. This dinner was about power and access and in that world, a widow from Buckinghamshire just didn't cut it.

I suddenly felt incredibly homesick for my beautiful farm, my beautiful life, and what I had thought was my beautiful, wonderful husband. I ached with missing him—I just wanted to put my head down on the table and sob my heart out. I wondered if he was sitting on a terrace overlooking the same Mediterranean, just miles around the same coastline, sipping a scotch and missing me, wondering if I was all right. Or was he simply figuring out the best way to trap me and bring me to justice? Sometimes the whole affair—the happiness, the marriage, the desertion—felt surreal, especially on an evening such as this when the bay danced with lights from the yachts, and the hillsides sparkled with villas and their dinner parties, and brightly lit cruise ships traversed the horizon as though out of a dream. I envied the people on those ships, probably as much as they envied those of us on shore. It was an evening for lovers.

The imported French chef's dinner menu was designed to catch attention, and it did, more for its bizarre riskiness than for its palatability. It got people talking. The first course was lightly seared foie gras chaud, perfectly prepared and served on a bed of watercress. Liver in any of its incarnations is not especially one of my favorites, although I ate it, washing it down with several healthy sips of a gorgeous 1986 La Tache. Next came a broth that looked suspiciously as though it had something's little tiny heart floating in it. Not only was this fellow knocking himself out to get talked about—he'd gone overboard. The main course was sweetbreads three ways—grilled, fricasseed, and baked. Thank God for whoever had selected the wines.

I kept a pleasant expression on my face, in case the conversation between the two men lagged and a lighter touch was required, which it was from time to time. Even a country farm widow can come in handy to help ease those conversational transitions that, without the proper segue, can become unspannable crevasses. Otherwise, I occupied myself by thinking about the two giant cabochon emeralds here this evening—one on Sissy McNally and one on Lucia. What if one of them actually was l'Empresse? I had to assume one of them was—there weren't that many 255-carat cabochon emeralds around.

I looked down at Sissy. She was the flash point for her section of the table, among good friends, telling Texas tall tales, keeping things bubbling along. Unless she had a completely opposite side to her personality, I couldn't picture her breaking into anything. She lived her life in a fishbowl—she wouldn't risk it by stealing jewelry, even on a lark. And if she suffered from kleptomania, it would have been on the front pages of the tabloids ages ago.

Marjorie was seated between Giancarlo and the chairman of the board of a Japanese car manufacturer, one of the evening's main underwriters. She was earning her dinner—she never took her attention off the industrialist who smiled at her as though he were hypnotized.

On Giancarlo's other side was the chairwoman of the International Refugee Foundation, a powerful, wealthy woman in her sixties who made no pretense at youthfulness. Her hair was gray, her face had not been tampered with since the day she was born, and she was unfazed by the few extra pounds around her midriff and hips. She was one of the most persuasive, effective fund-raisers in the world because she was one of the most generous people in the world—she put her money where her mouth was and gave away millions every year. She was unquestionably the most respected philanthropist in the room.

Lucia was at the opposite end of the table and from a distance seemed to be enjoying herself.

Between sips of the Château Margaux, I worked up scenarios of my plan to steal the biggest perfect diamond in the world. There weren't very many of us who could do that. Would my nemesis make a move tonight just for the fun of it? There were some very precious stones here. For someone like me, it would be easy to take a necklace or bracelet or two and have them vanish into my deep pockets before the targets were even aware they were missing, even with all the security. No. Nothing would happen here this evening. Other than the emeralds, I hadn't seen anything that could qualify as a trophy. The burglar had his eye on one thing and one thing only. I knew he was here at this table—I could feel it.

Unless it was Alesandro, of course.

A trio began to play on the terrace.

I looked in Giancarlo's direction at the same time he looked in mine. Our eyes connected and he gave me a wonderful, intimate smile. 'Do you want to dance?' he asked silently.

I nodded.

"These affairs are hell," he said. He was a superb dancer, much better than Thomas. "It will be over soon."

We glided around in the moonlight without speaking.

"Bella," he said shortly. "I know this is a late invitation, but would you consider letting me escort you to the gala? You would be doing me a great favor."

I didn't take a deep breath, but I wanted to. The camel was in the tent. I opened my mouth to reply, but he kept talking.

"I'm embarrassed to invite you in this way, but the truth of the matter is Consuelo's family is still in a mess and I need someone who can be my hostess. I can't ask any of these starlets or girls, I need someone with some maturity and elegance who won't spend the entire evening trying to get a famous director to put her in his next film. I can't think of anything more delightful than spending another evening with you. And I promise, we'll sit together at dinner."

I laughed. "I'd love to, Giancarlo."

"*Bene. Bene. Grazie,* Bella."

Then he kissed me. And it absolutely took my breath away.

My mind and body exploded into conflict—I was instantly flooded with desire and at the same time afraid of where that could lead, and would lead if I let it. One part of me was saying, childishly, "See, Thomas, someone wants me." While another part reminded me that I did, indeed, want to be kissed, but by Thomas, not a stranger. I felt exhilarated and ashamed. I looked into Giancarlo's eyes as he began to kiss me again and pushed him away.

"I'm sorry, Giancarlo," I said. "It's too soon. I just lost my husband. I'm not ready, even for kisses. I hope you understand."

He nodded. "Of course, I do. Come, let's tell our guests good night."

TWENTY-EIGHT

It was early, not even eleven, when I got back to the hotel. Some people, true café society types, were just going into dinner. The bar was quiet. There were a few couples on the terrace sipping Prosecco or liqueurs. One table in particular caught my eye.

Alesandro. With a woman approximately my age. Beautifully groomed and dressed, and wearing what I considered to be major-league jewelry. Maybe that was my problem in attracting him: In spite of all my tennis diamonds, I wasn't showy enough. I had too much taste.

This particular woman had on a diamond necklace, ruby cuffs, ten-carat-plus stones on four of her fingers, and a cross-shaped ruby and diamond brooch that looked like it came off the top of one of the English royal family's ceremonial crowns.

She had a kind, soft, sad face that could not conceal her vulnerability. She was a sitting duck. She didn't deserve to get robbed. What should I do?

I went upstairs and got Bijou and took her for a quick walk and then she and I went into the bar and were seated at a table near Alesandro's. Bijou jumped up onto the chair next to mine and sat down.

There's nothing like a dog to break the ice. Especially a precious little white fluffy one like mine.

"Oh," Alesandro's lady friend said. "Look at your darling Westie." She got up and came toward me. Her eyes filled with tears. "May I?" She reached for Bijou. The rubies sparkled from her wrists. "She looks just like my baby. My Sugar. I had to leave her at home and I'm miserable without her." She sat down and kissed Bijou and buried her face in her fur and began to cry.

"I'm so sorry," I said. I kept my eyes away from Alesandro. I knew there'd be a look of total bewilderment on his face and I didn't want to let him see I knew I'd rescued a victim from his clutches.

The woman sat up and took a hankie out of her purse and dabbed at her cheeks. "I'm so sorry. I'm just so homesick. Isn't it silly?"

"It's not silly at all. Why didn't you bring her with you?"

"You know how these travel agents are. Mine told me some of the hotels I'm staying in don't allow pets," the woman said. "I wanted to change hotels but my son convinced me my little Sugar would be fine staying with him and his wife. I didn't know what to do. I'm traveling alone for the first time." She looked at me and the look on her face broke my heart. Like me, she was waiting to get her life back. Waiting for someone to come along and fix it, put it all back the way it used to be. "I lost my husband a year ago and decided I needed to try to strike out on my own."

"I'm so sorry." I put my hand on her arm and looked in her

eyes. "I understand exactly how you feel. I made my mind up a long time ago that if I can't take my dog, I won't go. That way you're never alone. Besides, there isn't any place I want to see that badly anyway."

"I agree."

"I love to be at home."

"I do, too," she said.

We smiled at each other. We were kindred spirits. I could tell, neither one of us cared if we ever left home again, but she had, because she felt she had to give it a try, and I had because I didn't have any choice.

"This trip has been the worst experience of my life. What's your puppy's name?"

"Bijou," I answered.

"Bijou." The woman kissed her again before placing her back on the chair. "She's absolutely precious. I'm so glad I ran into you. I think I'll just forget the whole thing and go home tomorrow." She retrieved her purse from her table. "Thank you so much for the champagne, Count de Camarque," she said to Alesandro, who'd gotten to his feet. "It was lovely meeting you."

"And you, signora," he said charmingly. *"Buona sera."*

We both watched her make her way across the terrace and disappear into the main lobby. Alesandro turned to me. He looked stupefied, at a total loss.

"I'm so sorry," I said. "I hope I didn't ruin your evening. I didn't mean to make her cry." Bijou had jumped onto my lap and returned his gaze innocently.

He gave a small shrug and stood there, not seeming to know exactly which way to go.

"Won't you join me and finish your drink?" I said. "Really. It's the least I can do."

"No. *Grazie,* Priscilla. I'll hope to see you tomorrow. *Buona notte.*" He turned and walked off.

I didn't hear it go off, but just before he entered the lobby, Alesandro took a small cell-phone out of his pocket and studied it as though he'd just been paged.

A pager in Portofino? How unbelievably cheap.

How unbelievably Colombian.

TWENTY-NINE

I didn't sleep all night. All I did was think about Giancarlo and his kiss. It was so gentle. So familiar. So sexy. So practiced. So unsettling. I played that part of the evening over and over again, dancing on the terrace in the moonlight with Portofino twinkling all around us. I would have given anything for it to have been Thomas. Giancarlo's kiss was sweet and tantalizing— like a spritz of champagne. Thomas's, on the other hand, had depth and passion. They were as complex and alluring and satisfying as a fine bordeaux.

I also thought about Alesandro.

His laid-back style was an act. He gave the impression that he had not a care in the world, and that was part of his talent. It took energy, creativity, drive, and discipline to break into a museum. And the robbery at the Ritz had required long-range planning and nerves of steel. And the Riviera robberies? Well, it took an enormous amount of stamina to rob two ladies in two different hotels on the same night. All you had to do was see Alesandro on the tennis court to appreciate his level of energy and concentration. But the personality he put on was feline, magnetic. He just watched and watched, and waited for his victims to come to him, for the time to be exactly right to slip upstairs for a nightcap. Then, I imagined, he handed off his loot to the girl he'd been having lunch with at Splendido Mare. I assumed she dressed as a hotel maid and waited in the hall for him to come out.

I further assumed his accomplice had paged him because she'd had another bird on the wire.

By seven o'clock, I gave up on sleeping and called the front desk to see about an eight o'clock tennis lesson. Eight o'clock in the morning in Portofino might as well be the middle of the night, but the pro, my darling Guilberto, could not have been more courteous or accommodating, even though he smelled slightly boozy. I don't think he'd been home yet from whatever he'd been doing the night before.

The exercise felt good and the focus the game required took my mind off my problems for a while.

"Brava! Brava, signora," Guilberto called across the net.

I'd returned six shots in a row, including a lunging backhand that he'd raced to return. And missed.

The hour flew past.

"Tomorrow, I will teach you to serve," he said.

"I can't wait."

I think I am going to become a fitness nut.

Alesandro was waiting for me, courtside, with a towel. "You've improved impressively. Did you practice all night while the rest of us were sleeping?"

"Beginner's luck," I answered. "Isn't it the most beautiful day?"

He nodded. "It's going to be warm. You were smart to come out early before it gets hot. Will you join me for breakfast?"

"I'd love to."

He followed me down to the main dining room where we were seated in the shade. The ocean breeze was cool and fragrant.

A waiter poured our coffee and placed a basket of steaming hot, miniature orange muffins in the center of the table.

"Have you been following the Shamrock Burglar's antics on the Riviera ?" I split a muffin in two and spread it with butter. The muffin had flecks of lemon zest and chopped pecan—it practically melted in my mouth.

Alesandro nodded. "He's very busy. I think he must be very young. Two ladies in one night? *Dio.*"

"I think he has an accomplice."

A large smile crossed his face. "Two people? Very intriguing. You might be right. Perhaps it's an entire gang. Probably Russians, I hear they're very successful at robbing people."

"I've heard Colombians are better," I said.

"Really? Where did you hear that?"

"I don't recall. I read it somewhere."

"Interesting." His expression was totally unreadable because he had on his dark glasses and I had on mine. If I took mine off, he'd take his off. But then he'd see what I really looked like in the morning with no makeup and then, I'm sorry to say, the jig would be up and he would lose interest quickly. My eyes were puffy—they are every morning—not so bad that they look like I have flapjacks pasted on them, but well, maybe little silver dollar-sized pancakes. There was no possibility I was going to take my glasses off.

"I'm sorry for those women," I said. "It's sad."

"You should be careful yourself, Priscilla." Alesandro dropped three sugar cubes into his coffee and stirred it slowly. "Be on your guard against such men. You are an uncommonly beautiful, desirable woman traveling alone. You have beautiful jewelry. You're exactly what these men look for. There's no shortage of scoundrels, men who prey on lonely, wealthy women."

"Well, thank goodness I'm not lonely." I laughed.

"Oh, that's right," he grunted. "I forgot. You have your little dog."

We smiled at each other.

THIRTY

After breakfast, I took a shower, wrapped a towel around my wet hair, pulled on a soft cotton summer robe, and stepped out onto my private terrace to plan my day. The view never failed to give me pleasure—the natural beauty, the busyness of the small port, the quiet privacy. The heady daytime fragrance of petunias. I looked across the hillside to just below the Giolitti palazzo at the little house I'd bought. I could only see the corner of the covered terrace—the rest of it was hidden by shrubbery.

I was looking forward to lunch with Lucia Giolitti, not just because it would put me back inside the palazzo, but because I liked her. And I would have liked her whether or not she could serve my purposes. She was special. She reminded me of myself—she was alone. But not lonely.

While I was bathing, the maid had placed a bottle of Panna Water, a small pot of coffee, and a folded morning paper on the patio table. I opened it up. The headline was huge:

LADRO TRIFOGLIO! IN SAN REMO!

The Shamrock Burglar had struck again. This time right up the road, around the Corniche at the magnificent Hotel

Excelsior in San Remo, just east of the French-Italian border.

I took a deep breath. This person was on a joyride. Who was it?

I turned on the television set. Before long, Thomas was on the news, talking to Giovanna McDougal who was following the robberies at the same leisurely pace he did. They were stopping off at all the Riviera's most beautiful watering holes, for a robbery, a story, and a cup of coffee or a *coupe de champagne*. I know theirs was supposed to be a professional, adversarial relationship, but when you really looked at the facts, she and Thomas were having a most luxurious, all-expenses-paid vacation. Together.

"A fifth robbery, Commander Curtis. How do you explain this?"

"We're dealing with a very sophisticated criminal, Giovanna," Thomas responded, and I couldn't help but notice he'd called her by her first name. "This individual, we're not sure if it is a man or a woman, has a plan to which I am not privy. However, we have some very solid leads. I'm confident the Shamrock will not remain on the loose for much longer."

I felt as though I were looking at a stranger.

"You think the Shamrock Burglar could be a woman?"

Thomas nodded. "You seem surprised."

"Well, the impression has been that there has been seduction involved."

"Impressions can be misleading." I knew he was about to get patronizing, something he was inclined to do when dealing with what he considered to be lesser human beings, meaning

basically anyone who didn't hold a doctorate from Oxford,
preferably two. One in law and one in philosophy, as he did.
Or anyone who couldn't tell a fresh, young merlot from a
slightly oversized burgundy. "And frankly, Miss McDougal,
those seduction implications have come only from you and
your colleagues in the media. Not from the authorities."

"Has a pattern emerged?" She ignored his tone.

"Not particularly, but the burglar is taking very fine and distinctive pieces that will be easily identifiable."

"Such as?"

"I don't think it would serve our case to become specific."
Thomas smiled paternalistically.

"You haven't provided any specifics at all, Commander,
about any of the robberies." Not only was Giovanna un-
daunted, she was a crackerjack reporter and she wasn't going
to accept any brush-off answers. "Since the original burglary at
the museum in Paris, the police have not released specifics of
anything that's been stolen. Why won't you give us some idea
of the sorts of jewels—especially if they are as distinctive as
you claim. Perhaps one of our viewers will see one of them and
call you."

I expected Thomas just to turn and walk off at her sheer
naiveté, at her sheer audacity for questioning his judgment, so
what he said next caught me totally off guard.

"All right."

Any number of factors could have contributed to Thomas's
relaxation of his professional demeanor—maybe the seductive
Mediterranean climate that seemed to put the world in a different

perspective. Or maybe it was the seductive Giovanna herself. Whatever it was, they were starting to seem awfully chummy to me.

"Although it's against our policy," he said, "I think in this instance, you might be right. Perhaps we will get a tip from one of your viewers. Among the pieces stolen in Beaulieu were two matching diamond bracelets and an extremely rare diamond and turquoise blackamoor brooch."

"Blackamoor?"

"Yes," he answered slowly. I could tell he was trying to choose his words carefully, so the uneducated could comprehend them. "In the nineteenth and twentieth centuries, when the British Empire was at its peak, with new frontiers breeched almost on a daily basis in the Near and Far East and Africa, it became stylish to have exotic black slaves, although some were classified as indentured servants. Indentured means . . ."

"Yes, Commander. We all know what indentured means," Giovanna said.

"Of course. Some were Nubian, some were Indian, all were men, most were eunuchs. As it inevitably does, fashion followed this trend and many elaborate sculptures and pieces of jewelry were created with black faces, generally made out of ebony or onyx—hence, blackamoor."

Thank you, Kick Keswick, I said to myself. Thomas—Mr. Television-Jewelry-Expert—didn't know a diamond from a dingbat until he met me.

———

"The brooch that was stolen in Beaulieu was about three inches tall, and had an onyx face, with a gold bib and gold turban studded with diamonds and turquoises."

"Sounds beautiful," she said.

"Very striking," Thomas answered. He smiled at her again.

What was going on here? Just because I lost my bearings for a moment or two under the spell of Giancarlo's sensuous lips, it never occurred to me the same thing could happen to Thomas. Was he having a fling with this girl? Had he been swept away by romance and glamour? By a blond with a good tan who had unlimited access to airtime? Which we all knew Thomas thrived on. Was *he* kissing *her* on a terrace over the Mediterranean? Dancing with her in the moonlight? Feeling exhilarated and ashamed? Never! Thomas would never kiss anyone but me.

"Do you know where the Shamrock is likely to strike next?"

"I have a good idea," Thomas said.

"Portofino." She said it as a statement of fact. I didn't care for the look on her face—it seemed lascivious to me.

Thomas didn't answer.

"Son of a bitch," I said.

Time had run out for me. If I didn't move quickly, I would be in handcuffs before lunchtime.

I pulled out all my suitcases and started packing.

THIRTY-ONE

I waited as long as I could before calling Villa Giolitti. My watch said ten-thirty and I knew it was still too early but I needed some fast decisions. I was counting on Giancarlo's inborn sense of hospitality, and the hope that our delicious, sexy kiss burned in his memory as intensely as it did in mine. If I put it the right way, he would invite me to come stay at the palazzo before Thomas got to town and mucked everything up. But he needed to invite me right now, otherwise not only would I have to scrap my plan to prevent the Star from being stolen by my copycat, but I also wouldn't have time to get off the peninsula before Thomas—and his media groupies—headed in and spotted me trying to escape. The road was too narrow and, unless I disguised myself, I was too noticeable to slip past them and I'd be trapped. I couldn't use my little cottage as a hiding place. That was for later, when all this had blown over. I had to get out of the hotel and possibly out of town. Now.

It wasn't as though Thomas could arrest me for anything legitimate. Even if he wanted to go whole hog and reveal the truth about my life, and our life, and claim I was the real Shamrock Burglar, he had no proof of anything. The only piece of incriminating evidence I had, the Queen's Pet, was gone, and now presumably in his possession. No. He couldn't pin any of this on me. I didn't have any of the goods and I hadn't been in any of the locations except the Ritz. The only thing he could prove, if he really decided to go for me, was that I was traveling under an assumed identity. And even at that, the most he could get me for was renting a car with a fake ID—not an insurmountable problem. The bigger problem was, if he did detain me, I would miss my shot at the Star and I'd be back at square one.

"*Pronto,*" a man's voice answered.

"Count Giolitti, please. It's Signora Pennington calling."

"One moment, please, signora."

It took Giancarlo a couple of minutes to pick up. "*Buon giorno,* Bella." He sounded as though he'd been asleep.

"I'm so sorry, Giancarlo. Did I wake you?"

"No. No. Not at all. What a lovely way to begin my day. Lucia and I are looking forward to seeing you for lunch."

"That's why I'm calling, Giancarlo," I said. "I'm not going to be able to join you for lunch or the gala."

"What?! Why?" Now he sounded awake. I could picture him sitting straight up in what was probably an ancestral bed that had a canopy and bed hangings and was four feet from the floor. I imagined he slept in the nude. Something I wouldn't consider doing under any circumstance.

"I have done the stupidest thing," I lied. "I completely forgot that when I booked my rooms at the hotel they told me they were sold-out for the nights around the gala. At the time, I didn't think anything of it. But I have to check out by noon, today. I'm already packed."

I wanted to say eleven, because noon was pushing it for me with Thomas's arrival, but I knew eleven would push it too much for Giancarlo. I had no choice but to risk the hour.

"Where will you go?"

"They've made arrangements for me to spend two nights in a perfectly lovely spot in Genoa—as you can imagine, everything on the whole peninsula is booked solidly. I'm so sorry, Giancarlo. I'm so disappointed—I had such a beautiful time with you last night."

"Genoa?" I could see his nose wrinkle. "There is no 'perfectly lovely' spot in Genoa. No. You will move to the villa."

I smiled. Steady, Kick. Steady.

"I can't do that, Giancarlo. You have too much going on. You've already got a house full of guests, you don't need to add another. We'll have dinner when I get back."

"Don't be silly. I will call for you at twelve o'clock. You will stay at Villa Giolitti. There is plenty of room."

"Are you certain?"

"Sì. End of discussion."

"Well, if you insist, I'd love to stay. That is very generous of you. And you don't need to send a car for me. I have my own."

"Perfetto. Come whenever you are ready. Ciao."

"Ciao, Giancarlo."

THIRTY-TWO

As I drove up the hill toward the palazzo, I had to pull over to the side of the road to make way for an armored truck that was on its way down, which signaled to me that the Millennium Star and the jewelry for the gala had just been delivered.

The road wound past the lane to my little pink bungalow. Just knowing it was there, safely tucked away in the hillside invisible behind the trees, gave me a sense of well-being. I'd tucked the front door key into my pocket in case of emergency.

Security at the main villa's gate had been beefed up significantly from last night. A black-and-white striped barrier blocked the road and two uniformed officers examined my papers and checked my name on their list before calling to make certain I was still expected and that someone would come out to meet me. They were extremely polite—they even gave Bijou a little cookie—but I had the feeling that if I said or did anything untoward, they would shoot me. And my little dog. I had no idea how many officers were on the Portofino police force but their squad cars had caused a complete traffic jam in the villa's courtyard.

I guided my Mercedes to the front steps where a tiny houseman in Giolitti livery introduced himself as Vesuvio. He looked like he was one hundred years old and didn't weigh more than ninety pounds dripping wet.

"*Benvenuto*, signora." He held out his hand toward the open front doors. "*Prego.*"

The huge lobby/foyer and terrace, where we'd had cocktails last night, swarmed with activity—people with clipboards, people pushing around palm trees on dollies, people pointing, and people ordering people about. Everybody had on a headset with a microphone. A piano tuner kept hitting the same note over and over again and the orchestra sound man was doing sound-checks, high-pitched electronic squeals added unpleasantly to the cacophony. The lighting designer was throwing a tantrum, red-faced and screaming at his weeping helper who teetered on top of a high ladder. It was chaos.

Over in one corner, a dozen dark-suited men and women wearing earphones were gathered around Melissa Carrington, the Refugee Foundation's director, and the security chief having a staff meeting, checking and cross-checking their plans to make sure they'd covered all contingencies for the priceless jewels that the ladies and movie stars would be wearing. Judging by all the firepower, I gathered that I'd been correct about the armored truck: The Star had been delivered and stored in what Giancarlo had referred to as the "Jewelry Room." The fact that the ladies would put their pieces on when they arrived for the party and give them back when it was over—all on the premises—made for a very clean, smart, and completely controllable operation.

At least they hoped that was how it would go. That was their plan. The difference between the security contingent's plan and mine and the actual burglar's was: The thieves had only one or two schemes but the security people had to be ready for five or six. Except for their guns, they were always at a disadvantage because they didn't know what was going to happen. We did.

When I stole pieces from Ballantine & Company, pieces that had come in for auction, I'd always spent weeks in my secret workroom at home creating a perfect replica of the brooch or necklace. I worked from huge color, close-up photographs of the piece, the photos taken by the house photographer for the catalogue. A few days before the sale, I'd FedEx the finished item to myself at the office and store it in my desk drawer.

Typically, when a jewelry auction begins, the actual pieces are in jewelry cases in the exhibition room and the house security guards bring in rolling jewelry vaults that resemble armored stacks of safe deposit boxes. In the sale room itself, only photos of the pieces are shown on large screens. The displays are dismantled by what are known as the Jewelry Ladies as the auction proceeds nearby in the sale room. I always helped the Jewelry Ladies move items from the cases to the safes, my perfect replica ready in my pocket. As soon as the gavel fell on "my" piece, if it were bought by a private party, not a dealer— I'd never try to trick a dealer—I'd make the swap. Just as smooth as could be. Out of one pocket into the other.

So, based on my experience, if I were going to steal the Star, I would do it with a sleight-of-hand swap. In a controlled environment like this, a smash and grab would be far too crude and risky, especially because these guards, unlike bank guards, were armed and, I assumed, they had bullets in their guns.

I hated to admit it, but the thought of all the jewelry in such close vicinity made my mouth go dry and my fingers tingle.

"*Mi dispaccio,*" I apologized for the tenth time to Vesuvio, who'd just completed his third trip carrying my luggage to my room. "Please let me help you with that."

"No, no, signora." He smiled, showing me what looked to be newly restored teeth. "You want to know the truth?" His watery eyes looked at me conspiratorially from beneath their droopy lids. "Signora Sissy has *vente* suitcases, just like this, big, heavy suitcases. And *two* dogs!"

"Twenty?"

"*Sì.* Big, big cases like this. Every year she almost kills me, but I love her. She's so kind and gracious. She's from Texas in the United States. Her maid, Bessie?" He flipped his thumbnail on his front tooth in a sign of contempt. "She's a snob. She does nothing to help us. So"—Vesuvio shrugged philosophically— "we do nothing to help her. You understand?" He disappeared out the door to make another trip.

"I do."

My bedroom room was an extravaganza—a wonderland of pastel-painted rococo furniture, a crystal chandelier and sconces and gilt-framed paintings. A huge, smoky-with-age mirror in a frame that must have weighed five hundred pounds hung above a marble-topped sideboard upon which sat a number of candlesticks and two topiaries in painted-metal jardinières. A bouquet of shell-pink hydrangeas utterly overtook the fireplace, filling the opening completely. Linen slipcovers had been installed for the summertime: The canopy and bed hangings on the four-poster were of pale melon and white, in an almost tropical pattern, and the sofa was covered in the same crisp, sunny fabric. The carpets had been rolled up for summer, as well, leaving only a shiny glazed white tile floor.

A bottle of Dom Pérignon sat in an ice bucket on the coffee table, along with two flutes, a plate of cheeses, and a plate of chocolate truffles.

It was a fresh sun-filled room fit for a visiting dignitary—done up exactly the way I'd decorate a guest suite in a palazzo. Anything less would have been disappointing.

"*Mi dispaccio,*" I said to Vesuvio again. What more could I say? I guess he was grateful I traveled with only one dog, no maid, and only five heavy-duty Vuitton suitcases. None of this soft-sided, lighter-than-air, roll-along baggage for we ladies of means with taffeta evening gowns and silk afternoon dresses packed in tissue paper.

"I will send Sophia to see to your unpacking," he puffed, once he'd hauled the last piece of luggage.

"That's not necessary, Vesuvio. I prefer to do it myself."

"*Prego,* signora. In here . . ." He directed me to join him in the dressing room where five white gardenias floated in a carved crystal dish on the mirrored dressing table, filling the air with their lush, hypnotic scent. Vesuvio opened one of the closet doors. A hotel-type safe sat above the built-in drawers.

". . . is a safe. You can make your own combination. Do you know how to work it?"

"I do, thank you." This sort of safe was designed only to instill confidence in the naive traveler. It certainly wasn't designed to protect anything valuable and anybody who put anything of value in one of these things was just asking to be robbed. You could practically open them by saying, *Boo!* Their only benefit was that if you *didn't* put your jewelry in the safe and you were robbed, your insurance wouldn't cover the stolen pieces because you hadn't tried to protect them, as the cashier at the Ritz had pointed out so succinctly when the White Tiger Suite was stolen. I was certain that, here at the villa, all the houseguests' jewelry of consequence was stored either in a main vault or stashed in hiding places in the rooms themselves.

"There is also a large vault down the hall which you are welcome to use, if you like. It is attended."

"*Grazie,* Vesuvio."

"*Bene.*" He checked his watch. "Conto Giolitti and Principessa Lucia will greet you at twelve-thirty on the family terrace."

"*Grazie.*"

"*Prego.*" He began to close the door.

"Oh, wait! I left my dark glasses in the car."

"I'll send them up *pronto,* signora."

"No, no. I'll go get them—I probably forgot ten other things. Just point me in the direction of the garage."

"*Prego,* signora."

THIRTY-THREE

Forgetting my glasses was a ruse, of course. I wanted to see where my car was in case I needed to get out of here in a hurry.

I followed Vesuvio along the upstairs corridor past other bedroom doors, some open, some closed. An army of maids moved quietly around the hallway, some carrying stacks of linens and fresh towels, others carrying fresh flowers, others clothes. I saw two spectacular evening gowns come out of one room on their way downstairs for pressing, and jackets and slacks brought back up to another in time for lunch. The maids' rubber-soled shoes squeaked on the terra-cotta tile floor. Arrangements of snowy white hydrangeas billowed from side tables beneath yet more wonderful paintings, most of them of the region. Watercolors, oils, pastels, collected by generations of Giolittis, formed a record of centuries of Liguria and the villa.

"Here is where you may store your jewelry," Vesuvio said. "This is Armadio."

Armadio, a formidably sized fellow, sat at a desk, looking for all the world like a concierge in a fine hotel. What looked like the door to a bank vault loomed behind him. I studied the door as best I could—it was a serious thing. Not uncrackable, but if I was going to try to break into this vault, it would certainly draw upon all my skill and gadgets. Security cameras covered the entire area and I was confident these were hooked up, unlike the bogus ones at the Paris museum. It also looked as though Armadio had a big gun under his jacket.

"*Buon giorno,*" I said.

"Signora." He nodded, his big, flat face expressionless.

I followed Vesuvio to a back service staircase that took us down to the main floor, ending up near the library where I'd had cocktails the night before with Giancarlo and Lucia. All the woodwork gleamed with fresh wax and smelled like cedar.

"*Prego,*" Vesuvio said and held open a heavy door that led into a long, dark hallway that led to yet another ancient door, this one banded with thick iron strips, as though it had originally been in a dungeon. Finally, we emerged into a large square courtyard. Two walls of the yard were parking stalls—maybe twenty of them, separated by ancient stone walls, their tile roofs covered with thick vines of blooming wisteria. This must have been the stableyard and box stalls at one time. Now it looked like a luxury car dealership. Vesuvio consulted with a guard, took me to my car, and waited while I retrieved my glasses and a lipstick that had fallen on the floor. I was relieved to see that the keys had been left in the ignition. I grabbed them as well.

Then he escorted me back to my room. I could tell that wandering at will around Villa Giolitti was politely, but efficiently and effectively, discouraged.

———

I went out on the balcony off my sitting room and lay down on the chaise to catch my breath. Between the lack of sleep last night, my early morning tennis game, breakfast with Alesandro, and the last-minute packing and move—I was tired. I closed my eyes and stretched out in the sun. I didn't know precisely what would happen next, but I knew I was in control of what mattered. For instance, I knew which one of us—Alesandro or Giancarlo—would get to the Millennium Star first. There was only one Shamrock Burglar.

There was a knock at the door.

"Signora," a woman's voice said. "It is a quarter to one. Are you all right? May I help you dress?"

Oh, my God. I'd fallen asleep! And now, I was late for lunch and I hadn't even opened my suitcases.

"I'll be down in five minutes."

THIRTY-FOUR

The unplanned catnap had had a completely revitalizing effect. My mind was clear as a bell and I moved quickly but without rushing—stopping long enough to turn on SkyWord to see if there was any update on Thomas's progress toward the peninsula. I turned up the volume enough that I could hear it in the dressing room while I unlatched my bags. I quickly found what I was looking for: one of my favorite dresses that matched the color of my eyes almost perfectly, an aquamarine shantung silk sheath with a jewel neck and cap sleeves.

Around my neck I put another favorite: a fifteen-strand torsade of Burmese peridot and deep blue South American tourmaline beads. The gold clasp was studded with a large lapis cabochon.

Peridot, an especially delicious lime-green gemstone, has been in continuous use since 4000 B.C. Many Egyptologists claim it was Cleopatra's favorite stone, probably because it is said to have many mystical properties including the ability to enhance awareness, insight, and intellect. It also imparts wisdom, relieves anxiety, depression, and insomnia, and provides enthusiasm, self-confidence, and inspiration—all characteristics Cleopatra had in spades. Tourmaline is also said to do many of these things including being helpful in treating eye and brain disorders, and helping to regulate metabolism and the digestive process. Both stones are said to bring good luck.

Why would anybody ever wear anything else?

When the ropes of tourmaline in my torsade were twisted with the ropes of peridot, they made the most refreshing summertime combination—like limeade and blue birds.

The television news droned along. They replayed the earlier interview but evidently nothing new had happened.

I added large gold earrings encrusted with peridot mêlées and my own blackamoor-style bust brooch—a much finer piece than the one Thomas described that had been stolen. Mine was a work of art—a shining coral face framed by a carved emerald turban and a dazzling bib of carved rubies, amethysts, cabochon sapphires, pearls, topaz, and lapis.

I stashed my jewelry cases, stepped into aquamarine, slingback Manolo pumps, touched up my lipstick and blusher, and tucked one of the gardenias into my French twist. A quick fifteen minutes after the knock on my door, I looked in the mirror. I looked like a contessa. *The* contessa, to be exact. Of this palazzo. I was a little bit late. But? *No problema.* This was Italy. No one did anything on time.

The gala preparation maelstrom was still in full swing when I got downstairs. I said *"Buon giorno"* to the guard at the Jewelry Room, and then passed through a series of sitting rooms and out onto the family terrace. A round, glass-topped luncheon table was set for seven with delicate yellow Madeira linens and a low, tightly packed bowl of creamy roses. Marble urns and planters, filled with red geraniums and pink petunias, framed the patio. The terraced garden spread below us like a postcard with everything in full bloom: banks of magenta azalea bushes and hydrangeas as big as beach balls. The petunias perfumed the air.

Lucia wasn't there yet. Giancarlo was talking to Sissy Mc-Nally and Marjorie Mead.

And Thomas.

And Giovanna McDougal.

THIRTY-FIVE

I wasn't nearly as surprised to see Thomas as he was to see me. And I was extremely irked to see Giovanna. In person, she was even more beautiful than she looked on television with her clear, healthy tanned skin, a slim Armani pantsuit, and perfectly done television makeup. She was young enough to be his daughter.

Thomas's and my eyes met. I'd been prepared to see him but I was unprepared for how it would effect me—for a moment I forgot anything had gone wrong between us and almost rushed over and grabbed him. He looked so handsome, so distinguished and solid. His blue eyes took me in with a look of complete appreciation, a compliment at how beautiful I looked. I don't know if my return gaze portrayed any of the confusion of emotions I felt. I hoped not. But we knew each other well. Then I remembered, he *used* to be my Thomas—now he was a traitor. I dropped the curtain, letting an Arctic blast replace the warmth that had been there.

Giancarlo strode toward me with his arms wide open—a champagne glass in one hand, a cigarette in the other. Movie star dark glasses hid his silvery blue eyes. He looked like a matinee idol in his loose gabardine trousers, white cotton shirt, and pink linen sports coat. I don't believe there was an ounce of fat on him he was so fit.

"Ah, my *bella* Bella, I'm so glad you're here. I've been missing you terribly." He put down his drink and cigarette and took my face in his hands and kissed my cheeks. His cologne was tangy, made from oriental spices. "Let me look at you. You look *gloriosa, magnifica,* as ever." He made it sound as though we were old friends, even lovers. Good. It would let Thomas know I hadn't been sitting around sobbing my heart out because he'd deserted me. Dumped me like a sack of potatoes. Oh, I hate you. You bastard.

"I'm sorry to be late," I said. "I got totally carried away with the view. My room is so beautiful, Giancarlo, I hated to leave it. And thank you so much for the bottle of champagne—how did you know that's my favorite?"

"You are always worth waiting for, *cara mia.* Always." He kissed my hands. "Besides, you aren't late at all—this is Italy."

I might have blushed a little. "*Grazie,* Gianni." I took the liberty of using the diminutive of his name. "Thank you so much."

The expression on Thomas's face was a combination of confusion, fascination, humor, jealousy, and complete shock. I glanced at him ingenuously.

Giancarlo handed me a flute full of orchid-colored bubbles. "Prosecco with a dollop of elderberry wine from one of my vineyards. Let me introduce you to my very important visitor. Commander Thomas Curtis, from Scotland Yard. Commander, this is my dear friend, Mrs. Priscilla Pennington."

Thomas and I greeted each other as though we were actually meeting for the first time.

"Commander," I said. I looked straight into his eyes, as bold as brass.

"Mrs. Pennington," he said. "I'm so pleased to finally meet you. I've heard so much about you."

"Really," I said. "Well, ditto, Commander. I've heard a lot about you, as well."

We each smiled winningly.

"Who's your friend?" I asked.

He paused before replying, probably because he wanted to say something like, *Speaking of friends, what's with you and Romeo?*

"This is Giovanna McDougal," he finally answered. "From SkyWord."

"Of course. I'm sorry I didn't recognize you," I smiled and took her hand. She had a good, firm grip and a direct, intelligent gaze. This girl was no bubblehead. "I always enjoy watching your reports."

"Thank you." Her tone was moderately gracious but not forthcoming. She was obviously accustomed to praise, and had no interest in a middle-aged woman who could not possibly have any effect on her life one way or another.

"Are you vacationing in Portofino or do you live here?" Thomas asked me.

"I would love to live in Portofino but, actually, I live in Buckinghamshire."

"Buckinghamshire," he said, drawing the word out. "I see.

Well, isn't that interesting. It's very beautiful there, as well."

I nodded. "My husband and I have lived there for years on his family manor, but now he's dead and I'm here to recoup myself." I tried not to put too much emphasis on the word "dead," but I couldn't help putting some, and I was rewarded with a flinch.

"Aren't we fortunate she chose Portofino?" Giancarlo said. His gushiness was starting to irritate me.

"Very," Thomas replied. "I'm sorry about your husband, though."

"That makes two of us, Commander. He simply dropped where he stood. No indication. No warning. Just . . . dead."

"It happens that way sometimes. People just steal away. I'm sure he's sorry he's gone."

"One hopes but I'll never know."

"What I hope"—Giancarlo put his arm around my shoulder and gave me a little squeeze—"is that you will stay as long as you want, Bella."

Thomas looked perturbed.

The six of us chatted convivially about the gala for another twenty minutes until Lucia arrived. She swept in, as only a six-foot-tall princess can, wearing a beautiful cerise silk blouse and slacks, and a gold necklace and bracelet.

She accepted a kiss and a champagne cocktail from her father and as she took the glass, I saw it. She was wearing my ring. The ring I'd fabricated myself with one of my Kashmir sapphires. The ring that was stolen out of my living-room safe at home. The ring I'd accused Thomas of taking. How on earth did Lucia get it? Conversation was going on all around me but I felt as though I were observing it from the sky as the pieces began to fall into place. I thought back to the charity picnic at the farm. So many people came, they'd been in the garden, the orchard, and in and out of the house. Sissy McNally had been there but she was too hopped-up to be an effective thief. Was it possible Lucia had been there as well? Of course it was. Just as it was possible, even likely, we hadn't even laid eyes on each other. And how easy it would have been for an accomplished thief to find and open the little wall safe in the living room. There was nothing special about it, if you knew what you were doing.

I looked at her and I knew without a doubt that Lucia was my impersonator. Not her father. Not Alesandro. I studied her as she visited with Sissy, oblivious to the fact that she'd been found out. I looked at Thomas to see if he'd made the connection, noticed the ring. But I could tell he hadn't, and he wouldn't, because he wasn't looking for it. He didn't know it was missing. And besides, he was busy chatting up Giovanna and Marjorie. I wanted to pull him aside and say, *Get the stars out of your eyes, old boy—the burglar is right in front of you.* But I didn't because I wanted to be sure, and also, because I didn't want Lucia to end up in jail. She needed a chance to redeem herself.

Also, and this might sound strange for me to say, but I was proud of her. I had a secret protégé. With more experience, she could really be good. She could be as good as I was. But she wasn't there, yet.

I took a sip of my champagne. Something about the jolt of the bubbles and the elderberry went down the wrong way and gave me a coughing attack.

"Do you need a Heimlich, Mrs. Pennington?" Thomas asked. He stepped toward me with his arms spread.

I shook my head, unable to speak.

THIRTY-SIX

"Come," Giancarlo said shortly, directing us to the table.

He ran his hand over my bottom as I passed him and when I turned to look at him, he winked.

"*Mangia!* Chef has prepared a beautiful luncheon for us. Priscilla, you sit here by me." He held out a chair, and then seated the rest of his guests, putting Sissy next to me, then Giovanna, Thomas, Marjorie, and finally Lucia on his left.

One of the main keys to being successful, at anything really, but especially a criminal activity, is nerves of steel. I had been in situations in the past where my detainment might have been imminent, but I was able to move my way through it unscathed because I didn't blink. Lucia was cool as a cucumber, calm as an angel, not a feather out of place. But she'd made a fatal slip—worn her loot in public—and she'd fallen into my lap. What a silly mistake. She was obviously a very talented thief. I could picture her pulling off all these robberies, perfectly. But why? Why would Principessa Lucia Giolitti want or need to steal? Why risk everything? I'd stolen because I needed the money and it was the only way I could see to make the sort of living I envisioned for myself. But for Lucia? I assumed she did it because she was bored or it was a test of her abilities to manipulate her world and her father. Or perhaps in spite of outward appearances to the contrary, they were like much of the world's aristocracy, they needed the money.

"This gavi is from my vineyards in Gavi," Giancarlo announced, halting all conversation at the table. The butler filled our glasses with a beautiful pale gold white wine. "*Gavi di Gavi!* To my old and new friends." He raised his glass and looked at me.

We all sipped. The wine was crisp and flinty, the perfect complement to the first course of crisp, garlicky crostini and grilled fresh sardines.

"Tell me, Commander," I said, "aren't you the one we've been seeing on television who's in charge of finding the Bean Sprout Burglar?"

"Shamrock," Thomas said. His eyes sparkled across the table at me. He wanted to laugh as badly as I did.

"Excuse me?" I said.

"Shamrock," he repeated. "It's the Shamrock Burglar."

"Oh, of course. Shamrock. I knew it was something like that. Watercress or something."

Everyone laughed. Ha. Ha. Ha. Glasses clinked to the Bean Sprout Burglar. The butler opened another bottle.

"And yes," Thomas said. "I am in charge of that investigation."

"That's what I thought I'd heard you and Gina talking about on television."

"Giovanna," he said.

"Excuse me?"

"Giovanna. Her name's Giovanna."

I looked at the girl. "I am so sorry. I knew that. I don't know why I said Gina."

She smiled, tightly, as though she'd just bit into a lemon. She really was very, very attractive. And cold as ice.

"Do you expect the burglar to be at the gala?" I asked.

Thomas nodded. "I do. I'm certain of it." His expression was portentous—a subtle warning obviously meant for me.

Ooooh, everyone chorused.

"This is just like one of those murder stories, isn't it?" Sissy drawled. "I love those stories. Do you think the crook could be sitting right here at this table and during the afternoon and evening we'll all get bumped off one by one except for the actual killer? And then you'll grab him."

"I certainly hope not." Thomas laughed. "In the first place, this is a burglar we're dealing with, not a murderer."

"Well," Sissy said. "You know what I mean."

"But it is exciting, Commander." I rallied to Sissy's side. "Do you think one of us could be the Shamrock Burglar?"

"Well . . ." he began.

"Don't say such a thing." Lucia frowned. "Don't even think it. We want no robberies at Villa Giolitti. We've never had a robbery here."

"We don't want any robberies, either," Thomas answered. "That's why I'm here, to prevent one. And to answer your question, Mrs. Pennington: I don't know if the burglar is here at this table. If I did, then I'd make an arrest and the entire affair would be over."

"*Grazie,* Commander." Lucia gave him one of those calm, transforming smiles. "We are in your care."

"Marjorie," I said, "are you really going to wear the Millennium Star to the gala?"

She looked sensational in a tight black T-shirt and a broad-brimmed straw hat with a red band. Her skin glowed with youthful good health and I could tell her makeup had been applied by a member of her entourage. "I am. I got to see it this morning. It's as big as a baseball. And so beautiful. I've never seen anything like it. And"—she paused and turned to Thomas; she put her hand on his arm—"the commander is going to be my personal bodyguard."

Patches of red bloomed at the corners of Thomas's eyes.

Ooooh, we raised our glasses in a toast.

"He's not going to leave my side all evening. Are you, Commander?"

Thomas laughed and shook his head. "Not for one second."

Ooooh, we all raised our glasses again.

"The commander, as well as a number of policemen, are staying here at the villa," Giancarlo said. "So I would say we are all in very good hands. Ladies, you and your jewelry could not be more well protected anywhere on earth. There's more security here for the next few days than even at the Vatican."

"Good," I said. But I didn't mean it.

Thomas gave me a look but I ignored him.

As the butler cleared the table, Giancarlo leaned close. "You look so beautiful, Bella," he whispered. "I can't take my eyes off of you." And then, he put his hand on my knee and ran it up under my dress much, much, much higher than he should have.

THIRTY-SEVEN

This simply wouldn't do.

Giancarlo's hand was warm. And completely disconcerting. I was glad no one could see what was going on under the table. But, still. It wouldn't do.

I put my hand on top of his, lifted it off my thigh, and placed it on the table.

"Giancarlo." I looked into his eyes.

Why did he have to be so handsome? All my life I'd wished Cary Grant would make a pass at me, and now someone who looked just like him was. But there were a couple of flies in this ointment: He might have looked like the late actor but as lunch had progressed, I'd begun to find him a little too much of a braggart and bon vivant for my taste, especially in direct comparison with my husband. Thomas had more than good looks. He had class, presence, and elegance. He had restraint. Well, he was British, of course. Giancarlo was Italian. He was all hands. There it was.

Also, I'd been down this sort of road before with a man who was much more worldly than I. A handsome, vigorous, youthful man who lived in the fast lane and spent his evenings with world famous models but who was then, inexplicably, all of a sudden smitten with me. Consumed with me. And for quite a while, I fell for it. He turned out to be a man with an agenda in which I was a mere cog, a stepping-stone, a means to his end. He had no compunctions about my humiliation, just as I knew Giancarlo had no real feeling for me.

Look, I know I am a beautiful, wealthy, charming woman— but who's kidding whom? Count Giancarlo Giolitti—a well-known Italian aristocrat and playboy, a jet-setter of the first order, a vintner of the finest Italian wines, who had a chef and a villa and a shiny black Lamborghini Testarosa, and a string of polo ponies—didn't suddenly take one look at me and decide I was the woman for him. No. Giancarlo had a plan, although I couldn't imagine what I would be able to offer that he would want. Unless he and Lucia were in it together.

I scanned the table. Was there anybody here who *didn't* have a plan?

"You can keep your eyes on me all you want," I said very quietly so only he could hear. "But you simply must keep your hands to yourself."

He put my fingers to his lips. "Priscilla, you are *magnifica.*"

Everyone had been glued to our private tête-à-tête even though they couldn't hear what we were saying. "Oooooh." They all giggled and clinked their glasses. "*Amore.*"

Thank God the arrival of the *primi piatti* distracted us. Fresh green pea *agnolotti*—tiny raviolis filled with green pea puree in pasta so fine it was almost transparent and dressed with curls of shaved Parmigiano. I think we were all getting a little tipsy, myself included.

"This Barbaresco is from my vineyards in Barbaresco," Giancarlo bragged as our glasses were filled with the beautiful translucent ruby-colored wine from Piemonte. "It is one of the finest wines in Italy."

It was absolutely superb and I had to bite my tongue from saying, *Thomas, can you believe how beautiful all this is?*

"Commander," Sissy said, "you're almost as famous as Sherlock Holmes. I've read about you for years. What's the hardest case you've ever done?"

Thomas considered for a moment. "I'd say it's this one."

"Oh, come on." Sissy frowned. "These little podunk jewelry robberies? I'd think they'd be nothing to you compared to all the serial killers and so forth that you've caught. I think you just said you'd do this case so you and Giovanna could get a little vacation on the Riviera! And come to the gala."

I raised my eyebrows. "Ooooooh," I said. *"Amore."*

"Amore." Everyone joined in.

Thomas gave me a dirty look.

Giovanna's cheeks colored and she looked at him. A familiar sort of look, I thought.

Thomas didn't crack a grin. I could tell he thought we were all idiots and Sissy was an empty-headed dope.

"Not at all. This is especially challenging because this particular burglar is so brilliant."

"Really?" I took a bite of the *agnolotti*. It melted in my mouth.

"Brilliant, how?" Lucia asked.

"Somehow, the perpetrator is befriending the victims without their even being aware of it, and gaining their trust enough to get into their hotel rooms without causing any suspicion, which has led me to believe the robber is a woman."

"A woman!" Sissy exclaimed. "I heard you say that on TV. Well, doesn't that take all."

"If they make a movie about her, I want the part!" Marjorie laughed.

"It would be a good one," Thomas acknowledged. "If you really want to glorify crime."

"Well, it could have a happy ending. She could get saved. Go straight. Live happily ever after." Marjorie said.

"Yes, she could." Thomas nodded.

Lucia kept her eyes on her plate and shook her head almost imperceptibly. She looked incredibly sad, and alone.

"Tell me, Commander." Sissy put her hand on Thomas's arm and leaned close to him. "Is there a Mrs. Curtis?"

"Yes, there is."

"Well, damn," Sissy said. "All the good ones are always taken."

Giovanna didn't look any too pleased with this news flash. Was it possible Thomas hadn't told her he was married? Or separated? Or whatever it was he was.

"This chardonnay is not from one of my vineyards," Giancarlo announced as the *segundi piatti* was served, a filet of sole with lemons and capers. "It is from the vineyard of a friend who is married to one of my cousins. But the olive oil is my own and it is the finest in the world. Here's what you must do." He drizzled a healthy amount of the beautiful dark green oil over his plate and then raised his glass. "This fish was caught this morning by my chef's assistant. *Buon appetito.*"

"*Chin. Chin,*" we all said and clinked our glasses for the millionth time.

Three more courses followed: grilled rack of lamb with fresh lavender and rosemary and la Massa Super Tuscan that was so huge it looked like blood in the glass. An arugula salad lightly dressed with oil, lemon, salt, and pepper. And a dessert of Panne i Pesche Caramello—a cinnamon bread pudding soaked in hot caramel sauce, covered with sliced fresh peaches, and sprinkled with pecans crisped in maple syrup. It was one of the most sinfully delicious desserts I'd ever had.

"I wish Mrs. Curtis would learn to cook like this," Thomas said.

"And then perhaps you'd be here with her, instead?" I teased.

"I'm here on business, Mrs. Pennington," he answered sternly.

Finally some espresso. But by then it was too late for any chance of sobriety. Everyone was ever so slightly, and politely, smashed. Thank God there was no limoncello or the whole day would have been lost.

Giancarlo didn't put his hand on my leg again, but it did graze past my left breast a couple of times, accidentally on purpose, and linger there.

Italians. I can see them coming around corners.

THIRTY-EIGHT

"I hope it's not too late for my tour," I said to Lucia as we all stood up from the table.

"No, no. Not at all." She'd been quiet for most of the lunch and now seemed relieved and flattered that I'd remembered. "Would anyone else like to join us? I'm taking Priscilla on a tour of our paintings collection."

"I'd love to come along," Marjorie said. "Do I have time?" she asked Giancarlo. "What am I doing this evening?"

I listened attentively, not sure what the plans for the evening were and whether I'd be included or not.

"You're going to a dinner party on the Constantine's yacht, the *Venus*. We're going out on the *Ercole*."

"Right. I forgot." She turned to Thomas. "I hope you'll come with me."

"By all means."

"He's the best bodyguard I've ever had." She beamed at the rest of us. "Don't worry," she said to Giovanna, "I'll give him back when all this is over."

Giovanna simply smiled, a tolerant little smirk. She was condescending and arrogant and I didn't like her. And I'm not just saying that because she was there with Thomas and evidently they were having a thing of some sort. I wouldn't have liked her anyway.

"I'm going straight to a massage and a nap," Sissy said. "Some of us have to work harder at looking beautiful than others." She kissed Giancarlo briskly on each cheek. "Thank you so much for a beautiful lunch, Gianni. I'll see you later." She took my hands. "You, too, Priscilla. Ta-ta, y'all."

"I'd like to come along on the tour, if I may," said Thomas.

"*Bene,*" Lucia smiled. "Let's begin in the chapel."

For two hours Lucia led us through a brief history of the villa and its collection, touching only on about ten percent of it in any detail. The collection was so complex, it took that long just to go through the chapel and three other rooms. Thomas and I asked questions incessantly. This sort of thing—tours of art museums and ruins and so forth—was such a mutual passion, it was as though we were trying to communicate with each other secretly, in the only way we could. I was trying to tell him how much I loved him and how innocent I was and how I would consider forgiving him for leaving me if he'd consider absolving me of suspicion and come home. I was sure he was doing the same. We were afraid to stand next to each other, the pull between us, the desire to touch each other, was so strong.

Oh, for heaven's sake, Kick. Get a grip. I was obviously getting carried away by the romance of the villa. I might have still loved him, but I hadn't even begun to forgive him and the truth was: If I stood next to him, I was much more likely to slap him silly than fall into his arms.

"This Michelangelo of *The Annunciation* is extraordinary for a number of reasons," Lucia said. "Not least of which is that it is still privately owned by the original owner."

We stood, openmouthed, gazing up at a monumental oil painting. It took our breath away. Light radiated from the Virgin and the Angel—the blue of her robe and white of his gown were translucent, opalescent, from another world.

"I've never seen anything like this," I said. I was so caught up in the painting that I didn't realize how close Giancarlo had gotten to me until I felt something poking my backside.

"Oh!" I jumped about ten feet in the air.

Thank God it turned out to be his hand, pinching my bottom. He winked. I thought Thomas was going to hit him.

I take back what I said about Giancarlo being a braggart and a bon vivant. The fact was: Giancarlo was a jerk. It suddenly became clear: He didn't have some big secret plan to use me— I was the only one left who'd go out with him.

THIRTY-NINE

Lucia looked at her father and shook her head. "Papa, please."
She was clearly angry. She checked her watch. "Unfortunately,
we'd better not do more today—it's getting late."

"Is there time for just a quick visit to the Jewelry Room?" I
asked. "I'd love to see it."

"Of course." Giancarlo tucked my arm through his. "Come
with me. Everything's all locked up in safes. But the guards will
show you whatever you want to see."

"Perfect," Marjorie said. "I'd love for Priscilla to see the Star."

"Skating a little close to the edge, are we?" Thomas muttered
as we passed. But I ignored him. He stepped aside to let Giovanna move ahead of him, and she bumped into me, brushed
past without even excusing herself. I was getting to hate her.

Giancarlo led us down the hall to the closed double doors
where there were now two armed guards on duty. A panel of
lights, presumably for the alarm system, blinked next to the
doorway. One of the guards opened the doors and after we'd
passed through an airport-style security check, we entered the
large, window-less reception hall. Antique tapestries draped
the paneled walls. Dressing tables stocked with makeup and
hair spray rimmed the room and there was a bank of full-length

mirrors in the center. Each table had a list of two or three names in large type as to who would be at that particular station to receive her jewelry and a last-minute touch-up. Next to each table sat a rolling jewelry safe, similar to those we used at the auction house, with stacks of drawers and multistep locking systems.

At the end of the room, behind velvet ropes and stanchions, were two more guards sporting the DeBeers LV logo discreetly on the breast pockets of their blazers. Their vault was state-of-the-art, inky gunmetal blue/black with a fingerprint scanner and digital electronic lock. It was a three-foot square cube, had five drawers and was bolted on to a solid block of marble. A spotlight directly above it shone down intensely and gave the whole affair a sort of showy, dramatic James Bond effect.

The place was as fortified as Fort Knox. The Tower of London. I scanned the walls to see if there was any telltale sign of a secret door or panel but if there was, it was invisible. Only one way in and one way out. In my opinion, unless a burglar had a great deal of creativity, skill, and courage, it was unrobbable. Completely burglar-proof. Well, almost.

Giancarlo walked up to the DeBeers guards. "*Buona sera,*" he said to them.

"*Buona sera.*"

I got the impression that Giancarlo had already spent a great deal of time in this room, getting to know everyone. "One last peek, *per favore, signores. Per lei signoras.*" He shrugged his shoulders and indicated Marjorie, Lucia, Giovanna and me with outstretched hands as though we poor silly women could not keep ourselves away from the Millennium Star.

The guard smiled. "By all means, Count Giolitti." He had a precise British accent.

After an efficient drill of unlocking the safe—fingerprint scan, followed by the combinations—they slid open a deep, velvet-lined drawer and lifted out a large dark velvet box, approximately the size of a laptop computer but about five inches deep. One guard held the box while the other undid the small latch and lifted the cover. The guard knew exactly what to do, how to display the contents to their best appearance. He tilted the container so the stone caught the light. We all gasped.

I'd seen the Millennium Star from a distance in London, and my synthetic replica from Zurich was perfect and shone with a radiance unrivaled in any synthetic I'd ever seen before. But seeing the real thing at a distance of only two feet was like looking at the sun. It burned with life. I had never seen a stone of such extraordinary beauty. Originally 777 carats of sheer brilliance when it was discovered by an alluvial digger in the Congo in 1996—the carat weight signified extreme good luck—DeBeers's top cutters studied the Star for over three years before they painstakingly shaped it with lasers into what is the most beautiful flawless blue diamond in all history.

The stone was not quite as big as a baseball, as Marjorie had claimed. It was more correctly described as the size and shape of an Anjou pear. And because of the way it had been faceted—I had no idea how many facets there were altogether but it was in the hundreds, possibly even a thousand—it sparkled in a way that was unlike anything else. The stone was suspended from a pavé diamond and platinum necklace, graduated in width from approximately one half inch at the clasp, to one inch at its chevron point. By itself, the necklace would have been a major attraction, but incredibly it became almost an afterthought, an incidental backdrop for the Star.

Giancarlo was the first to speak. "*Permisso?*" he said and lifted the necklace out of its case and placed it around Marjorie's neck. "*Dio.*" Then he took her in his arms and began to twirl her around the room in a sweeping waltz while we all watched in silence. They were beautiful to behold—the dashing older man, the magnificent young beauty. I know everyone, but Lucia and I, was thinking the same thing: That maybe Giancarlo was the Shamrock Burglar and was testing the possibilities—not of Marjorie. But of robbery. Possibly he thought he could waltz her right out the door.

Lucia stood still, as though she were watching them, but her eyes were on the diamond. I wondered what she had in mind for it.

The guards watched comfortably. The necklace was going nowhere. At least not out of this room. There was no way the Star would be stolen from here.

After a brief applause, Giancarlo let the guard remove the necklace from Marjorie's neck and place it carefully back in its case.

I was probably the only one who noticed they did not return the case to the safe while we were still in the room. It would be stored in a different drawer than the one from which they'd removed it in our presence.

FORTY

Lucia and I walked upstairs together. I was exhausted. Just as we reached the landing, the burglar alarm went off—a huge, screaming, brain-numbing piercing wail and everyone went running in different directions. The main floor looked like a lifeboat drill.

Lucia and I looked at each other, perplexed. She and I both knew she was the burglar and she was covering it with such a cool façade.

"Do you suppose we're being robbed?" she asked guilelessly.

"I have no idea."

We stood and watched, fascinated, over the rail. Thomas rushed past, followed closely by Giancarlo. Shortly, the din stopped and a voice echoed throughout the entry hall. "False alarm. False alarm. Sorry."

Lucia shook her head. "What a monstrous noise."

I agreed.

"Would you like a cup of tea?" she asked.

"I'd love one."

"Come. My room is right down the hall."

Lucia's "room" as she called it was in fact an apartment, almost the size of my beautiful flat on Eaton Terrace in London, with a wide, wisteria shaded porch that wrapped around two sides. Unlike the opulence of the rest of the villa, her rooms were like her—spare and uncluttered. A combination of classic and modern masterpieces lived comfortably together on the walls. All the furniture was slipcovered for the summer in pristine white linen. There were two collections besides the paintings: about a dozen and a half small Greek and Roman marble busts sat on one sideboard and a display of ancient Roman malachite horses sat on another. She rang a bell and her maid appeared.

"Sì, Principessa?"

"Tea, please. Do you have any preference, Priscilla?"

"No. Anything will be welcome."

"Earl Grey, then."

"Your room is beautiful," I said. "It's so peaceful."

"Thank you. I love it. I would be happy never to leave the palazzo. Please make yourself comfortable." Lucia sat in a straightbacked arm chair and indicated I do the same across the tea table. "Have you been in Portofino before?"

"No." I shook my head.

The maid returned with a tray of silver teapots, cups and saucers, and little tea cakes, set it on the table, and then vanished.

"What brings you here now?" Lucia tucked a strand of hair behind her ear and picked up the hot water and poured it into the teapot.

An edge to her tone got my attention. "I recently lost my husband and decided I needed a break. I'm glad I chose

Portofino—I think it's the most beautiful place I've ever been."

Lucia nodded. "Sì."

"Why do you ask?"

"Just curiosity. Forgive me, I'm very jumpy and suspicious of everyone at the moment. Sugar? Lemon?"

"Just lemon, thank you. Jumpy and suspicious, how?"

She picked up one of the delicate cups and began to pour but stopped. The brew was still too weak. She put down the pot. "Because of the robberies. Truthfully? I've never approved of holding this gala here in our home. I don't approve of the spotlight it puts on my family and I don't like having strangers wander through our rooms."

"I don't blame you at all. It must be very disconcerting."

"You have no idea. Fortunately, most of them have no interest in the collection, they're only here to see who else is here, or try to get close to the celebrities. As you know, they pay dearly, and it's for an important cause." She shrugged. "But still, these events tend to attract a number of undesirables."

"And you thought I might be the burglar?"

Lucia laughed. "I'm sorry. I think everyone's the burglar."

"Well, you're right, of course. It could be any of us. But let me assure you, it's not me. I've come by all my jewelry honestly."

"Who do you think it is?" Lucia said. "That's the question."

"I haven't a clue and I'm glad I'm not in charge of figuring it out."

"Me, too."

We smiled at each other. Two world-class liars.

She poured again. The tea was darker. "There, that's better." She handed me my cup. "I'm sorry to be talking so candidly about how I feel about the party. I should be more gracious; after all, you are our guest and I should keep my private feelings private. Please forgive me. But you have a way of making me feel very comfortable, as though we've been friends for a long time."

"I feel the same way. It's nice, isn't it? How old are you, Lucia?"

"Thirty-four."

Younger than my daughter would be, I realized. Maybe Lucia was a second chance for me to make up for that act of cowardice so long ago, for refusing to look at my child's face, for not even inquiring if it was a boy or a girl. I'd forgiven myself—after all, I'd been a child myself at the time—but now I was being handed the opportunity to make a difference, especially in Lucia's life.

"What happened to your mother?"

"She died when I was a little girl. I don't even remember her."

"Well, I suppose you're comfortable with me because I'm your mother's age. It's always nice to have someone older to talk to. I didn't have anyone when I was growing up, either."

She looked at me. "You didn't?"

I shook my head. "No. Just myself. I know exactly how you feel."

She looked at her hands and nodded her head slightly. "Most of the women my father goes out with are younger than I am—they're the only ones who will put up with his behavior.

Wait until you see the way they act around him tonight. It's laughable—they all want to be the next contessa. I usually just make a quick appearance at the party and then excuse myself."

"Sounds like a reasonable approach," I said. "It's easy to see that you're a very private person. But I imagine with Marjorie here as guest of honor, you'll stay longer. She seems to be a very close friend."

"My oldest and best. You're right, I'll stay longer this year. Marjorie and I always have a good time together—we had the best time at school. We were always in trouble." She paused and sipped her tea. "Do you think Commander Curtis is right? That the burglar will try to steal the diamond?"

I shrugged. "I hope not. I know he'll catch whoever it is one of these days and then that person's life is going to be a mess. Well, let's leave it up to Commander Curtis, and instead think about these little Russian tea cakes. I can't believe I'm actually considering eating one after the lunch we just had."

"They're delicious." She took a large bite. Powdered sugar crumbled onto her fingers. "Our cook makes the best in the world."

Russian tea cakes are one of my weaknesses. There's just something about the combination of pecans and butter and powdered sugar all in one little two-bite ball that makes me lose all resolve. I bit into one. The shortcake evaporated in my mouth like butter-flavored gold dust. "Umm," I said.

We each reached for another.

"Tell me," I asked between bites. "Do you have a sweetheart?"

"I did. Until last week."

"What happened to him?"

"He couldn't handle who I was. He got bored with my scholarly life."

"Then he wasn't the right man for you."

"I know, but I thought he was. I fell in love with him—he was supposed to escort me to the gala." Her eyes filled with tears. "I've decided I'm finished with men. I'm going to be an old maid."

"Do you want me to tell you something, Lucia?"

She nodded. The tears spilled over and she brushed them away with the back of her hand, leaving a streak of sugar on her cheek.

"I used to feel exactly the same way. I never thought I'd find the right man for me, but that was all right. It didn't matter. I loved my life and my world. I was complete as I was. Then, one day, when I was, well, never mind what I was, let me just put it this way, I was a great deal older than you are now, I met my husband. And he was worth the wait." And he *was* worth it, or so I thought. I'd adored Thomas. I still adored him. I felt like crying along with Lucia. "But if he hadn't shown up, that would have been all right, too. The secret is, don't compromise anything about yourself for love. If it's meant to come, it will. So stop worrying about it and enjoy your life. You're a very talented, special young woman. You require someone equally special."

She regarded me gravely. "No one ever told me that before."

"Not even your father?"

"Especially not my father. To him, women are for sex and

babies." Her cheeks colored. "Oh, forgive me, Priscilla. I didn't mean . . ."

"I know you didn't. And that's his problem, not yours. You seem to be happy with your role as curator of the collection."

She nodded. "Very. I love it. I'd love never to have to leave the grounds of the villa, but it's a very costly undertaking. I'm not sure we can support it much longer."

"I know this is blasphemy, Lucia, but you could consider selling a piece or two. That could carry the collection and the villa a long, long way." I wanted to add, *Instead of stealing pieces of priceless jewelry you can't do anything with anyway but that could end up putting you in jail for the rest of your life.*

"No. Selling would not be feasible." She looked at her watch. "*Dio.* It's after six. Are you coming with us tonight?"

"I don't think so," I answered. "Your father hasn't mentioned it to me."

"I'm sure he meant to."

"I don't even know what it is."

"Just a casual dinner," Lucia said. "On the *Ercole.*"

"The *Ercole?*"

"Yes, our yacht. The *Ercole. Hercules* in English. It's the calm before the wildness of tomorrow. Just a few friends. Very casual."

"I'd love to come along."

"*Bene.* We'll leave about eight."

I stood up. "Then I'd best have a nap if I'm going to look like anything by eight o'clock. Thank you so much for the afternoon and the tea and for showing me a little of your collection."

"Thank you, Priscilla." Lucia kissed me on both cheeks. "You made me feel so much better. I've never finished a whole plate of cakes before—everyone's always so worried about their weight."

"Well, that's another thing you need to know: If you want to have a life with meaning, which you do, then there's so much more to it than your waistline."

"I wish you could stay with us forever."

"Well, I'll be here for a couple of days, anyway," I said. "Do you know what you're wearing tomorrow night?"

"I can't decide—do you want to see? Maybe you can help me."

"I'd love to."

Lucia's bathroom was spacious with oversized period fixtures and solid, pure white marble walls and floor. In comparison, her dressing room was surprisingly compact. She opened one of the closet doors and pulled out three evening gowns—shell-pink silk, black chiffon, and copper organdy and held them up one at a time.

"It's between the pink and the black," I said. "Save the copper for fall."

"You're right. I never thought of that."

When she removed the organdy gown, I briefly glimpsed the hinges to the door of a wall safe on the back wall of the closet and I was relieved to have an idea of where she stashed her loot. It would save me precious time and guesswork.

FORTY-ONE

The maid had closed the drapes against the afternoon sun, and like the rest of the grand palazzo, my suite was cool and still. I wandered into the dressing room and thought about my conversation with Lucia. It had moved me. She reminded me so much of myself, not the princess part, of course. My own rearing, if you could even call it that, had been haphazard, at best. But the independent part. However, she hadn't reached the mature conclusion, yet: That we're alone in this life and it's up to each one of us to choose if we're going to be happy or unhappy.

I wondered about my long-lost child: Happy? Sad? Living? Dead? For years, I'd checked the Internet adoption sites in the hopes the child would want or need to find me. Born: Florence Crittenden Home, Omaha, Nebraska, August 1965. Mother, unknown. Father, unknown. But no such query had been made and I stopped checking. What a coward I'd been not to leave my only child a clue.

Lost in thought, I put my torsade back into its case, then my blackamoor brooch, stepped out of my dress and hung it up, and pulled on a peach silk peignoir with handmade chantilly lace trim. I needed a nap and I had an hour before I had to get up and start the whole deal all over again.

I'd just climbed into bed when there was a knock on the door. Thank God. It would be Thomas. So like him to wait until he knew the house would be asleep, and we could meet privately. I pulled my robe back on, checked myself in the mirror—hair and makeup still looked fine. I sprayed on a little scent and went to the door. I hated to admit it, but in spite of my anger and all the issues between us that needed explanation and resolution, I was excited to see him. I couldn't wait. My heart pounded. I took a deep breath and gathered myself. I threw open the door.

"Well," I said, "it certainly took you long enough."

FORTY-TWO

"Bella."

"Giancarlo!" I gasped. My face froze. "What are *you* doing here?"

He stepped into my outstretched arms and put his lips on mine and closed the door with a swift, slamming, cavalier, Zorro-like kick of his foot.

No. No.

No. No. This would not do.

I put my hands on his chest and pushed him away. "Stop. What do you think you're doing?"

"Priscilla. I know you want this as much as I do." He pulled me to him again.

"No. No. I don't." I freed myself from his clutches and stepped back.

He stepped forward. I stepped back again. Around to the other side of the bed. He came after me and caught my arm.

"Priscilla." He laughed. "Surrender."

"No, Giancarlo. Get out of my room."

"You are my guest."

I couldn't believe my ears. Or what was happening. What was this? Droit du seigneur? It was like a bad swashbuckling movie. I broke away from him again and he dashed after me. He was actually chasing me around the room. It was insane. I headed for the dressing room and Giancarlo leapt up on the bed, ran across it, and leapt to the floor to block me, placing his hands on either side of the door, like John Barrymore. He was laughing the entire time. Like this was a game. He was a complete and total idiot. At least Bijou had figured out it wasn't a game. She locked her little jaws onto his pants' leg and started growling and tugging.

"Get the hell away from me, Giancarlo, or I'll scream," I said.

"Yes, yes. Scream." His eyes rolled with pleasure. "Scream. Scream."

Bijou growled.

"Get away from me, little doggie." He shook his leg trying unsuccessfully to dislodge her grip and at the same time he got a hold of my arm and pulled it out of my negligee, ripping my gown and exposing one of my breasts.

I slapped him. As hard as I could. "Get a hold of yourself," I said.

There was a knock on the door. I literally lunged for it and threw it open.

Thomas.

He looked completely astounded.

"Thomas," I said breathlessly.

"Terribly sorry to interrupt."

I realized what this must look like. I was half-naked, in complete dishabille, my lipstick was smeared, my hair was ripped to shreds, and Giancarlo was standing close to me with a big smile on his face and his hand on his just-slapped pink cheek.

Bijou jumped into Thomas's arms.

"No," I said, clasping my robe to my throat in an attempt to pull myself back into some sort of presentable shape. "Not at all. You aren't interrupting anything. Giancarlo was just leaving."

Thomas smiled. "I'll come back later."

"No. You'll come in now," I ordered.

"Very well." Thomas stepped inside, leaving the door open. Bijou squirmed in his grasp, whimpering with joy at seeing him and licking his face. He stuck her under his arm. "Friendly dog. Cute. I'm just making the rounds to make sure everyone's jewelry is secured for the evening. Please put your valuables in the safe down the hall before you go out. That is . . . if you do go out."

"Absolutely," I said. "Is that all?"

"I believe it is."

"Lovely." I put my hand on Giancarlo's back and guided him out the door and removed Bijou from Thomas. "Then I'll tell both of you gentlemen 'good afternoon' and see you later."

I didn't care if they heard the deadbolt turn once they were out the door. I was furious. Thomas had come to my room for a reason and I'd missed it because of that idiot, Giancarlo. What in the hell was his problem, anyway?

I went into the dressing room and almost screamed when I saw myself in the mirror. I looked like I'd escaped from an insane asylum. My eyes were wild, my lipstick was more than smeared, it was all over the place and my hair stood out like I'd been shocked. Worst of all: The white gardenia was sitting right on top of my head like a silly little hat.

"Oh, my God." I started laughing. "Oh, my God. What Thomas must have thought."

I drew a deep hot bath and sunk my head, gardenia and all, beneath the bubbles.

FORTY-THREE

There was another incident with the burglar alarm while I was dressing—I could hear Giancarlo screaming that the security company had better get things in order, or else. My head was splitting from the noise.

By the time I went downstairs, the giant house was quiet. It seemed almost empty except for an electrician and his helpers who were trying to locate the short in the alarm system—I could have told them to save their energy, that the alarm was going to keep going off no matter what they did. The Jewelry Room guard was changing and I overheard one of the DeBeers men say, "We'll be in the shift room. Call us if you need us." The security chief thanked them, saying they should go ahead and bunk-in, he anticipated a quiet night. "Get some rest," he told them. "Tomorrow's going to be a long day. It'll be a zoo."

Lucia was waiting in her red Ferrari convertible at the bottom of the front steps. The beautiful machine rumbled with the low-throated growl of an impatient lion.

"I'm sorry to be late," I said. "I've been on the phone with my banker in the U.S."

A complete lie. The truth was, I'd had a terrible time getting dressed. What did one wear for a little dinner party on a boat?

I had no clue. I'd never been on a boat of any size before, well, except for a water taxi in London, once. Once was enough for me. I've never really had much, or frankly any, interest in the ocean. And interestingly, there were very few society magazine pictures of what guests wore at dinners on yachts because they were so very private. The same way you seldom see pictures of what people wear on their private jets. They don't want outsiders to see into their world because it just opens them up for more abuse by people who don't have private jets and yachts and who are jealous and have a lot of time on their hands for criticism.

Lucia had said it was casual. Casual means different things to different people and this was such a generally flashy crowd, I imagined anything would go. All I knew about boating clothes, at least all I thought I knew, was that people wore lots of white and shoes that don't skid. White is really not a good look for me, or any big girl, so after an inordinate amount of thrashing around, I put on what movie stars wear everywhere: black slacks, a black T-shirt and a black blazer. Lots of gold jewelry and a spray of red oleanders in my hair.

The fact was, I also needed to dress to be able to do a little business after dinner.

"You aren't late at all," Lucia said and revved the engine. She wore white jeans, a loose silk tunic, and rubber-soled es-padrilles. A single eighteen-millimeter, gray, South Sea pearl was suspended around her neck from a black cord, possibly the same cord that had held the large emerald cabochon the night before that I now knew was the actual Empresse. "They won't leave without us."

The second I was in the car—my door was scarcely closed—
she let out the clutch and we screamed away in a cloud of
burning rubber and shot down the hill as though we'd been
launched from a catapult and were being chased by demons.

"Whoa," I said and grabbed for the handhold.

"Don't worry. I won't hit anything," she said with conviction.
And I believed her.

One of the things that most endeared Lucia to me was her
quiet confidence, her indomitable sense of entitlement, and the
fact that she—no one else—controlled her world. But she'd
been so protected and so spoiled, she was still amazingly unfa-
miliar with—actually completely innocent of—the reality that
consequences exist. In her realm, consequences were fixable.
But now—if she were able to follow through with whatever her
plan was for this gigantic heist—she would be stepping through
the veil. I loved the contained security of her world, as much as
she did, and I would do everything in my power to make sure
she didn't have to leave it. She thought the life of a jewel thief
was glamorous, dangerous, fun. And it is. But the consequences
are not—she only saw the fantasy of stealing jewelry to under-
write her family's legacy, not the repercussions of getting
caught. The reality was something else altogether. That's why
I'd stopped. I didn't want to get caught. I didn't want to go to
jail. I'd made a beautiful life and I wanted to enjoy it.

Lucia's innocence had touched me and I knew I was risking
everything to let her keep it. But I had experience, options,
workable escape plans and escape routes. She had none of those
things. She had youthful invincibility, great reflexes, and a lot

of style. She had no idea how lucky she was that I'd come into her life.

Most of the roads around Portofino are one lane wide, at the most, and consist of one hair-raising, hairpin corner after another. Lucia was an excellent driver and I thought, What the hell. If this is where I'm meant to die, so be it. It could be worse. She slowed slightly as we neared the town proper, and when we reached the entrance to the piazza, she stopped while an ancient fellow crept out of an unobtrusive little shed and removed the bollards, staggering under their weight. We then proceeded with impunity across the cobblestone waterfront, where cars were not allowed. Lucia was, after all, the *principessa*. Carbinieri saluted as we rounded the docks, past the diners at Splendido Mare, the colorful apartment buildings, and storefronts. She stopped next to her father's Lamborghini at the bottom of a very disappointing little gangplank that led up to what looked to me to be a very disappointing little boat.

I don't know what I was expecting, something like the *Britannia*, I suppose. Something with a little oomph, a helicopter, and a couple of lifeboats. I imagine, in the boating world, this brand—Ferretti, according to what it said discreetly on the side—would be considered a substantial thing. It was maybe a hundred or so feet long, and white with lots of wood (I couldn't help noticing a number of rust spots around the railings and portholes). It was quite lovely, I suppose—a sort of miniature *Britannia*.

"*Bienvenuto al Ercole*," Lucia said.

"What a charming boat," I said casually and mounted the wobbly gangplank as though it were something I did every day.

FORTY-FOUR

"Priscilla." Giancarlo, dapper in white flannel trousers and a navy blazer, took my hand and kissed it. No trace of my slap remained on his cheek. "You're coming along with us. What a pleasant surprise."

"I hope you don't mind. Lucia invited me at the last minute."

"I'm delighted. I meant to invite you myself but I wasn't given the opportunity." He smiled as though his afternoon chase around my room had been fun—an acceptable form of exercise. "Welcome on board our little *Hercules*. My father had her built in the 1930s by Mr. Ferretti himself, so she is a treasure. Let me show you around."

I was now completely immune to Giancarlo. I was on to him. When I looked back on the episode this afternoon, I saw how comical it was. No matter what he might think, he wouldn't get to me twice. The truth was: He was now simply a used-up cog in *my* plan. I was in, and I was set to go. As a matter of fact, once I got my "business" done later this evening, I intended to relax and enjoy the next twenty-four or so hours. I knew exactly where I stood and what I was going to do.

I followed him around the boat. There wasn't really that

much to see, except that it must have been very beautiful at one time. But now, the *Ercole* was a relic, in need of restoration and refurbishment—a testament to Lucia's earlier allusion to the cost of their lifestyle and the justification for her misguided solution of stealing irreplaceable and virtually unfenceable pieces of jewelry. I realized she obviously hadn't gotten to the stage of trying to sell any of it yet—if she had, she would have changed targets. The living room and dining room were good-sized and appointed with highly varnished yachting-style furniture but the fabrics were stained and worn and the varnish marred by years of use. The small staterooms still had rudimentary 1930s baths. I would have no interest in having anything more than dinner aboard this boat. It should be sold to someone who could afford to take care of it. If they didn't sell a painting or two and get some cash flowing, they and their collection would all go down with the ship. Literally.

"Here we are," Giancarlo said as we exited onto the aft deck, which was quite pretty, outfitted with a bright blue canvas awning and matching cushions, and a dinner table set for eight now being quickly reset for nine—Giancarlo, Lucia, Sissy, two other couples, and not especially surprisingly: Alesandro. "Let me get you a cocktail. Scotch?"

"Please."

"Signora Pennington." Alesandro kissed my hand. "How nice to see you. Do you know my friend, Sissy McNally?"

Sissy put down her half-full martini and we bussed each other's cheeks.

"Oh, honey, I'm so glad to see you. You look positively gorgeous." She sounded relieved I was there and after the runaround in my bedroom with Giancarlo, I understood why. I was sure she'd been chased around the bed a few times herself. "I was so afraid you weren't going to make it." She gave a quick roll of her eyes and whispered, "Look out for Giancarlo tonight. He just gets to be too much for me to handle sometimes. He's all hands."

"Tell me about it." I laughed. "Don't worry—I can handle him."

"Well, be my guest." She tossed off her drink and handed the glass to the maid. "I'd like another, please. *Grazie*."

Poor Sissy. Her life, which looked so glamorous in the papers, was empty and unhappy. She had on enough jewelry to blind an eagle and I'm sure Alesandro had it tallied up to the last euro. Even though I knew he wasn't the Shamrock Burglar, he was a thief nevertheless, and Sissy would be an easy roll. I hoped she didn't get drunk and invite him back to her room at the villa. It could complicate matters for me, extremely.

"Lucia, darlin', come over here and talk to me." Sissy put her arm around Lucia's waist and said to me, "Do you know, I've known this girl since she was an itty-bitty thing. Didn't she turn out to be lovely?"

Lucia looked uncomfortable.

"Your daddy used to get so mad at you and Marjorie when you girls were in school. Always in trouble. He was always having to get on the train to Lausanne and have a meeting with the directrice to beg her not to throw you out. You girls were terrible! And now look at you. You're a world-famous art historian and Marjorie's a world-famous actress. I never thought either one of you'd amount to anything. When are you going to get married, honey?"

"Sissy, stop. You're embarrassing me," Lucia said kindly.

"I just hate to think of you rattling around in that big place all by yourself. We both know your daddy's about as useless as tits on a bull."

"I'm really very happy."

"I suppose you are. You've always been happy. You and your collections." She couldn't keep the envy out of her voice. Sissy's problem was that she needed to get a life—cruising around the world half drunk and drugged all the time didn't qualify. She turned to me. "Lucia is a born collector."

"I know."

The sun was setting as we pulled away from the dock and headed into the ocean and cruised along the coastline. Giancarlo, Sissy, and Lucia pointed out various villas that dotted the steep hillsides and told funny stories about the people who lived in them.

I wondered where Lucia kept the speedboat she'd used to get up to Beaulieu, Saint-Tropez, and San Remo and back. I could picture her, all in black, roaring across the open sea to the Riviera and changing into dinner clothes before she docked at her destination, where she would probably be a familiar patron, there to meet friends for dinner. How would it go?

Principessa, the headman would say. *What a welcome surprise. We weren't expecting you.*

You weren't? she would answer. *But I'm supposed to meet the Mountbattens here,* she would lie.

Oh. He would check his book and not see their name and make a mental note to have words with his reservation manager. *Let me offer you an aperitif while you wait.*

She would pretend to wait while she checked out the guests, specifically, the older, solitary, bejeweled women. After a while, she'd approach one of them. *I feel uncomfortable sitting in a cocktail lounge by myself,* she'd say. *Do you mind if I join you until my friends come?*

Then what? Well, if it were me, I would slip something into her drink, wait until she was woozy and asked me to escort her upstairs, where I'd tuck her in and steal her jewelry. I don't know if that's what Lucia did, but in my opinion, it would be the only humane, ladylike way to approach it. And Lucia was most certainly a lady. I couldn't picture her conking people on the head or rappelling down the façade of a hotel and through an open window.

I studied her as we stood along the rail, watching the moonlit coastline slip past. She had such poise and self-possession.

Her profile was classic, her high cheekbones, arching nose, and full mouth mirrored the antiquity of her heritage. She could have been a Roman emperor.

She turned and caught me staring at her. "What is it, Priscilla?"

"Oh," I said. "You just reminded me of someone. An old, old friend. Someone I love very much."

Lucia smiled. "Oh? Who?"

"My daughter, actually."

"How flattering. Thank you."

What I wanted to say was, *You remind me of myself*.

FORTY-FIVE

We spent a completely relaxing, convivial evening aboard the *Ercole*, and after a delicious supper of antipasti, osso bucco, and several bottles of Chianti—of which I drank very little—we returned to the dock after one o'clock in the morning. I was glad to be back on dry land. I didn't want to make any hasty judgments, but based on this experience—even though it was, as I've already admitted, a convivial sojourn on a small craft—boats weren't my thing. A bigger boat? Possibly. But I doubt it.

I rode back up the hill with Lucia. She drove at a somewhat calmer pace.

Sissy rode with Alesandro and I was relieved to watch them turn into the hotel drive instead of returning to the villa.

"That was great fun," I said. "Thank you for inviting me."

"It was a fun evening, wasn't it? Poor Sissy. I worry about her."

"She can change if she wants to," I said.

Lucia glanced over at me, surprised.

"I don't mean to sound unsympathetic, but I do get impatient with people who have great financial resources and complain about how hard and empty their lives are—I just don't understand it. It's like people who complain about the consequences of their actions—people who go out and break the law and get caught and then complain when they get sent to jail. It's beyond me."

"Umm." She nodded and put her foot on the accelerator, indicating the end of the conversation. I knew she was thinking about the Star and how she would steal it tomorrow night and how she wouldn't get caught. How her actions would have no consequences because she was above the law. She was the *principessa*. She didn't know it, but time was up and she was out of the running. She'd picked the wrong brand name to plagiarize and she wasn't ready for the big leagues anyway. But she'd figure that out for herself soon enough.

Evidently, all the other houseguests had already gotten home. The house was dim and quiet. Giancarlo escorted me to the top of the stairs where he kissed my hand. "Guilberto tells me you've become an excellent tennis player," he said.

I laughed. "Far from it."

"Would you like to play in the morning?"

"I'd love to."

"*Bene.* How's ten o'clock?"

"Perfect. *Grazie,* Giancarlo. It was a perfectly lovely evening. *Buona notte.*"

He put his arm on the doorjamb and leaned toward me. His lips were very close. "Wouldn't you like for me to come in? Just to visit, I swear. No funny business. No chasing. Just a sip of champagne."

"No, Giancarlo. Thank you, but I wouldn't. I'm going to get some sleep."

He came closer, heat radiated from his body like a nuclear reactor. "I know you want me, Bella. I can feel it." He put his body next to mine and began to kiss me.

The burglar alarm went off.

Giancarlo's head jerked up and he spun around. "God damn it! God damn it!" he yelled and headed for the stairs. "*Basta! Basta!* Off! Off! This is over. We need to sleep."

I laughed and took my finger off the innocent-looking Palm Pilot in my pocket that had been responsible for setting off all the false alarms—part of my order from EKM Elektronika. The gizmo could identify alarm codes and activate alarms up to a distance of one-hundred meters, through cement walls and floors. For one hundred thousand dollars, it should also be able to cook your dinner.

It was time to go to work.

FORTY-SIX

I waited a couple of moments outside my door and looked down toward Lucia's bedroom to make sure her end of the hall was still dark, and then I dashed into my suite, fastened my tool belt around my waist, slid my copy of the Millennium Star into my pocket, and tiptoed down the back stairs. Giancarlo, the electrician, and the security chief were shouting and arguing in the middle of the cavernous foyer—their angry voices echoing throughout the hall and up the stairs. Even the Jewelry Room guards had joined the fray, leaving the Jewelry Room door closed and locked, but unattended.

My lock pick hit the mark and within seconds I slipped in, closing the door silently behind me. The room was dark except for the DeBeers vault squatting at the far end in its spotlight. It looked like a giant, hulking, impenetrable black rock on top of an iceberg. I pulled on my night-vision goggles and skintight latex gloves. On the wall just inside the door was a switch panel. I quickly unscrewed it, and then, using a wire with an electrical current, I shorted out the switch. The room fell into inky blackness. The acrid smell of burning wires had evaporated by the time I reattached the switch plate.

I was energized. My blood flowed through me in a smooth,

powerful current, like a fast-running river. I'd missed this high, this living at the edge of danger, and tonight I was really out there with minimal preparation. I hadn't had the opportunity to study what times the guards did their rounds, so I had no clue what sort of timeline I was on. Sixty seconds or sixty minutes. It didn't matter. My mission was specific and my focus complete. It was thrilling—like an adrenaline shot that sharpened my senses and filled me with the power of a freight train.

I made my way quickly to the safe and examined it thoroughly before touching it. It was freestanding—no cables or wires emerged from it or from the marble base. The fingerprint reader was behind a small panel on the side, next to the keypad. I lifted the cover and it beeped a couple of times before stopping. Its red light glowed back at me. I flipped down magnifying lenses and studied the glass on the reader itself. I shook a whisk of black powder into the palm of my hand and blew it gently on the front corner and top of the safe, revealing three or four clean prints. I applied a strip of wide double-stick tape to my finger, and then, being careful not to let the tape adhere tightly to the metal, I rolled it across the cleanest-looking print and lifted it off the black steel.

The reader needed not only the right print to connect, it also needed the right pressure and heat. If I made the wrong selection, there would be sticky tape and black powder all over the glass and the system would take a few minutes to reset itself after I'd wiped it clean with acetone. So if this wasn't the right fingerprint, I'd really be way, way out there.

I took a deep breath and shook my shoulders around to loosen them up. The print looked sharp. I pressed it firmly onto the glass. The red light blinked and blinked and finally turned green and started to beep. I had less than thirty seconds to enter the correct combination into the electronic lock.

Electronic locks can be very temperamental, daunting and usually defeating, unless you know what you're doing.

In the mid 1990s, when electronic safes became available for residential use, they were considered crackproof, and essentially they still are. You get three tries at an electronic lock before it freezes for a minimum of fifteen minutes, sometimes more—a demoralizing situation in the high-speed, smash-and-grab life of a jewel thief. You can rip off the keypad, but it doesn't make any difference. The brains of the mechanism are sealed between layers of armor, cooked in there like a little pancake, nowhere near the keypad. You can try a blowtorch, but the second the vault feels the heat, the locking bars freeze themselves into place. So, even if you were to cut an opening big enough to put your hand through and try to open the safe from the inside out, it wouldn't do any good. At that point, your only recourse is to try to cut a hole big enough to remove the goods through—but then you can only take what you can get, like reaching into a party grab bag.

On a safe as sophisticated as this one, I assumed the locking bars were the latest thing: flexible rods that circled the entire box like a mesh of ribbons around a package, not just across the door. I'd never tried to crack one of these safes with the flexible rods. We'd gotten one at Ballantine & Company just before I left, but there'd never been a reason or opportunity for me to try to break in to it. All the safes I'd cracked were residential and had either a regular combination lock or a standard electronic one.

On the plus side, the availability of black-market, digital-scanner technology had kept up with industry electronics, and I've always kept myself up-to-date on what's new. It was serendipitous that also shortly before I left Ballantine & Company, I'd purchased a new, state-of-the-art, high-speed scanner from EKM for forty-five thousand dollars. It would disarm this vault's state-of-the-art lock in about two seconds.

I held the scanner right next to the keypad and pushed the button. The lights flashed and almost instantly the web of flexible locking tubes inside the black armor begin to retract—the most beautiful sound in the world. To a jewel thief at any rate.

Five drawers.

I started with the top one and moved down. They held a king's ransom in diamonds and pieces of jewelry—even without the Millennium Star, this heist could rank among one of the biggest in the world. But, like Lucia, I was on a trophy hunt. I found the Star in the fourth drawer. All by itself in its navy-blue velvet box. Even in total blackness, complete absence of light, looking at it through the eerie green of goggles, the diamond looked alive, as though it would burn me if I touched it. It was the most beautiful stone I'd ever seen. I pulled the replica from my pocket—gave it a last, quick polish—and made the switch, attaching the real Star onto the thin platinum chain around my neck next to the Pasha. I tucked them both into the top of my bra, next to my heart. I took one last look at my stone, it was only slightly less lively than the real thing. Without detailed scrutiny, no one would spot it as a fake. I slid the box back into the drawer, closed it up, swabbed the reader with acetone and reset the lock. Finally, I pulled a soft cloth and a tiny spray bottle of fine gun oil out of my back pocket and began to polish the black powder fingerprints off the vault.

The door flew open. A shaft of light cut across the room.

"What's happened in here?" one of the guards said. "It's pitch-black." He stepped around the open door to the wall and flipped the light switches up and down. "Hey! The lights are out."

Covered by the darkness, and the fact that the guard was concealed by the partially open door, I ran as quickly as I could across the room and crouched close to the floor near the entrance. The second guard came, flashed his large beam around the room, saw everything was in order, and then held it on the panel while his cohort kept flipping the switches.

"Look at this," he said. "The wall's burned around the plate. Maybe this is where our alarm short has come from. Go get the electrician."

I waited until the guard left and then, while his partner continued to fiddle with the switch plate, I crept out and made my way back up the stairs to my suite, and after checking to make sure I was alone, that Giancarlo hadn't returned and was hiding under my bed, waiting to ambush me, I locked the door.

My face was aglow. I'd forgotten how much fun this was. I undressed slowly, luxuriantly. The lights turned my mirrored dressing room into a blaze of stars as the Millennium Star sparkled from between my breasts—it was like being caught in a shower of sparks. I put on a sexy black satin nightgown and robe and admired how beautiful the diamond looked—how beautiful I looked. I wished Thomas could have been there to see me.

I slept like a baby. My dog and my diamonds kept me warm.

FORTY-SEVEN

When I arrived at the tennis court on the villa grounds at ten o'clock the next morning, I discovered, much to my relief, that we would be playing mixed doubles: Giancarlo and Marjorie versus Guilberto and me. Before we began, Guilberto pulled me aside and gave me a quick tutorial on serving, which I had never done. It was hugely fun, but if I had thought for even one second that Guilberto and I would win, even if he was the pro, I would have to have been extremely naive. He would never beat Count Giolitti, the patron of his village. We were giving it a good go, though.

"Deuce!" Giancarlo announced gleefully. "I am going to break your serve, Guilberto."

"Not today, *Conto*."

It was the first set and we were behind, two games to four. My first and second services had been quick nonevents, but by some miracle, Marjorie had won hers in the second round. But now Guilberto was up. He tossed the ball high in the air and slammed it as though it were a recalcitrant nail and he was an angry hammer. It went so fast, it screamed invisibly past Giancarlo's racket.

"Add in." Guilberto beamed.

He made quick hash of Marjorie, who played only slightly better than I, but she did have on a beautiful white eyelet tennis dress that was lined in only the strategic places, which gave her a distinct advantage.

I, on the other hand, had the Millennium Star tucked securely into my bra. So I had my own sort of smug supremacy.

"Four-three!"

Giancarlo took his place along the service line, bounced the ball a couple of times, and then spun it slowly past me as though it were a special trick ball of some sort. It landed gently right in front of me and then made a sharp right turn. A graphic example of age versus experience: Guilberto's game had power and speed. Giancarlo's, finesse.

"Fifteen-love."

He aced Guilberto, as well.

"Thirty-love."

Out of the corner of my eye, I saw Thomas arrive courtside, wearing his wrinkled, rumpled linen suit and dark glasses. I know he was amazed to see me and I struggled not to laugh. He'd gotten to know a whole new Kick Keswick in the last twenty-four hours.

Giancarlo served to me again. I returned it! Solidly! An actual volley ensued. I didn't participate in it of course, neither did Marjorie. We stood by, pretending to be ready and watched the men charge back and forth—I've got it! I've got it! I've got it!—and Guilberto won the point.

"Thirty-fifteen."

Guilberto's return was out.

"Forty-fifteen."

My return was nonexistent. The ball simply zoomed right past me.

"Five games to three," Giancarlo crowed.

My serve.

"If I get this in, Giancarlo," I called. "You'd better be nice to me."

"*Si, amore.* Very, very gentle. *Como siempre.*"

Oh, shut up, I wanted to say. But I was glad to see that Thomas, who had sat down under an umbrella, had crossed his arms over his chest. There was a scowl on his face.

I tossed the ball above my head and thank God, it didn't fly out of control. It went exactly where I meant it to. I swung my racket over my head at just the right time and the serve sailed across the net and landed in the right box. I was so astonished, I forgot to hit back Giancarlo's powder puff return.

Love-fifteen.

Up the toss went, way off to the side, where it bounced list-lessly and slowly rolled away to the fence. I retrieved it, keeping my eyes firmly off Thomas. Up it went again. I missed. Oh, this was hell.

Love-thirty.

Guilberto came over to me. "Remember what I told you, Priscilla. Take your time. Toss the ball firmly but gently. Keep your eye on the ball, bring your racket around smoothly and hit it squarely at the top of the arc."

I took a breath. "*Grazie,* Guilberto."

Somehow, probably due to fury—because just as I was

about to try again, Giovanna showed up and kissed Thomas before sitting down next to him—I fought and fought, and I won my serve. Thomas's mouth was hanging open. Everyone clapped and cheered. Except Giovanna who looked put out that anybody would care what I did when they had a world-famous television reporter right there in front of their noses that they could be paying attention to, instead.

When all was said and done, Giancarlo and Marjorie won the match.

"Nicely played, ladies," Thomas said to Marjorie and me.

"Thanks," I said and draped a towel around my neck and flipped my racket around as though this were something I did on a regular basis. "I'm thinking of going on tour." We all laughed. "Good morning, Giovanna. Did you have a good sleep?"

"It was all right. Once all the alarms stopped going off."

"That was awful," Marjorie said. "I had a terrible time getting back to sleep."

"Marjorie," Giancarlo said, "how was the Constantines' party last night? Dreadful? You beat us home."

She looked at Thomas and then at Giovanna. "It was just like all the rest of the gala parties. The anticipation is more fun than the real thing."

Giovanna tilted her lips. Let her, I thought. Let her have her little smirk and my husband. She was welcome to him. The biggest heist in the history of diamond heists had gone on right under their noses while they were asleep in their beds and they didn't even know it. In spite of all the hype and hoopla, she wasn't much of a reporter. And he wasn't much of a detective.

FORTY-EIGHT

The rest of the day was spent at leisure—nothing scheduled, a day given to beauty treatments and walks. I stayed in my room and napped and read my book and didn't see Thomas, Lucia, Giovanna, or Giancarlo, which was fine. I didn't really need to see anybody until this evening. The ball began at eight o'clock.

At about four, I took one of my big Hermès canvas tote bags out of the closet and started to get organized. I think these sacks were originally designed to carry saddles or tack, but they're invaluable for overnight trips or major shopping forays. Sturdy. Unobtrusive with their natural canvas sides and saddle leather trim. Like most Hermès bags, they have a deceptively large capacity.

All my jewelry except what I planned to wear to the ball— and the Star that I kept around my neck—went into the bottom, followed by two pairs of slacks and sweaters, soft-soled walking shoes, a package of dog food, lingerie, scarves, small toiletries and makeup kits, my passport, driver's license, credit cards, various other odds and ends, and dark glasses. On top I placed another identical tote bag and closed it all up. Then I dressed in a light shift dress and sandals, shouldered the tote, and went down the back stairs to the garage courtyard.

"*Buona sera*," I said to the guard. "I need to get something out of the trunk of my car."

He began to accompany me.

"It's all right," I told him. "I know where it is."

He opened his mouth to insist, but thankfully, another guest appeared, wanting to make sure his car had been washed properly and that it would be ready for his departure first thing in the morning. I crossed the courtyard as quickly as I could without sprinting, and popped open the trunk of the Mercedes, which contained only Bijou's travel bag and the car's heavy touring blanket. I pushed the dog's case aside and set down my satchel, unlatched it, pulled out the extra tote, and stuffed it with the car blanket. Then I closed the trunk, leaving my packed satchel inside next to Bijou's bag, slipped the car keys back into my pocket, and went back in the house, tote slung over my shoulder.

The deadbolt was securely in place when I climbed into the bathtub and lay there peacefully, enjoying the view across the bay. I'd be sorry to leave Portofino. But it would just be for a while. I might be back soon to start my new life—it all depended on how the next forty-eight hours went. I was not, however, sorry to be leaving the company and the antics of the count. I really had the most terrible judgment in men. I closed my eyes and let the hot water soothe me while I focused my mind on what lay ahead.

The knock on the door was faint and far away. My heart

stopped. I lay silently to see if it came again. It did. If this is Giancarlo, I will slap him to death. But it might be Thomas.

Reluctantly, I climbed out of the tub and pulled on a terry-cloth robe.

"Who is it?" I asked through the bolted door.

"It's me, Kick. It's Thomas," he whispered.

I opened the door just enough for him to slip inside. "What do you want?"

"To talk to you," he said. He looked extremely distinguished in his evening clothes, a white dinner jacket and black-ribboned tuxedo pants. A small red rose in his lapel, presumably a security-related designation so they could all recognize each other easily.

I crossed my arms over my chest and stared at him without speaking.

"What are you doing here?" he said.

"Clearing my name."

Thomas studied me.

"It's not me, Thomas." I felt cold. Angry.

"Don't do anything stupid, Kick. I . . ."

The sound of his voice was suddenly drowned by the clanging of an alarm bell. "God damn it! Not again!" he yelled over the din and threw open the door. He headed for the stairs.

"Maybe it's the Shamrock Burglar," I yelled back at him. "You, you *shit*."

That stopped him midstride and he turned to look at me. I might as well have punched him in the stomach he was so shocked at my language.

"And I mean it." I slammed the door as hard as I could and locked it tight.

There was a split of Cordon Rouge on my coffee table, which the maid had very thoughtfully delivered to my room, along with an accompanying note from Giancarlo.

"Till this evening. Baci, baci, Giancarlo."

"*Baci, baci,* my foot," I said and filled my flute right to the top.

I got back into the tub. I should have been happy and excited, but I was fuming. It took two glasses—the whole little bottle—for me to calm down and continue my toilette. I couldn't afford to get upset, I had a long way to go and no one to help me.

The fact was, I could leave right now if I wanted to. But my absence would attract attention and put matters in motion way too soon for me to make a clean getaway. Besides, there were a couple of other steps to complete. I wanted to see what Lucia did, see how she had planned to steal the Star. The replica I'd left in its place was so fine, it would remain undetected for quite a while, but I wanted to see what she did about it.

And, I wanted to tell Thomas good-bye.

FORTY-NINE

I selected a very special dress—a strapless, salmon-pink taffeta ball gown with a wide taffeta shawl that framed my face and shoulders like a portrait collar. I chose important, attention-getting jewelry—a necklace of white and pink diamonds and oriental pearls; earrings with pearl centers and eight-carat, pink diamond drops; diamond combs in my hair—along with another gardenia from the crystal dish on my dressing table. They were such a nice touch, I decided it was something I'd continue doing, wherever I ended up. I jimmied my fingers, hands, and arms into elbow-length, white kid gloves that were so tight it was like adding a second layer of skin, and once I'd gotten the little pearl buttons done up—which really almost sent me into a lather, they were so tiny and frustrating—I added the final detail, a wide diamond cuff, similar to the Queen's Pet.

I then dropped a few pertinent items into my pockets and tucked the Star into a secret compartment in the corsage of the dress.

I'd be lying if I said I didn't feel a little like a princess as I descended the wide staircase, my gown billowing around me. Giancarlo waited at the bottom of the stairs and he looked so, so handsome in his white dinner jacket and black tie. His silver hair was perfectly combed and his silvery blue eyes lit up when he saw me. It was easy for a moment to forget what a nitwit he was.

"*Bella, bella* Priscilla." He took my hand. "People are just starting to arrive. Come help me greet them."

The media were everywhere, their white flashes and video camera lights giving the feeling of a Hollywood premiere. Giovanna was in the center of the action, lovely in a plain black Armani sheath, live on the air, interviewing celebrities. I watched two ladies enter the Jewelry Room and two exit, sparkling like Christmas trees, and join their escorts who had waited uncomfortably alongside the stone-faced, armed guards who were now backed up by wary German shepherds.

The set and lighting designers had transformed the area from the main entrance to the terrace into an ethereal corridor of breezy white. Instead of trying to inject color into a space that was already as white as it could be, the designers had emphasized it, creating a walkway of floor-to-ceiling panels of snowy gauze that concealed the dinner tables, the way the curtain hides a stage set. I peeked behind one panel. The cloths were persimmon, the chairs gold, with sumptuous arrangements of Casablanca lilies, roses, and hydrangeas in the center of each table. Dozens of candlesticks and votives waited to be lit. Each setting had five sparkling crystal wineglasses of various sizes and shapes and an array of silver flatware.

I took my place beside Giancarlo at the central archway to the terrace and greeted people as they passed us, through another media phalanx, and into the classic Riviera evening for cocktails and hors d'oeuvre. A jazz trio played softly. The huge golden ball of the moon had just appeared over the silhouetted ridge of hills.

Shortly, Alesandro, looking very energetic and snappy, arrived with a nicely done-up woman who I think was the same woman he'd been with at the museum in Paris—the older woman who I now assumed was one of his accomplices. "Priscilla!" he said. "Allow me to introduce you to my wife, Contessa Sophia de Camarque. Sophia, this is Priscilla Pennington. From London."

I took her gloved hand. It was as limp as a bad baguette. She was no more a contessa than I was. "Contessa de Camarque, what a pleasure to meet you."

"We love London," Sophia said, without the slightest indication that she loved London, or anything else.

"It is a wonderful city, isn't it?"

"I hope you'll save a dance for me later," Alesandro said. "You won't mind, will you, Sophie?"

"Not in the slightest."

"Well then, by all means," I answered. "I'd love to." I looked around for the third in his trio, the tough-looking girl he'd had lunch with. I knew she'd be lurking around here somewhere.

Sissy McNally accepted kisses on each cheek from Giancarlo. She looked sensational in a slinky black satin sheath and a suite of diamonds and rubies that were so big they could choke a horse. Her eyes were bright as Roman candles, boosted up on something.

Not surprisingly, Lucia was the epitome of elegant understatement in her shell-pink peau-de-soie gown and pearls and long white kid gloves. She simply appeared, without calling any attention to herself, and joined her father and me in the receiving line.

We kissed each other. "You look stunning, Lucia."

She smiled. "Thank you. So do you. Oh, my, look at your bracelet." She picked up my arm and examined it closely. "Remarkable. Do you know it looks almost exactly like the one Queen Victoria is wearing in the Winterhalter painting *The First of May* with Prince Albert and the Duke of Wellington."

At least she's done her homework, I thought, and appreciates what she's got. "How wonderful."

"It's a beautiful painting. I'm surprised you aren't familiar with it since you're British. It's in the British Museum."

"Well," I sighed. "There are lots of paintings in Britain. I'll look for it the next time I'm at the museum." I stepped aside to make room for her. "I've been standing in for you, but now that you're here I'll let you take over your official duties."

"No, I like having you here. Please stay."

I spotted Alesandro's young woman—she was dressed as one of the caterer's cocktail waitresses. Between Alesandro and Lucia, there was going to be some action tonight. Who would get there first? Oh, sorry. I mean, second.

I looked around for Thomas but he must have been with Marjorie. Giovanna and her cameraman were roving the crowd on the terrace, interviewing celebrities she'd missed in the foyer. The more I saw of her, the less I could picture Thomas being interested in her. She was such a cold fish. Thomas didn't care about glamour, he cared about substance. But, the fact remained, he and Giovanna seemed to be an item. Oh, well, he was no doubt just as baffled by Giancarlo and me—talk about a superficial relationship.

A trumpet fanfare sounded and Giancarlo stepped into the center of the archway. "Ladies and gentlemen," he announced. "Our guest of honor has arrived."

All the lights went out, leaving the party in the silvery glow of the moon. Suddenly a shaft of bright light blazed down at the far end of the white-draped corridor, illuminating Marjorie, a solitary figure on an otherwise dark stage.

The gasps were audible, and she paused there for a moment, letting the effect sink in. She looked like a goddess. Her strapless black gown followed every curve of her body and a full train, gathered from the small of her back, fanned out behind. She stood straight as a stick, head held high, black hair pulled back. She wore no jewelry but the Millennium Star and diamond stud earrings. She began a slow stroll down the walkway, boxed by four lockstepping armed guards in DeBeers LV uniforms. It was like watching a ball of fire roll toward us.

"Doesn't it just make you hate her guts?" Sissy whispered in my ear.

Thomas appeared close by me, his eyes scanning the crowd.

Now, here is the difference between a detective and a criminal—we watch completely different things. (I know he'd been the Samaritan Burglar and all, but I didn't consider that really very challenging or risky criminal activity. After all, he'd been an insider—what he'd done was like stealing candy from a baby.) He was watching the crowd to see if he could spot someone suspicious.

I, on the other hand, was watching the Millennium Star—it was no wonder the firm in Zurich charged so much. I'd paid a quarter of a million dollars for this replica and it was perfect.

Lucia stood next to me, calm and detached. Reviewing her plan.

FIFTY

The cocktail hour whizzed past—I stayed close to Marjorie and Thomas, which wasn't too hard to do because so did Giancarlo.

I didn't know about Thomas, but I felt sad. All we needed was an honest conversation to solve our estrangement, but he would have to initiate it. I was surprised that no one seemed to sense the tension or feel the electricity between us. I couldn't wait for the evening to be over and to get out of here.

Dinner was finally announced by another dramatic trumpet blast commanding our attention be directed indoors where the white panels now glowed with illumination. Then, one by one, just as though it were a Busby Berkeley movie musical, attendants peeled away the stanchions holding the curtains, revealing the gold and red candlelit dining room. It was dazzling.

Dinner proceeded very smoothly, especially for such a large gathering. While the entrée was being cleared, Marjorie dabbed at her lips and laid her napkin alongside her plate. "Excuse me for a moment, will you?"

"I think I'll powder my nose as well," I said and stood up. So did Lucia.

"All three of you?" Thomas said. "I'd be more comfortable if you just went one at a time."

"Why?" Marjorie said. "Do you think one of us is the Shamrock Burglar?"

"That's not the point," Thomas replied, avoiding an answer. He gave me what I knew to be a warning look. "It's just better security-wise."

"Oh, don't be an old fuddy-duddy, Thomas." Marjorie put her arm around him and he and the guards walked us—the hostess, the star, and the princess—to the powder room and locked us in so no one could get in and steal the Star.

The powder room had two white marble sinks set in a long, dressingtable-like counter with a pleated, red satin-damask skirt. Lucia opened a drawer in the counter and pulled out a package of cigarettes and a lighter. We all had a smoke and fixed our makeup. All three of us acted a little tipsy, but I'm not sure if any of us really was.

"This is a wonderful break," Lucia said. "Evenings like this are torture to me. You're so good at them, Marjorie. I envy you, and you look so beautiful. What a wonderful idea not to wear any other jewelry. The diamond by itself is surreal."

"Isn't it?" Marjorie took the fake stone between her thumb and forefinger and twisted it back and forth, making it sparkle.

"I wish I could try it on," Lucia said.

"Do you want to?"

"I don't dare. What if I dropped it? Or broke it?"

"Don't be silly. You can't break diamonds. They're the hardest substance on earth. Come on. I want to see what it looks like on you."

Lucia reached her hands behind her neck and removed her necklace. "Truthfully? I'd love to." She placed the pearls on the dressing table where they clattered like marbles.

I pretended to concentrate on applying my lipliner but I watched the whole operation in slow motion, knowing every move that was to follow.

Marjorie unclasped the diamond chevron necklace with its priceless pendant. She handed it to Lucia who took it gently, gingerly.

"*Dio,*" she said. "It's heavy!" She lifted it to her neck but the ends slipped from her fingers and the piece fell to the floor, disappearing beneath the edge of her gown and the damask table skirt. "Oh, no!" Lucia knelt to retrieve it and I watched her make the switch beneath the masses of fabrics. I could not have done it more smoothly myself.

Blushing and flustered, she handed the necklace back to Marjorie. "I can't believe I did that. I'm so sorry. Please put it back on before anything happens to it."

"You didn't hurt it. See? It's fine." She reclasped the piece behind her neck.

It was a very good copy. Very, very good. Of course, the necklace itself was a regularly available commercial piece, Lucia could have bought it at DeBeers LV or Cartier or Graff, but the Millennium Star was a challenge she had met cleverly—just as I had. It was synthetic. But evidently, she couldn't afford to pay the going rate for the finest replica possible. She'd cut corners.

Not as drastically as on the copy of the Empresse emerald that was clearly a fake, but with professional scrutiny by an experienced naked eye, this stone would be spotted as paste. I needed to move along shortly.

Marjorie rapped on the door, signaling we were ready to come out. The guard unlocked it and opened it up. Thomas was waiting.

"Come, Inspector." Marjorie put her arm through his. "I love it when you squire me around."

FIFTY-ONE

Giancarlo asked Marjorie to dance, and she accepted. Thomas stood on the side of the dance floor, hands in his pockets, watching them whirl around.

I walked up to him. "Inspector," I said. "I know you need to stay close by Marjorie and I'm quite sure you don't want to clunk around the dance floor after her like a trained monkey. Would you like to dance with me?"

He smiled. "I'd love to dance with you, Mrs. Pennington."

I tried not to feel comfortable in his arms. I stood stiffly, far away from him and stumbled over his feet a number of times, scuffing the shoe shine he always took such prudish pride in, even if his clothes were always a rumpled mess. He tried to pull me closer and I resisted. "Mrs. Pennington," he said. "You're a surprisingly dreadful dancer."

"I refuse to laugh, Thomas. But I do have some information for you."

"Oh?" His eyes brightened.

"The Shamrock Burglar is Alesandro de Camarque," I said, hoping that if he'd gotten any inkling that it was Lucia— he *knew* it wasn't me—this would head him off in another direction.

"Alesandro de Camarque?" He looked surprised.

"Yes. He's a Brazilian count who's really from Colombia and he's got a ring of thieves here tonight."

"He does?"

"Don't say I never did you any favors."

Thank God, the music stopped and we all sat back down.

Once dessert was over—a banana chocolate concoction, not worth the calories—I excused myself and went upstairs and got Bijou.

"I'll bet you're ready to go out." I picked her up and kissed her on top of her head and clipped her rhinestone leash to her "diamond" collar with the big emerald drop—the copy of the Empresse I'd bought in Paris.

Upstairs was quiet and deserted. The sound of the orchestra could be heard, echoing far in the distance.

I went down the hall and around the corner to Lucia's bedroom. Her door was open. Two lights burned dimly on either end of the sofa, giving the suite an aura of calm. I carried Bijou through to the dressing room and looped her leash around the bathroom doorknob, last replaced in 1922, according to the big red log book.

I was so at home, it was positively luxurious.

Lucia's dressing room was immaculate, no typical last-minute jumble of makeup or shoes. Not surprisingly, she was extremely meticulous. She had left a marker—an almost invisible strand of her hair closed in the top of a closet door. The strand would fall out if the door was opened—letting her know if anyone had tampered with anything. I pushed on the door, activating the spring-latch, and caught the strand as it fell. I carefully noted the location of the hangers. Then I shoved them aside, starting with the bronze ball gown. There was the safe, secured with an electronic lock, for which I was terribly grateful because it is aggravating as hell to try to crack a safe wearing gloves, even if they are of the finest, sheerest kid.

I pulled the scanner out of my pocket and opened it up.

They were all there, arranged like trophies in a showroom: the Empresse, the White Tiger Suite, the blackamoor brooch, the matching diamond cuffs, an incredible pink diamond brooch of three elephants—was it the famous Pink Elephant Diamond? I didn't even know it was missing. The vault was packed with other one-of-a-kind pieces there was no time to appreciate, except for, unfortunately, the Queen's Pet. I would have liked to have taken the old girl with me. But it was not to be seen.

I struggled with my conscience. Oh, what the hell, I muttered under my breath and reached in and grabbed. Before closing the safe, I pulled the gardenia from my hair and laid it lovingly inside.

All of a sudden, Bijou barked and I heard footsteps crossing the bedroom.

FIFTY-TWO

"I'm so sorry, Lucia." I was on hands and knees on the floor, rubbing it with a tissue. "Bijou escaped and ran down the hall and had an accident in your bathroom. I'm so embarrassed." I dropped the perfectly clean tissue in the bowl and flushed. "But I think I've got it all cleaned up nicely."

Lucia's eyes had gone first to her closet door and her marker that was exactly as she'd left it. "Dogs." She laughed. "Aren't they wonderful?"

"Well, they certainly have their moments." I got to my feet. "Are you all right? Your face is flushed."

In truth, her face gleamed with energy, just as mine did when I'd made a perfect score. Elated. Triumphant. She was a talented girl with a lot of promise.

"Yes, I'm just fine. I had to get away from the hubbub for a minute or two. I don't know how people go to parties like this all the time." Her words came out in a rush. She was anxious to get the Millennium Star out of the hem of her dress and into her safe. "Some of these people—that's all they do all year long. They have no lives at all except getting dressed up and having dinner with the same boring crowd, night after night."

I nodded. "Well"—I picked up Bijou and stuck her under my arm—"I'll see you back at the party."

"Wait," she said. "Let me see Bijou's collar. Isn't it wonderful?" Lucia held the emerald cabochon in the palm of her hand and rolled it slightly. "It looks just like the Empresse." She studied it more closely.

"Isn't it a treasure? I bought it on the Rue de Rivoli right after the robbery—the day I met your father, actually. But I rather feel I need to get her something new, now. I think we're all finished with the Empresse, don't you? She's had her fifteen minutes."

Lucia laughed and continued to examine the stone. Then she let go of it. "It is a remarkably good copy, though."

I nodded. "It's amazing what they can do with faux these days, isn't it? It looks *exactly* like the real thing. I'll see you downstairs." When I reached the doorway, I paused. "One more bit of advice, Lucia. If you want to play in the big leagues—be sure you're prepared to pay the price. I've saved you from yourself tonight, but I won't do it again."

Her brow wrinkled. "I don't understand what you mean, Priscilla."

"You will." I disappeared around the corner.

FIFTY-THREE

"Priscilla! Priscilla!"

I could faintly hear her calling my name—her voice echoed almost imperceptibly down the back stairs and through the narrow passageway as I stepped into the now-chilly night and the parking courtyard.

"Just taking my dog for a quick spin," I told the guard, who smiled and went back to the soccer game on his miniature TV set. He was accustomed to rich people doing silly things like taking their dogs for midnight, moonlit drives. I pulled my shawl more closely around my shoulders and crossed the cobblestones. It was hard going in my smooth-soled, high-heeled evening shoes. Halfway there, one of my feet slipped and I almost fell, twisting my ankle painfully. But I didn't let it slow me down. I was on my way. I gathered my full skirt up with my other hand so I could see the ground and paid closer attention to where I put my feet.

The big engine turned over smoothly. I forced myself to drive slowly out of the back gates of Villa Giolitti. Then, like Lucia, I gunned it and sped down the hill, removing my jewelry as I went, dropping it into the map pocket in the car door.

Before turning onto the A-12 in Rapallo, I stopped long enough to put up the top. It was freezing outside.

I could picture Lucia, move for move. She had no doubt made sure I was well down the hall before locking her bedroom door. And then, after peeling off her gloves, she'd taken a deep breath and punched in the numbers to open her safe and place her big prize safely inside with her collection of trophies. Instead, she saw the gardenia lying where the Empresse had reigned. And then, because she was a novice, she panicked and raced full speed down to my room, calling and calling my name. And when she found it empty, she pulled herself together, regained her composure, and descended the main staircase, slowly and regally as was required of her, and returned to the party to search for me. It wouldn't take her too long, maybe a couple of minutes, to realize I wasn't there, either.

I wondered how long it would take for one of the DeBeers people to realize the Star was a fake. I wouldn't think it would take them long. And once the robbery had been discovered, it would take Thomas no time at all to figure out I had vanished.

Between Genoa and Turino, I pulled into a roadside comfort area. The prostitutes, whose territory it was, first eyed my car enthusiastically—a man in a Mercedes SL500 could make a girl's evening. What a gruesome way to make a living, servicing truck drivers behind trees next to the Autostrada or in the back of their cabs.

When they saw a woman emerge from the Mercedes in a ball gown, they turned suspicious, a couple of them even looked a little hostile, as though they might take some pleasure in beating me up.

"Don't worry," I said in Italian to what looked to be the prostitute-in-charge, a girl of maybe twenty-two who was done up to look like an innocent fifteen-year-old. "I'm just here to change my clothes and be on my way." I ran into the women's rest room, and changed into slacks and a sweater. On my way out, I handed a thousand euros to the woman. "I was never here. Never. I've just left my husband—if he finds me, he'll kill me."

"Never." She smiled. "Good luck."

She and her coworkers understood better than anyone how dangerous it was to be sought by an angry man. They all waved good-bye as I pulled back onto the highway.

Thomas and his merry band of detectives would never match that amount of money. They thought a hundred euros was a big deal.

By now, Thomas had realized I wasn't at the party. He might even have gone upstairs himself to check my room. He would open the closets and drawers but the only clue that I might no longer be on the premises would be that Bijou was gone.

"Dammit," he would say. "I never should have let those three women into the loo together."

No. You shouldn't have.

And Lucia would blame the switch on me. And the whistles would start to blow.

I headed up the A-26 in heavy traffic, almost all of it trucks, and after an hour was relieved to be out of the coastal hills with their sharp turns and tunnels. Now I could really turn on the afterburners. I appreciated the Mercedes's heavy, steady, powerful ride. Like my Jaguar, it was a car that had to be driven every second, which helped me stay awake and alert. I stopped only once for gas and a coffee—north of Turin in a roadside farmers' market where the produce trucks from the countryside were being unloaded. I put on a scarf and zipped Bijou into her travel bag so she couldn't be seen—people might not remember me when questioned by the police but they would certainly remember the dog. From there, I continued up into the Alps to the Valle d'Aosta and finally through the Mt. Blanc Tunnel into Switzerland.

It was just a little after six when I reached the Geneva airport, where I made a stop at a roadside DHL Overnight Courier kiosk before turning in my car. I locked the door to the Hertz ladies' room and bid Priscilla Pennington a fond farewell in a little bonfire ceremony, incinerating her passport and driver's license. Then I dug out one of the cans of temporary hair color I'd brought from my stock at home—an execrable product that is supposed to turn gray hair black—not that I have gray hair—

and sprayed it onto both Bijou and me. The thick coating gunk did as advertised in the theatrical supply catalog, turning me into a tired-looking middle-aged woman with bags under her eyes and dingy hair, and Bijou into an unhappy, ill-tempered, dirty little Scottie.

At eight o'clock, American Lucy Templeton and her sulking dog, Jenny, boarded a flight to Paris.

FIFTY-FOUR

"Welcome to the Hôtel du Palais, Mrs. Templeton," the man at the registration desk said in English. His accented words lacked any modicum of sincerity or warmth. "One night?" He looked past me out the doors to where a tour bus had just pulled up and began to disgorge its contents—overweight Americans in tank tops, shorts, sneakers, and backward baseball caps. His nostrils flared.

"Unfortunately," I answered, trying to be friendly. "I wish I could stay longer."

He rang his little countertop bell for the porter, and that was that.

This was my first and last visit to the Hôtel du Palais, a great big, run-down tourist hotel that resembled a Soviet-era-style apartment block, near the Palais Royale. Without a fifty-million-dollar renovation and total overhaul of its staff, the Hôtel du Palais would never, ever be able to live up to its name.

The bellman, who needed to wash, took me to a dreary room—the carpet was worn and the closed curtains sagged—and put my bag down on the bed and stuck his hand out for his tip. I gave him two euros. He snorted and departed. What more could he expect from a bedraggled, broken-down American and her churlish little dog?

I turned on the television set, slid the security chain on the door, and pushed open the curtains, which made a flurry of dust fill the air. Even if the windows had been clean, there wouldn't be anything to look at, unless you were interested in the back wall of the Musée Montpensier.

Shortly, Giovanna appeared on the screen in front of what I assumed was the Portofino police station. She was still in her evening gown and had tied a sweater around her shoulders, covering her bare arms. "It's really so thrilling," she said. "One mystery solved and another one emerges. Just after two o'clock this morning, it was discovered that the world-famous DeBeers Millennium Star diamond—the largest perfect diamond in the world—203 carats—had been stolen by the Shamrock Burglar. We're here at the Portofino, Italy, police station waiting for Commander Thomas Curtis, actress Marjorie Mead, and Princess Lucia Giolitti to arrive. The ladies have volunteered to come and look at pictures of possible suspects."

Giovanna continued. "Inspector Thomas Curtis, who is the head of the international coalition mandated to capture the Shamrock Burglar, was trumped again last night by this incredibly talented burglar who's been on a crime spree that began three weeks ago in Paris with the theft of the Empresse de Josephine emerald from the Musée Montpensier.

"Movie star Marjorie Mead was wearing the Millennium Star diamond to the Gala di Portofino last night when the officials of DeBeers LV, owner of the giant stone, discovered it was a fake. Miss Mead admitted she'd accidentally dropped the necklace in the ladies' room and it was possible that it was switched at that time by a woman known to her as Priscilla Pennington who has since disappeared. Interpol has issued an international all-points bulletin for airlines and train stations to be on alert for a middle-aged blond Englishwoman— no photos were taken of the woman at the gala. Miss Mead, Princess Giolitti, at whose villa the ball was held, and Commander Curtis should arrive any minute at the Portofino police station to look at mug shots of possible suspects. Oh, here they come."

The screen filled up with a flurry of blinking blue police car lights and the blaring sound of sirens. A brawl of uniformed Portofino police jostled for camera position as the Mercedes limousine delivered Marjorie, Lucia, and Thomas. They pushed through the crowd like rock stars arriving at a concert. The girls were very collected. Marjorie even said something to Thomas and they both smiled.

"Well, Commander." Giovanna thrust her microphone into Thomas's face. He was still wearing his evening clothes. He was frowning and he looked baggy, tired, and in extremely ill humor. "Any progress on catching the Shamrock now that she has eluded you again? What do you plan to do next?"

"I haven't the faintest idea. Excuse me, will you?" With that, Thomas turned and disappeared from the screen. It looked as though his and Giovanna's Riviera romance was over.

———

"Come, precious," I said to my bedraggled little puppy after I'd had a tepid shower—the Americans had evidently used up all the hot water—and put myself together as much as I dared. I reapplied the hair darkener and only minimal makeup—I looked like hell, as unremarkable as could be. I spend a bloody fortune on my hair keeping it the soft, gentle blond it is and it practically made me sick at my stomach to turn it black, especially such a dark, cheap black. I caught a glimpse of myself in the mirror as I stuffed things into my tote bag. My face had a grim sort of fix to it, a focused determination and fatigue I didn't need to fake.

I fastened the real Empresse around Bijou's neck—I had to wrap the diamond necklace around a time and a half—which made her even unhappier. I slung my heavy tote over my shoulder. "Let's get some lunch."

The day was miserable—hot and muggy—and I was starving. I took a sidewalk table at a brasserie in Place André Malraux and ordered a baguette with butter and *jambon*. I smeared mustard on the lean country ham, reclosed the sandwich, and took a bite. The baguette was soft and chewy and the ham salty-sweet and mustard so hot it made my nose tingle and my eyes burn. I washed it down with a healthy swallow of beer. After a double espresso and a cigarette, I felt much better, restored and eager to get it over with.

FIFTY-FIVE

Evidently, the fifteen minutes was, in fact, over, not only for the missing Empresse de Josephine, but also for the Musée Montpensier altogether. In the last two weeks, their heyday had passed and now the place was really on its last legs. Their only legitimate attraction was long gone, as was any residual interest in its absence. The cobblestone courtyard was empty and Mme. DeBussy was no longer sitting on her chair at the door eager to tell her story for an extra fifty euros. She was nowhere in sight. They had not yet lowered the admission back to where it was prerobbery but I imagined that would be just a matter of time and when they did, it wouldn't make any difference anyway. No one was there and no one was going to come.

It was stuffy inside and I noticed the fresh shamrock bouquet hadn't been replaced for a number of days. It lay beneath the fake necklace like a pile of, well, dead shamrocks.

I wandered around. Nothing had changed. The exhibition room still had five ways in and five ways out. The security cameras were still disconnected. No other security was evident. I looked in all directions and stepped into the dark hallway that was blocked by the ACCÈS INTERDIT sign and went up the stairs.

Other than a small empty office with an antiquated adding

machine, an IBM Selectric typewriter, and a cigarette smolder-ing in a full ashtray, the rooms were dusty and deserted. I se-lected one that was filled with stacks of cardboard cartons and made a hiding place for Bijou and me behind a wall of boxes, next to the window that I told myself I could jump from if I had to. Who's kidding who? It was about twenty feet to the ground, and if the fall didn't kill me, it would minimally break both my legs, and probably my back.

No. I was going to exit via a regular door—I was too old to jump out of windows or onto speeding trains. I was too old for this business. I pulled a jacket from my tote bag and made a pillow, and Bijou and I lay down. My old life seemed as far away as Oklahoma. After a while I went to sleep.

I wakened at nine o'clock. It was almost completely dark outside and wonderfully cool. I lay quietly and listened. The only noise was the tinny sound of a radio or television. After about ten minutes, I sat up and removed my night-vision gog-gles from the tote, put them on and replaced Bijou's necklace with her regular collar and leash. I slid the Empresse into my pocket. Then I stuck the dog into the bag, zipping it so only her head was out, and hefted it over my shoulder.

I crept down the hall. Someone was still working in the of-fice. A TV set blared with another soccer game and a man was talking on the phone. I was grateful for the noise. I tiptoed past and went down the stairs. I wasn't worried about running into an after-hours cleaning crew because that had obviously been the first line item to be cut when their star fell from the sky. The place was even dirtier than it had been two weeks ago.

The salon was pitch-black, and after a cursory scan, I headed directly for the Empresse. My eyes and concentration were so fixed on my plan, I didn't pay attention to where I was going. Suddenly my foot hit something soft and there was a huge shriek. It was a cat. It screamed bloody murder and shot up the stairs. Bijou gave a loud bark and wiggled around, trying to escape from the satchel. I clamped her mouth shut and raced into the archway that led to the main entrance and hid behind a display for the shop, hugging my bag close to my chest.

A light came on in the stairway.

"Qui est là?" a man's voice said. His footsteps sounded like sandpaper coming down the grimy steps. *"Qui est là?"* he called again. He switched on the lights and circled the room, testing the doors into the garden that were locked. "Humph," he finally said, turned the lights back off, and went back upstairs.

After that, I wasted no time. It took only seconds to replace the piece, and even less time than that to add my own pièce de résistance, my coup de grace, my flourish and fillip: a formal card written with straightforward print, nothing frilly or scrolly, like those silly things Lucia had left for the Shamrock Burglar. No. This was a man's card, something for Thomas. I hoped it gave him a serious case of indigestion.

The Samaritan Burglar

I turned the Empresse's spotlight onto her, blew her a kiss, and walked out the front door.

FIFTY-SIX

The TGV Méditerranée raced at speeds up to two hundred miles per hour through the countryside all morning long, but I missed the scenery. I slept as though I were dead during the three-hour journey from Paris to Marseilles. I took a taxi to the airport parking lot and when I saw my trusty little black Mercedes wagon waiting for me, I felt like shouting for joy. Bijou jumped into the passenger seat and curled up and slept all the way home, probably the first decent sleep she'd had since we'd left—what was it? Two weeks ago? Three? I couldn't think, and it didn't make any difference, anyway.

Would Thomas be home? Come home? I had no idea. Did I even want him to? I had no idea about that, either. All I could think about was getting into my bathtub and getting my hair back to normal—I'd worry about the rest of my life after that. I knew my "Samaritan" caper had been discovered by now and I'm sure it made him laugh. I wondered if he'd received the overnight shipment I'd sent to him from Geneva, or if someone in his office had opened it. Either way, it would be the biggest story to hit the news in a long time. I was certain he was in either Paris or London right now, talking to Giovanna on the television set, he was such a publicity hound.

I turned onto my road and peace fell on me like a soft comforting blanket. Pierre had stacked all the mail neatly on the counter and left my daily baguette. Fresh eggs, milk, and butter were in the refrigerator. There were a few messages from Flaminia, but otherwise, that was it. I lugged my heavy travel bag into the pantry and heaved it onto the table—grateful to put it down—and opened the safe behind the cabinet and re-placed all my jewelry. I'd left some sensational clothes behind at Villa Giolitti but I could always get more clothes.

I didn't need fancy clothes anymore, anyway. I was never go-ing to leave my farm again.

After a delicious, gardenia-scented bath and a quadruple shampoo for me and Bijou, I put on my favorite pajamas—Chinese pink silk with gold frog closures and gold dragons embroidered on the collar and pink moiré slippers. I went into the kitchen. It was a warm afternoon—everybody and every-thing was asleep, even the bees. I padded into the living room and pushed open the shutters and looked across at Les Alpilles and at the church on the hillside. If Thomas came back, fine. If he didn't, fine. I had a lot of things to sort out—why he'd left me and why he hadn't admitted he knew the new Sham-rock Burglar wasn't me—and now I had all the time in the world. I took the phone off the hook and went back to the kitchen.

Everything glowed—the gleaming range, and white cabi-nets, the blue and white tiled countertops and floor, the yellow ceiling and walls. Pierre had also put a big bouquet of fresh lavender on the counter and the light filtered through it as though through gathered layers of tulle. I was home. Rooted to the center of the earth.

"*Bien*," I said out loud.

I popped open a bottle of Veuve Clicquot, poured a glass, and switched on the television set.

I wanted something to eat. Something special and delicious. Something complicated, complex, and challenging. I wanted bagatelles, the little chewy chocolate cakes I'd been working on the day before my world got dumped upside down. I draped my favorite chef's apron around my neck, secured the ties, and went to work.

From the pantry, I removed a block of unsweetened chocolate and set it on the cold marble cutting board next to my antique blue porcelain canisters of sugar and flour, *Sucre* and *Farine*. I went to the bar and retrieved bottles of kirsch, Grand Marnier, and Amaretto and after quite a lot of sniffing and a little bit of sipping, I settled on kirsch. The over-the-top, decadent combination of chocolate and cherries filled the bill for today's celebration. From the refrigerator, I removed one large egg and a slab of creamy farm butter. I turned the oven to 350°.

It wasn't long before the story came on. I watched while I buttered the miniature cake pans and dusted them with flour, banging the excess into the sink.

Giovanna had changed into her business clothes, a slim black suit and white blouse. "I'm here in front of New Scotland Yard, thanks again, to the Shamrock Burglar."

I placed the cake pans on a cookie sheet and slid them into the freezer because when it comes time to bake, and the frozen metal hits the hot oven, it forces a wonderful, smooth, buttery crust onto the cake that helps the silver leaf adhere, when they're done.

"Night before last, this brilliant thief, who now has achieved cult status throughout most of the Continent, somehow stole the Millennium Star—the largest, most perfect, and most protected diamond in the world—right out from under the noses of an army of security personnel at a charity ball in Portofino, Italy."

I used a butcher's knife to slice the block of chocolate into slivers and then slid them into a double boiler to melt with a good-sized piece of the butter. While that was in the works— melting chocolate and butter in a double boiler requires no attention at all—I poured a cup of sugar on top of another hunk of butter and turned on the mixer. I kept my eyes on the screen, watching for Thomas as the beater circled and circled, creaming the butter and sugar into a light, fluffy confection.

"Known only as Priscilla Pennington," Giovanna continued, "an identity which has since been found to belong to an eighty-five-year-old, retired schoolteacher in Leeds, the Shamrock Burglar has stolen many, many millions of dollars' worth of one-of-a-kind, irreplaceable, priceless pieces of jewelry."

I sipped my champagne.

Shortly, the butter and sugar were blended. I cracked in the egg, added a teaspoon of kirsch, and mixed all that together. By now the chocolate and butter were melted and using a rubber spatula I stirred them until they were well combined. I then poured the velvet like mixture into the bowl of creamed butter and sugar. I mixed some more. Once I was satisfied that the chocolate batter was properly blended and sufficiently smooth, I sifted on the flour, a quarter of a cup at a time, pausing between additions to fold it in thoroughly.

"An international dragnet was put out for her when the theft was discovered at the ball, but with no success, and so far, no pictures of her have been uncovered. This morning an overnight package was delivered to task force leader Commander Thomas Curtis at New Scotland Yard. We have been informed that the package contained all the pieces stolen by the Shamrock Burglar over the last several months, not only the Millennium Star and the well-publicized pieces from the last three weeks, but other items the police had kept unannounced. I understand the overnight box also contained a fresh bouquet of basil tied with an ivory ribbon—evidently, the burglar didn't have any shamrocks or any of her regular gold ribbon on hand."

"Oh, shut up," I said. "You try finding fresh shamrocks in an Italian farmer's market an three o'clock in the morning." Besides, the basil was gorgeous.

"I'm expecting Commander Curtis to join me here any minute now."

I ladled the batter into the little frozen cake pans, set them in the oven, and set the timer for twelve minutes.

I studied the TV screen impatiently in anticipation of

Thomas's appearance and then, without warning, felt myself becoming very emotional. I wanted to see him, hear what he had to say—but I didn't. There was more of him in this house, more of him in me, in our life, than I wanted to deal with right now. I looked out the window at the mountains.

"Good-bye, Thomas," I said and raised my glass.

"Kick?"

FIFTY-SEVEN

The voice so surprised me it almost gave me a heart attack. I grabbed my chest and spun around. It was Thomas. "My God, Thomas, you scared me to death."

He stood in the kitchen door, in a supplicating sort of way. He looked like hell—completely exhausted, and he clutched a large bouquet of what looked like at least three dozen salmon-pink roses. "May I come in?"

"Well, certainly. Come right in." I wasn't sure how to act. "I thought you were in London."

"Do you mind if I turn the television down?"

"No. Heavens, no. Do whatever you like."

He laid the flowers on the refectory table and crossed in front of me to the little television on the kitchen counter and switched it off.

I struggled against so many different emotions—predominantly joy and fury—I decided to keep my mouth closed, only speak when spoken to.

"May I sit down?"

"By all means," I answered. "Make yourself comfortable."

He took a stool on the opposite side of the counter. "Would you like to join me?"

"No, thanks. I'm pretty happy right here where I am." I took a swallow of champagne for a little fortitude. My hand was as solid as a rock.

"I owe you an explanation," he said.

Silence on my end.

"Just before our picnic lunch in the apple orchard, the Yard called and said it was an emergency—they needed me back immediately to work on a top-secret antiterrorist task force to develop an urban interdiction plan. I wasn't to tell anyone about it. Even you."

"Well, you've certainly become Mr. Task Force, haven't you? Mr. Terrorist Task Force. Mr. Jewel Thief Task Force."

He didn't say anything and the silence stretched between us like an unbreechable gulf.

"You could have told me you were leaving." My voice was even. "I would have understood, even if you couldn't say why."

"I didn't want to tell you because I knew you'd get stirred up and distracted and ruin the lemon meringue pie."

"If you're trying to get me to laugh, Thomas, you're failing."

"You're right. Sorry. I have feet of clay. It was supposed to be just an overnight meeting—that's what they said—and I thought I could get away with telling you I'd be in Marseilles and I could pick up that little painting you wanted on my way back home from London. But, after I got there, it became clear it would be an extended visit, and since there was no way you could contact me—our communication was strictly monitored, I decided to send you a note. There wasn't anything else I could do. And then this whole episode with the Shamrock Burglar broke loose and went public."

"You could have called and said you knew it wasn't me. You didn't need to ruin my life. Why did you call the police and turn me in? Why did you force me to run away from my home?" I was getting angry.

"Kick." Thomas was getting angry as well. "I tried and tried to call you for days—on your cell phone and at the house—and there was no answer. I called the police because I was worried about you, not because I wanted to arrest you. I asked Chief Bernard to come over and see what he could find out. Make sure you were all right. But you were gone. Where did you go?"

"I went to Paris to see for myself and when I came back the house was full of police. Police I assumed you sent to arrest me."

He shook his head. "That's why I was trying to find you—to tell you I knew you weren't the Shamrock Burglar. There'd been a series of unpublicized incidents over the last few months leading up to the museum robbery. We all knew the color of the ribbon was all wrong and that the real Shamrock Burglar didn't leave a note."

The buzzer went off on the timer and we both jumped.

I slid the pan from the oven.

"Here, let me help you," Thomas said.

"Just stay where you are. I don't need any help."

I put the little pans on a rack and immediately began to turn the cakes out one at a time, laying almost transparent sheets of silver leaf over them, sealing each one into a perfect little package.

"Why didn't you just leave me a message saying you knew it wasn't me?"

"Are you crazy? Leave you a message saying, 'Kick, all these Shamrock burglaries—I know you aren't doing them'? I couldn't do that. I couldn't get through to you, Kick. I didn't know where you were." He got up and took a champagne glass out of the cabinet and poured himself a glass. "Finally, we found your station-wagon at the Marseilles airport, Bernard said the Jag was in the garage—but the trail went completely cold at that point. I had no idea where to find you, but I figured you'd decided to take matters into your own hands. So, I volunteered to head up the task force. When you showed up at Villa Giolitti in Portofino—I was the one who almost had a heart attack." He downed the glass. "You and that stupid fop, Giancarlo."

I ignored the remark because I didn't want to begin that particular conversation. I knew if Giovanna's name came out of my mouth, flames would, too. But I couldn't help myself. "Really?" I said. "What about you and Giovanna?"

"Me and Giovanna? Give me some credit, Kick."

I helped myself to more champagne. Picked up the plate of silver cakes and went into the garden and sat at the table.

Thomas followed. "You know me better than that."

"I'll admit I was surprised—it did seem out of character." I picked up one of the cakes and so did Thomas. I still hadn't looked at him. I knew what I wanted to have happen, but I wasn't going to make the first move.

He took a bite of his bagatelle and out of the corner of my eye, I saw his face light up. The cake was so good he couldn't help it. I squeezed my lips tight to keep from smiling.

"I'm sorry I put you through what must have been an incredible escapade. I didn't mean to. Please believe me, I was trying to protect you."

"'Incredible escapade' doesn't even begin to describe it. But it's over." I felt my anger begin to dissolve. "The Shamrock Burglar is totally and completely retired. History."

"Quite a finale, I must say." He raised his champagne glass. "Brava."

I looked up and grinned. I couldn't help it. "I thought you'd be in London with Giovanna, posing for the cameras with all your recovered loot."

"No. I've posed enough. But I thank you, Kick, for returning all the jewelry—there are some very happy people now. And the Samaritan Burglar card at the museum in Paris? A very nice touch."

"Thank you. I hoped you'd like it. I did it just for you." We looked into each other's eyes and I could see we both wanted the same thing. We wanted each other. We wanted whatever stood between us to go away.

"You aren't interested in telling me where you found that jewelry, are you?"

I shook my head.

"I didn't think so. Well, would you like to give me a clue as to who the other Shamrock Burglar is? Or was?"

"As I told you at the party, I'm fairly certain it was a phony

Brazilian count named Alesandro de Camarque." I would bite off my tongue before I'd betray Lucia.

Thomas raised his eyebrows and started to laugh. "Alesandro? I know that's what you said, and it's so rich. He loved it."

"You know him?"

"Of course. He's the head of the Interpol Burglary Division."

"You're joking."

"No."

"Well, then I have no idea who it was."

Thomas nodded his head. I knew he didn't believe me and he knew there wasn't anything he could do about it. "Well, at least the pieces are in the process of being returned to their owners."

"Good," I said. "I hated that all those poor widows were being robbed. They didn't do anything to deserve it."

"Well, your retrieving them was all quite smooth. Must have been gratifying."

I smiled. "It was fun. But I wouldn't want to do it again."

Thomas smiled at me. "I love you, Kick. I missed you."

"I love you, too, Thomas."

"Can we get back to normal?" he said.

"Not quite."

"What does that mean?"

I pointed my cake past the row of cypress trees. "I've decided to put the tennis court over there. What do you think?"

"Do you want a partner?"

"Only if it's you."

EPILOGUE

SIX WEEKS LATER

"Kick?" Flaminia's Persian accent was unmistakable. "Can you and Thomas come for dinner on Saturday? Just a few friends and their summer guests."

"We'd love to."

Life had returned to normal at La Petite Pomme. Thomas and I had completely forgiven each other (although every time I saw Giovanna McDougal on the news it still made me frosty) and were back to our regime of brisk morning walks, long lunches, reading, cooking, wine, and love in the afternoon.

All the stolen pieces of jewelry had been returned to their owners, with one major exception. Occasionally, I wondered if Lucia ever wore the Queen's Pet, and if she loved it as much as I had. Perhaps one day I'd tell her its history. I also wondered how she was and if she'd heeded her lesson.

I'd reclaimed my Kashmir sapphire ring from her safe and decided to wear it to Flaminia and Bill's dinner party, along with the matching brooch. They were perfect midsummer pieces, rich and ripe, full of color. The brooch sparkled from my white silk evening pajamas like a succulent cluster of blue, blue grapes—its leaves carved from emeralds. I put a gardenia in my hair.

Thomas had on light gabardine slacks, a linen sports coat, and a regimental tie. That was my Thomas, a linen jacket and a heavy twill tie. I wouldn't change him for anything.

He put the top down on his Porsche and we roared through the summer evening to Ferme de la Bonne Franquette, Flaminia and Bill Balfour's hilltop farm in Les Beaux. Except for its yellow shutters, their low, fieldstone farmhouse was almost invisible behind masses of rosebushes and shrubs, and in back, the flower boxes along the top of the terrace wall were packed with bright red geraniums.

"Kick! Thomas!" Flaminia greeted us. Her black hair was in a tight, rose-covered chignon. "Anyone you don't know is a guest of a guest. I lost track after five or six. Just introduce yourselves. Bill, look who's here."

Bill brought us each a scotch and invited Thomas in to see the new piece of stereo equipment he'd just installed. It was a huge party, all the summertime grandees were there, and I moved into the group, greeting old friends and new. Until I came to Lucia— fortunately I saw her before she saw me. She was wearing the Queen's Pet. I must say, she handled my arrival very well. I watched her process it all. The sapphire ring that I'd liberated from her safe that matched my brooch. I watched her mentally make the connection between the bracelet and the ring that she'd stolen from a nearby farmhouse during a benefit picnic.

"Priscilla," she said. A tinge of fear shot through her eyes. "I'm so surprised to see you again."

"Actually, Lucia," I said. "My name's not Priscilla. It's Kick Keswick."

I watched the final piece drop into place in her mind, the final connection between being at Kick Keswick's farm and stealing her jewelry.

"I see." She swallowed.

"Are you enjoying your summer?"

"Very much. I'm here visiting my friends the Barnharts for the weekend. Priscilla . . ." Lucia saw Thomas wander onto the far side of the terrace and her concern intensified. "I mean, Kick. I . . ."

"You don't need to say anything. Your secret is safe with me, as I know mine is with you." I kissed her cheek. "You're a wonderful girl, Lucia. I hope you decided not to risk it all by stealing— it's not worth it. Just pick one or two of your paintings and sell them and get it over with. It's a safer, and eminently more honest way of generating income."

"I did. When I discovered you were gone and that you'd somehow actually stolen the Millennium Star right in the midst of such tight security and then cleaned out my safe, I realized I was over my head. I told my father that if he didn't agree to sell some pieces, I would move away and he could figure out how to support the collection. We sold two small Leonardo sketches, not too important, except of course they were Leonardos! And now we're fixed for quite a while."

"I'm glad." I smiled. "Tell me, are you enjoying your bracelet?"

She grabbed her wrist, covering the Queen's Pet with her hand. "Oh, *Dio*. I'm so sorry. Please let me give it back to you."

I put my hand on hers and shook my head. "No. I'm glad you have it. Someday I'll tell you its history."

"Are you really her? The real Shamrock Burglar?"

"I don't know what you mean," I said. She and I looked into each other's eyes. I put my hand on her cheek. "If you ever need anything, let me know."

"Kick." Flaminia appeared through the throng. "Come, there's someone I want you to meet."

A few minutes later, out of the corner of my eye I watched Thomas saying hello to Lucia. He was, of course, oblivious to any of the subtleties. He was delighted to see her and I could tell there was no subtext in his greeting. He hadn't a clue.

Lucia was seated at a different table for dinner and I didn't see her again.

"Did you notice Lucia's bracelet?" Thomas asked on the way home. "It looks just like yours."

"Really? I didn't notice."

He opened his mouth to say something and then glanced over at me. "You finessed me, didn't you?"

"I did."

Thomas shook his head and laughed. "You're good, Kick Keswick. You're the best."

I put my hand on Thomas's. "I love you."

We rode home in comfortable, companionable silence.

Ah, finesse, I thought. The mature art of being able to do something grand without appearing to have done anything at all.

It's not for children.